# Rocket Boy

John Wheatcroft

Stairwell Books

Published by Stairwell Books
161 Lowther Street
York, YO31 7LZ

www.stairwellbooks.co.uk
@stairwellbooks

Rocket Boy © 2019 John Wheatcroft

ISBN: 978-1-939269-88-1

Printed and bound in the UK by Imprint Digital

Layout design: Alan Gillott
Cover art: Sydney Luntz

**To Kay**
(Found in 1986)

# 1961

Thursday, July 13 (Manchester Evening Comet)

# Rocket Boys United!

Yuri Gagarin, the first man in outer space, wasn't the only high-flyer at Manchester Town Hall yesterday. Simon Waiters was launching a model rocket made for the occasion by his proud father, Harold. And didn't he look a real Bobby Dazzler in his CCCP sweater knitted by grandma Doris Waiters! Yuri spotted Simon on his dad's shoulders and the three-year-old was ushered through the police cordon to meet his hero. Yuri's the man with film-star appeal now, but one day Simon will be a real heartbreaker, too!

- **Full story of Yuri's visit, page 3**

# CHAPTER ONE

## The dawn of the millennium

What a swell party this is. You really should be here. Take your usual end-of-year bashes with the pledges to keep in touch, the commitments to lead a better, more industrious life, and the resolutions to be nicer to everyone. Imagine all that times 1,000.

Then, as Minster bells ring, see where the party spills onto the patio for a fireworks display across the common ground. Watch as people get together and cry, get engaged and cry, break up and cry. No one conceals the tears. You should be here.

And so should I. I'm at home, in the bath. I can lie here for ages as I'm doing now, thinking about the past, about Helen and the way she would perch on the side and talk to me while I was having a good soak.

Helen was a lovely girl whose misfortune was to settle down with the wrong guy at the wrong time. Not that there was ever a right time with someone like me.

Tonight, after watching a few acts on Jools Holland, I'm immersed up to my neck in water. With the window open I hear the bells and revellers and I know that 2000, a new century, has breezed in.

I'm not fey or prone to superstition. However, as I lie here, what I read in the Yorkshire Post business section appears to have been timed exquisitely to torture me, as if one of my inner demons had an eye for newspaper headlines: "Cohen Bros celebrate great year". There's a brief interview with the company secretary, Melanie Cohen. Though no picture, sadly; it would be interesting to see what sort of a figure she cuts these days.

Good grief. Melanie Cohen, the former (I assume) political agitator. Devoid of humour, too, unless you thought it was funny to call me Rocket Boy whenever I was being a trifle indecisive. Melanie Cohen, who tried to get me to a Communist Party meeting and attacked me publicly over my patronising attitude towards people from the Indian sub-continent.

I'll say this for her, she had confidence to burn; she knew where she stood and was ready to tell you so. She'd figured out the miseries in store for Planet Earth unless we mended our ways and she had a handle on what it was like to be a black person in Britain. And now, it would appear, she'd mastered her brief on the golden opportunities to be found by people seeking a new bedroom suite in Leeds. At what point, during the last two decades, had she turned into a capitalist and signed up to the family furnishings enterprise?

Melanie, 'a single mother', even talks about people's 'lifestyle'.

# CHAPTER TWO

## The persistence of memory

When Greg Hammond walked into the marquee the first thing I thought was: "What's happened to your tattoo?" It had made him look like an idiot and I'd told him so.

"No one will give ever you a job if they see that," I'd said: in the 1970s tattoos were mainly the preserve of sailors and criminals.

"You're so bloody bourgeois, Simon. What do you think I'm going to do for a living? Lifeguarding? Nobody's going to see it unless I'm wearing a t-shirt, it's not on me neck."

"And Rio, what kind of name's that? You'll be going out with someone else in a few weeks' time."

Hammond had given me a scornful look; he couldn't even be bothered responding to that one.

Today was the first decent day of spring. We were listening to a talk by Yorkshire writers, part of a book festival. The sun was shining onto the marquee which glowed bright yellow. The three scribes – Hammond, a science-fiction novelist and an investigative sports journalist – were sitting at what looked like a decorator's table, sagging in the middle below a green felt cloth. They screwed up their eyes as they peered into the audience. "Set the controls for the heart of the sun," said the sci-fi writer. Hammond had a hand across his forehead as he tried to pick out the woman next to me, standing up now and eager to ask a question.

So here he was, 17 years on from our final, angry confrontation in the car park of an Indian restaurant. In his Saturday slacks and crisp lilac t-shirt he looked tanned and relaxed. And why wouldn't he be at ease with the world? The acclaimed crime writer was meeting his appreciative audience.

The tattoo-free arm didn't deceive me, I recognised him straight away, even though it had been the best part of two decades. Some things about a man never change; he still had that Star-Turn-Has-Arrived air. In our church-going days, the minister had said that he could pick us out at a distance by the way we walked. "You've got an amiable lollop, Simon. Your mate Hammond likes to strut his stuff."

Well, you can wipe out a tattoo, but if you're a sarcastic bastard, you'll always be a sarcastic bastard, as my immediate neighbour was about to discover.

"Where did you get the idea for Even the Worm, Mr Hammond?"

"Let's see now, don't think I've been asked one like that before," Hammond said, a mirthless grin spreading across his face as he surveyed his audience. "In Belize, I think, for my last book. I was kayaking at the time."

"Gosh. And for the Fox and Finder characters?"

"No, that would have been in Colombia, when I was under fire from FARC guerrillas. That sort of thing tends to concentrate the mind, you know."

A ripple of nervous laughter around the marquee. The other writers shifted uncomfortably as if about to break wind. The Hammond devotee, with several Fox and Finder stories on her lap, was crestfallen.

"Oh dear," she said quietly.

Ought to stick up for her, I thought, but hesitated.

"Hard to say, the germ of an idea can come from anywhere," Hammond said as he realised that he'd gone too far. "It might be an item in a newspaper or an overheard conversation. Even something someone says to you, a throwaway comment."

"You always were an obnoxious twerp, Hammond," I slurred.

5

"Yes, sir, even a throwaway comment, executed with wonderful timing if I may say so," he repeated, before adding more quietly: "Do I know you?"

"Probably not. You're so up your own backside that you've probably forgotten life before you became a big shot," I said, not sure what point I was trying to make.

"The persistence of memory is a fascinating subject. I think we are all selective and this often informs our view of life. If something troubles you, would you care to enlighten me?"

His voice was quite posh. Like the Brazilian flag and 'I love Rio' on his arm, the flat northern vowels had disappeared without trace.

I'd had a couple of beers on an empty stomach. The stifling heat was making me feel queasy. I needed to get out. To do so, I squeezed past the arts writer from the local paper, a waif-like young woman who was padded out with two layers of clothes more than the weather called for. At the back of the marquee I saw no proper exit but managed, amid total silence, to wriggle through a gap where two tent pegs had come loose.

Hammond said: "What the chuffing heck was that all about?" in a cod northern accent, and something else I didn't catch. The audience roared.

# CHAPTER THREE

## An evening with Eusebio

In my head, I spend a lot of time with my lost girls, as I call them. Ah yes, old flames, you're thinking to yourself, that's the term people usually use.

Well, no, that's not what I mean at all. To me, old flames suggests early romances and all the soppiness, sighing and ups-and-downs of the "she loves me, she loves me not" variety. Then you get married to someone you meet later, live reasonably happily ever after if you're lucky, look back on all those false starts and smile.

But if, like me, you're pushing 42 and living alone, and if you never even went out with those lasses in the first place, it's a different kettle of fish. Believe me, it really is better to have loved and lost, than never to have loved at all. I've excelled at nothing but if they gave away Olympic medals for crying over spilt milk I'd never be off the podium.

So where do we start? Who was the first lost girl? Gill Todd, of course. Okay, I'm breaking my own rules now. We were seven when we met first time around and eight when we parted without a single word of farewell. But we were reunited briefly 11 years later. You could argue that Gill Todd is both old flame and lost girl.

Gill had arrived at Old Oak Primary School in January 1966. She had fair, closely cropped hair that was shorter than some of the boys'. I was smitten. I'd read somewhere about love at first sight and decided that this must be it.

7

She said: "Who are you?"

"Simon Waiters."

"Moy name is Gill Todd and Oi'm a tomboy.".

"What's a tomboy?"

"The dictionary says that it's a girl who acts loik a boy and loiks rough, outdoor games."

"Why do you talk like that?"

"Loik what?"

"Loik that. Funny."

"It's you that talks funny. Oi come from Portsmouth. Anyway you look funny 'cos your cap's too small for your head. You're loik a little Jew Boy."

She stamped her green sandals on my feet.

"That hurt."

"Serves you roight. But you can be moy friend as long as you aren't rude."

"Okay. Sorry, Gill."

I was impressed. Newcomers usually waited for the friendship invitation, but Gill Todd called the shots.

"There's a dead clever new girl called Gill. She reads the dictionary and she's got green sandals," I told Dad.

"Truly remarkable, Simon. Perhaps she'll be the first lady Prime Minister."

"Sarcasm is the lowest form of wit, Harold," Mum warned from the kitchen.

I had great expectations for my friendship with Gill. She was the only girl who played football with us. When she proved herself in goal by tipping a shot from the school captain over the bar (and, equally importantly, winning the dispute about whether it would have been over had there been a bar) she was promoted to outside right.

But her stay at Old Oak was short-lived. After a few months, their missionary work done or maybe they thought Manchester wasn't for them, her parents moved back down South. I missed the end of term with chickenpox. Gill never came round with a bottle of Ribena to wish me a speedy recovery and bid me farewell. I took it all very badly but wouldn't talk of what ailed me.

Mum and Dad observed my moody behaviour with concern. They took to watching very closely when my friends came round. Probably, I realised later, for signs that I was being bullied by people using Yuri Gagarin to torment me.

"Remember, when anyone makes jokes about you and Yuri, they're just jealous. How many people have met the first man into outer space?" they were always saying to me.

It was the summer of the World Cup in England. Dad, who wasn't especially a football fan, offered to take me to a match at Old Trafford.

"Portugal v Hungary, we could see that Eusebius."

"If you like. And he's called Eusebio."

"Right but it wouldn't do any harm to sound more grateful."

I only got the blues out of my system on the final day. I was too tense to think about anything but the match. We watched on ITV because the reception was better. West Germany's late equaliser had me close to tears. Extra-time was a nightmare until seconds before the end.

"Hurst, he could make it three, he has, he has," said the commentator, Hugh Johns.

"Well, we did it! 4-2!" said Mum.

"They only won because it's at Wembley," said my dad. He was a communist and had been upset when Germany beat the USSR in the semi-final.

"What would you know? You don't even like football that much," I said. "You only supported Russia because it says CCCP on the shirts."

This was a cunning ruse to get Mum on my side. Much as she'd loved the newspaper picture of Yuri and me, she was furious about my little Soviet sweater; she hadn't even been aware of its existence until she saw the Evening Comet.

"You can go to your room for a start if you're going to talk to me like that."

Half an hour later, sent upstairs to build bridges, Dad found me crying my heart out.

"Sorry, Simon, I'm really pleased our boys won," he said, reading from a script no doubt prepared for him by Mum, who had instructed me since I was five to ignore anything Dad said about Russia.

"It's not that," I sobbed. "I was thinking about Gill."

"The girl with the big dictionary and those fabulous sandals?"

"Yes. She must've been watching in Portsmouth, with her Mum and Dad. I'll never see her again."

"Dear, dear, Simon, why didn't you tell us that was why you were so unhappy? Better out than in," he said, as I buried my head in his old cardigan, with its reassuring smell of pipe tobacco; if I'd been smarter, I could have learned a vital lesson that day about not bottling things up.

I was back to my usual, chirpy self by the time the new term started, until I discovered that the largest eight-year-old I'd ever seen had taken Gill's old chair. He was called Michael Summerbell and he had a large, square head that was too big for his body. He was very pleased with himself and smiled a lot, revealing a ghastly set of teeth.

"Me dad's a dentist," said Greg Hammond, the classroom pin-up boy and all-round brightest spark. "You could make an appointment. Rocket Boy Simon Waiters is one of his patients."

At lunch time I tried to avoid Summerbell. His big head and bad teeth were an affront to the memory of lovely Gill whose seat should have remained empty as a tribute to her grace and beauty. However, Summerbell cornered me by the old oak tree that had given our school its name.

"Which are you then?" he said, nodding his head in the direction of a football kick-about.

"Which what am I?"

"United or....City."

Summerbell sneered over the last word to aid my response. I hadn't made up my mind. "Well, they're both Manchester teams," I said, as my dad always did.

"You can't be both."

"I think I might prefer City," I said. "Because of their light-blue shirts. My Uncle Andrew supports them, too."

Uncle Andrew had been promising to take me to see City in the Triumph Vitesse he called Alice but had so far failed to deliver.

"They're rubbish, they've only just got back in Division One. United will win the league again this year then next stop the European Cup. You can be my friend if you support us. Blimey," he interrupted himself, "who's that darkie with the ball?"

"That's Rupesh Ruia."

"He's nippy. They're not supposed to be good at football, you know, too languid, my dad says. He's read all about it in the Reader's Digest."

"Who are too languid?" I said. It was a new word to me.

"Indians and Pakis, but Pakis especially."

"Rupesh is okay," I said. "He's brainy, too."

Rupesh Ruia was one of only three non-white children in our class. When it poured down at going-home time, his mother would turn up in her old Ford Zodiac, cram in as many kids as possible and drop them off on their doorstep.

"Look, I tell you what," said Summerbell, digging into his pocket, "see these."

"Got, got, not, not," I said, as I examined the bubble gum card pictures of George Best, Bobby Charlton, Nobby Stiles and David Herd

"Herd's pretty rare," he said. "I was going to use them as swaps, but you can have him and Stiles."

"You mean, if I stick up for United?"

"No," he said, "you can have them anyway because I think you're all right. No obligation, they're yours to keep whether or not you choose to support the MIGHTY REDS."

When it rained at lunchtime we went into the school hall to read comics and magazines together.

11

"Have you thought any more about your football affiliations?" he said rather grandly.

"Not really. It's a big decision."

Michael sat quietly for a while reading an old copy of Charles Buchan's Football Monthly. From time to time he looked across at me as if searching for some indication that I was willing to put our friendship on to a proper footing.

Finally he said: "Take a look at this, Simon. There's a piece in here about someone with the same second name as you."

"Jonathan?"

"No, *proper* second name. Waiters. It says here that it's not very common."

Michael handed me the magazine.

*"When Tony Waiters, Blackpool's giant goalkeeper, plays away from home in a town he has never visited before, he always heads for the nearest telephone box. So why does he do this? Is it because he wants to ring a friend at home or because he would like to look up an old acquaintance?*

*"No," the amiable six foot two inches tall custodian explained to us. "It's because of my unusual surname. There aren't many of us Waiters around and I always like to check the directory to see if I can find any in a place I've never been before."*

"That's interesting," I said. "I always thought my name sounded ordinary. Yours is a nice one. Summerbell."

"I suppose it's not bad. Mind you, sometimes it's not always what you think with second names."

"How d'you mean?"

"Well, at my old school there was a boy called Bishen Patel and I thought that was an unusual name. But Dad said Patels are common as muck, like a darkie Smith. We don't like them very much."

"So you've said. Not even Eusebio?"

"Me dad says they're all right in their own country."

"Well, Rupesh is a really good lad," I said, trying to atone for not sticking up for him more decisively in the playground. "And his mum's great. You can't be my friend if you're nasty to Rupesh."

He thought about it.

"Okay, then, I'll be nice to Rupesh if you stick up for Manchester United."

"Fair swap," I decided.

# CHAPTER FOUR

## On the Elektra label

I teach in a prison. This is something that people tend to find interesting when I meet them for the first time.

I've heard all the jokes: "Are you resident or non-resident?" and "Must be useful to have a captive audience". If it's a nice-looking, unattached woman who's doing the talking at a party, say, I'll make a point of being amused. You might think that I'm too old to be behaving like that and you would probably be right.

My subjects are English, basic maths and current affairs, none of which gets my students very excited. Still, I persevere and try to find ways to keep them entertained while imparting a little knowledge along the way.

I've been ruminating over the mess I've made of things in my life and especially about those lost girls from my teens and twenties. It started on New Year's Eve, of course (the ruminating I mean, not the mess which goes back to the year dot). I've done my best to remain on an even keel during the first few months of the new century but today it all started to go seriously pear-shaped.

And history is repeating itself. Once again, Elvis Presley has been the catalyst. He's already played a big part in my life even though I've never been a fan. Now he's wreaking even more havoc. Thanks to Elvis, I'm all shook-up.

No, that's a cop-out. I'm the only person I can blame on this occasion. I gave away too much information; I talked about myself too much.

The day had started like any other. My first class was ten o'clock, so I'd missed the worst of the rush hour. It was mid-April, but had been more like May for a few weeks. Global warming if you believe in all that, which on balance I do, had put the cherry blossom on the trees a few weeks early. The gently rolling fields were green and the morning sunshine bounced off the golden stone houses in the village near the prison. Even the jail's wire-topped walls didn't look too intimidating. The buildings themselves, all single-storey, were barely visible from the outside.

It was almost possible to put that incident in the marquee the other week out of my mind. I don't really know what came over me. I mustn't blame Greg Hammond for the way I've wrecked my own life, even if he's been linked with some of the uglier moments.

I'd sweated on what the chilly waif from the local press would have to say about my bizarre behaviour during the Writers' Tales event in the marquee. Journalists have never done me any favours but I need not have worried. My exchange with Hammond (and unorthodox method of departure courtesy of the loose tent pegs) made for a jocular column. The journo speculated on my identity; but unless someone recognised me, I've got away with it.

It always puts me in a better frame of mind if I get the Good Screw, not the Bad Screw, when I arrive. They are lookalikes, both bald (whether by accident or design I didn't know) and stocky. But the Good Screw is a harmless cove with a small selection of weak jokes, usually a reference to my rare surname. The Bad Screw favours charmless greetings along the lines of "When are you going to get a proper job?" ("Like yours, I suppose," was the logical answer to that one although, inevitably, such smart responses came to me later).

"Morning, Mr Waiters. Hope you'll be serving the lads with some interesting fare today."

"I'll do my best to keep them entertained."

I walked past the small garden, on which a few inmates were working, to the education office. One man, a former student, waved, another brandished his fork as though it were a spear and the third chap stopped and stared because my arrival gave him something different to look at for 20 seconds.

The middle-aged women in the staff room (funny how I say middle-aged as though it didn't apply to me; I still see myself as a teenager at heart) clucked around me when my marriage broke up. Now I had reverted to the humble status they'd bestowed on me when I arrived eight years ago.

I was an oddity, a man who had chosen this strange non-career while they, living in featureless, modern palaces with rich husbands, were doing it for pin money. They also deemed too much sympathy inappropriate because I was a bloke. Their conversation centred mainly round the stupidity of men, a view of us based on the fatheads they lived with. People who chose to marry wealthy, bone-headed control freaks who determined which TV programmes they watched were not qualified to dismiss half the human race, but I smiled inanely and put up with it.

The only teacher in the staff room that morning was Vera Corbett, a large, graceless woman and the unofficial spokesperson. She was having trouble with her button-faced, teenaged daughter who rarely went out and showed no sign of attracting any boyfriends.

"I thought that our Diane could try the Internet, there's plenty of people using that as a way to meet up these days," she said to me.

"I believe there are, Vera," I said, as I spread some notes and lesson plans on the table.

"You could try it yourself, Simon. You've been on your own a long time now."

"Me?" I said, horrified.

"I meant Internet dating generally, I wasn't suggesting you take Diane out."

"I realised that, Vera, I just don't fancy it."

"But there's no stigma these days, is there?" said Vera.

"Unlike Internet dating in the 1950s?"

"No, blind dating. Lots of people meet their partners that way now."

"And there's plenty of nasty young blokes who have only one thing on their mind, even with someone as unappealing as your Diane," I didn't say.

"It's worth a try, I suppose," I said finally, before heading off to do battle with the inmates.

"Wonder what Melanie Cohen would make of my doing this job?" I pondered, as I sometimes did when I entered the classroom. Occasional idle conjecture had in recent months turned to fits of pique. Here I was, earning a modest income by trying to do something socially useful while, 15 miles away, there she was, the one-time great radical living the life of Riley. Was she selling the Socialist Worker in the Headrow? Was she under cover with Mossad? Was she an Israeli-Palestinian double agent? No, no and no. Well, okay, I couldn't say that for sure about the last two but I think it's highly unlikely. Especially as she had plenty on her plate as a single mother, a curious detail for the Yorkshire Post to have included in an article for the business section. No, Melanie's entire professional focus would be on persuading the bourgeoisie in Leeds to blow vast swathes of cash on new bedroom suites when the current ones were perfectly serviceable, thank you.

The wall was decorated with the lads' literary efforts: My Desert Island Discs, Keeping Tropical Fish, Boxing: For and Against, Who'd 'a Thowt It? Next to the blackboard there was a bell which would bring Screws Good, Bad and Indifferent running in the event of aggro, though it was never needed. The guys here are Category C, that's burglars, armed robbers, drug dealers, nothing really heavy. The presence of the occasional sex offender can create tension, because no one is segregated. But being On Education, as all the inmates put it, is a quiet life and they want to keep it that way.

"Morning, Guv."

This was the first arrival, Frankie, known as The Professor.

17

"Bob not with you this morning, Frankie?"

"No, Guv. He's had enough, he's switching to the kitchens."

"Any reason?"

"You were doing his head in, Guv."

All the men called me Simon, apart from Frankie who felt that Guv created a more seemly distance.

"Doing his head in. In what way?"

"Just doing his head in. Okay, Guv?"

"Yeah, okay."

I knew better than to get into any circular arguments with The Professor. It's like 1984; someone might say "Big Brother Ungood" but he can't build on the argument because Newspeak doesn't allow it. Guys like Frankie and his pal Bob are trapped forever by the poverty of their English-speaking skills.

Eight men in, the Elvis Presley-loving Trevor Smith arrived finally waving his exercise book at me. Trevor, by the way, is an armed robber. I rarely know what the guys are banged up for and it's generally best to be spared the details. But Trevor had been very keen to show me the clipping about his court case when we first met.

"I've been working on me memoirs, like you suggested. This is nothing to do with Elvis. Can you take a look, Simon?" The other men gave Trevor Smith a pitiful look.

Trevor, theoretically illiterate two months earlier, represented my greatest triumph. There's a waiting list to go On Education unless you've got literacy problems and I had my doubts about Trevor. It was just an instinct that he had pulled a fast one on my predecessor and was more capable than he was letting on. I tested this theory by leaving a copy of a film magazine on his desk. Later, we discussed famous folk.

"Who's Nick Drake, Simon? Brad Pitt's a big fan of his, got all his records."

"Fancy you being able to read that."

"I must have heard it somewhere," Trevor had said after the class without contrition. He was more quietly spoken and co-operative than anyone else, but he exuded an air of discreet menace and the rash of tattoos on his hand and arms didn't do him any favours.

"Come off it, Trevor, you've been rumbled," I said, as reasonably as I could.

"Give us a break, this is me third nick. I like writing. I couldn't take another decorating or woodwork class. I'm not very practical."

I noticed that the tip of Trevor's little finger was missing.

"Who's to know?" he added. "You'll look like a top teacher and me like a model student."

I saw the logic. To have an enthusiastic student who made great strides would be a feather in my cap.

"All right, we'll give it a go. Don't act too quick on the uptake, and we'll move you up to the intermediates in the autumn."

"You won't have to worry about that, Simon, with any luck I should be out before then."

Nevertheless, I did regret it. I'd been warned in my interview never to put myself in a compromising position with any inmates. The head of education felt it unnecessary to enlarge on this, apart from saying: "I'm sure you know what I mean." I hadn't brought dope or pornography into the nick for Trevor but I felt now that a hard-case armed robber had something on me. He had also found a way, part ingratiating, part menacing, of getting under my skin during classroom discussions. These could be hit-and-miss affairs as the blokes' views were basic on some subjects. Stray into any areas with even a hint of political correctness and you'd had it. I once put forward the idea that dressing animals as humans for TV commercials was tasteless. They looked at me as if I'd lost the plot. Desert Island Discs hadn't gone down brilliantly, either. Someone thought that asking for his favourite records and why he chose them was poking my nose into his private life. I'd suggested, to get the ball rolling, that they might have happy memories of a song because of an old girlfriend. "It's like yer spying on us, Guv," added Frankie, who obviously hadn't thought of the idea himself until then.

"You don't have to write about old girlfriends, that's just a suggestion."

"Fair's fair, Simon," Trevor had said. "You tell us your favourite record and who you associate it with, if you expect us to do the same."

"My favourite pop record's an obscurity, actually. On the Elektra label," I'd said, a detail that failed to impress.

"Which record, which girl?" said Trevor impatiently.

"Another girl, another planet," someone said.

"It was called Nevertheless and I think it was by a group called The Eclection. It came out in the late 1960s when I was about 10."

There was no mystery over the group's name. The other week, it had been played by Brian Matthew ("What a charming song, remembered fondly and requested by Simon Waiters of York") on Sound of the Sixties.

"You must have been an early starter then," said Trevor. "Someone at primary school?"

That got a laugh, even though Trevor wasn't liked.

"No, this wasn't about a specific girl, I just thought it was a good song."

"What a cop-out, Guv," said the Professor.

"You must have some tune you associate with an old flame," said Trevor. "You tell us yours, we'll tell you ours."

Oh, what the hell, I thought.

"Well, you know how it is when you mess things up and you don't even know where you went wrong. So Something Stupid really springs to mind when I think of several of my 'ex-es'. It was Frank and Melanie Sinatra."

"Think you mean Nancy, Guv," said the Professor. "Me dad liked it, how did it go again?"

"Actually, in a funny sort of way," I continued, ignoring the invitation to break into song, "I do associate that other record, Nevertheless, with a particular girl I met much later. She was called Wendy and I wanted to ask her out but I kind of lost my nerve. You know, sometimes you think that perhaps a girl is too classy for you, a bit out of reach."

"That's more like it, Guv," said the Prof. "It's just as well that doesn't put us off. They're all too classy for us."

I'd got their full attention now. But I didn't want to sound too much like a wimp, so I added: "I wasn't usually in the habit of doing that, it was a one-off. On the other hand, you can't help thinking about what might have been can you? For all of us there must have been cases where we feel we missed the boat but there's no point in crying over spilt milk, is there?"

"Some people do though, I guess, Simon," Trevor said, eyeing in me in that disconcerting, surly way.

He looked as if he'd scored a point; maybe he was still smarting because I'd uncovered his illiteracy scam. The lads eventually settled to some writing, softened up by the promise of a TV documentary after their cigarette break. I felt that I'd given away too much about myself although only Trevor, appraising me from his desk at the front of the class, seemed to have taken in my words.

Some of the men are obsessive about their favourite subjects, such as UFOs, and it can be difficult to shift them; with Trevor that subject, you've probably guessed, is Elvis.

I once quipped that modern telescopes are so strong they've discovered a London double-decker bus on the face of the Moon. But they're not yet powerful enough to see whether it's Elvis in the driver's seat. Trevor was not amused; he doesn't like jokes about his hero.

Have you noticed that the Elvis Presley population is growing? My local paper is full of Elvis impersonators. They walk the city walls in character and hold 24-hour karaokes. On Red Nose Day, 'kind-hearted' Elvises sit in bathtubs full of baked beans or, if they are really imaginative, spaghetti hoops.

I reckon that, one day, the world will be split 50-50 between Elvises and non-Elvises. The non-Elvises will make a belated attempt to stem the tide and the Elvis War will begin. History will record this as Elvis War One, if the conflict does not prove decisive.

Trevor Smith had been giving me reams of stuff about Elvis. "It's fine," I said cautiously, "but can't you write something else?"

"Such as?" he said, more aggressively than the question required, I thought.

"How about yourself?"

Trevor made a fist with his hand and I thought he was going to hit me. He shook his head, moved back a few inches and said: "Why would you want to read about me?"

"We've all got a story or two to tell. I used to have a mate who became a successful writer."

"Who was that, then?"

"Greg Hammond."

"The one who does the stories where a couple working on a newspaper solve the mysteries together?"

"Tom Fox and Sophie Finder. That's him."

"Are you in them, Simon? I mean, has he written anything about you?"

"No, I don't think so, I knew him mainly when we were kids."

Trevor scratched his favourite tattoo, a heart with the words 'Lucy Our Mam' running diagonally across it.

"All right, Simon, I'll give it a go."

So I've only got myself to blame for what happened next.

## MY LOST LOVES, By Trevor Smith

*I was on association the other night and one of the blokes said to me that there have been three loves in his life. There was his childhood sweetheart. Her parents went to Australia when she was a teenager. There was his first wife and then there was his current missus.*

*This made me sad when I started thinking about myself. Which I tend to do a lot. Believe me, there's no shortage of time for it when you're banged up here of a night.*

*The thing is, the women who might have meant most to me passed through my life very briefly. I missed some boats. Or I didn't take my chance when the big moment arrived. They were my lost loves.*

22

*The funny thing is, they are gone but not gone, if you see what I'm driving at. They continue with a life just as real as your own. But you will never know what form that life takes.*

*I read the other day that some scientists believe there are 'multiple realities being played out in an infinite number of universes'. Some of these universes might exist in the same spot where I'm standing now.*

*Maybe Elvis is still with us in a world where Colonel Tom Parker looks after him properly. Or – better still – the colonel never existed at all. So maybe a few millimetres away the King is still around. Could be that he even toured Britain. Yes, in that same parallel universe where I've got together with Annabel Barnes, Elaine Foster, Gillian Hay or Claire Daniels. Makes you think, doesn't it?*

Well, I guess it was asking too much for Trevor to keep Elvis entirely out of the picture. I read this while the lads were doing a spot of writing. As I looked around, one or two scratched their head and pulled funny faces to indicate concentration. Frankie stared even more vacantly at the walls than usual. He was due for release soon, he'd been allowed out for a couple of days to make sure everything was okay at home, and was probably nursing a hangover. If there was an inmate who, on weekend release, took his girlfriend for a quiet meal over a bottle of crisp Chardonnay with vanilla notes then I'd never met him. It was an opportunity to get hammered. Trevor looked disdainfully at Frankie, although I was sure that he would get equally wrecked on a home visit. He turned his attentions to me, as if he were evaluating my work, rather than the other way round.

"That's a lot of names you're throwing at me there, Trevor," I said. "All those girls. A lot of information to absorb in one go."

"They're very important to me," he said. "I can't possibly leave anyone out."

I continued reading...

*"When I was in my late teens, I was a regular in the public library. There was a shy girl with big, pebbly glasses who worked there called Claire. She was clumsy and short-sighted. I don't think anyone rated her very much. But I could see that*

*she had something. If she'd got herself some decent specs, and spent more time thinking about her appearance, she'd have been all right. I must have had a chance. But I never did anything about it even though she half-smiled at me a couple of times when I was returning books. One day she wasn't there and I never saw her again.*

*"Funny to think that there's a last time in life when we will see everybody. Or when they'll see us. Unless it's a dying relative or someone who is emigrating, you are unlikely to know when that moment will be. As I left the library that day, Claire Daniels was putting some reference books back on the shelves. That's a crap final memory of her. I never saw her again and someone told me later that she'd gone to university in Southampton. I often wonder where she is now. She'd be well and truly gobsmacked if she knew that a bloke whose only words to her were a muffled 'Just returning these two, don't think there's anything to pay' still thought about her 20 years on. I even invented a life for her. She did history and stayed in Hampshire. She taught in a school, then a sixth-form college, and now does that part-time. Her husband's a local solicitor, so there's no shortage of money. Her twin daughters have just started at secondary school, a posh one."*

I put Trevor's work down on my desk and stared vacantly into space.

"Is it all right, Simon?" said Trevor.

"Er, yes, fine. Nicely expressed and some interesting ideas in there. I'll take it home, have a closer look at it and make a few observations."

"Course, that's just a starter for ten. There's plenty more where that came from."

"Yes, I'm sure, I look forward to reading more. I can see now why the names are so important to you."

I walked out of the class later in a state of shock which I couldn't hide from the Good Screw as he saw me off with a cheery wave.

"Given you a difficult time have they, Mr Waiters? An indigestible serving of current affairs didn't go down too well with them, I take it."

"Something like that," I said. "See you tomorrow."

I just wanted to be alone. I might have been reliving my own teenage diary, spiced up with a dash of crime. I had a string of non-loves, whom I had more or less buried deep in my memory, but who now paraded mercilessly before me as I drove home. Lesley Linnell and Anna Florenski, for starters. There's even one whose name I've forgotten, a girl who wanted to go with me to see the Electric Light Orchestra. Although in the end it always comes back to Wendy ('Nevertheless') Thomas, first among equals in the Simon Waiters pantheon of lost girls from my youth.

# CHAPTER FIVE

## The Rocket Boy Winner

I idolised Grandpa Pal, my mum's father. He was called Asa
Tomlinson. I added the Pal tag when he explained that his first name
was a palindrome. Grandpa Pal had been a bricklayer with steady work
but he never seemed to have much money, perhaps because he was
excessively fond of a flutter. I usually had to wait until pension day
came round for special treats; but when he'd made you a promise, he
never forgot it.

A few years before I was born, Grandpa Pal developed a system that
couldn't fail to win the football pools. Meanwhile, best mate 'Uncle'
Alfie Clegg was equally convinced that his approach was a sure-fire
winner. A gentleman's agreement was reached. The two men would
split any spoils. When Grandpa Pal, a man of his word, won £500, he
paid up on the spot.

Uncle Alfie bought a terraced house but my grandfather was less
wise. Half the money was whittled away on holidays, extravagant
nights-out and gifts for friends and relatives. Grandpa Pal could afford
to be generous. He was going to get back the original sum and more
because he had spotted a gap in the market. There was no one in his
neighbourhood exploiting the law against high-street betting. Sadly, his
career as a pirate, off-course bookie turned out to be short-lived; he
lost the lot in double-quick time. Terrified of telling my grandma,
Grandpa Pal left the empty building society pass book on the kitchen

table and disappeared for two hours, to give her time to read, absorb and accept, all of which she accomplished with ease.

Mum explained to me: "He was such a loveable chap. Your gran forgave him almost immediately, but he had to go down on bended knee and promise that his gambling days were over."

My dad has always placed a few small bets on the Grand National. When I was 15, I liked the sound of Red Rum; Red for United, naturally, but also because (a habit picked up from Grandpa Pal) I read it backwards as 'Murder'. Dad agreed to stake my pocket money. ("Each way, mind you, son, and don't tell your mother"). The truth came out when I was seen brandishing £25. I've never seen Mum so cross. I told her that the money had come from helping Rupesh Ruia's dad to build a garden wall.

"I must have inherited some of Grandpa Pal's skills."

"You – you can barely construct a wall with Lego, you soft 'aporth."

But gambling never ruined my life, even though I went to university in a city with a race course and spent too much time reading the Sporting Life; I haven't got one of those addictive personalities. When my self-imposed £20-a-term betting pot was empty (I'd be ahead for a while but lose it more often than not a few weeks before we broke up) I would simply stop until my next grant cheque came through. I had little time to think about betting, or much else, during my early days as a desperate, one-lesson plan-ahead-of-the-kids teacher, though I did have the occasional punt outside term time and 1982 was the summer that I got lucky.

"Just done a £5 footie accumulator," I told Michael Summerbell in the pub one night. "Liverpool for the League again, Yawnsville, Tennessee…"

"Yawn City, Arizona," confirmed Michael. We were both sick to the back teeth of Liverpool, Bob Paisley, Kenny Dalglish and Graeme Souness.

"QPR for Div 2," I said.

"Also clear favourites, I'd have thought," said Michael.

"Yes, those two could get me up to £60. But now we have the medium shot and the long shot."

"Go on."

"United for the Cup."

"Well, it's certainly time we won something and it sure as hell won't be the League. And?…"

"City."

"For the League?"

"No, the drop. Relegation."

"Bloody hell, lovely thought but pushing it," he said. "I reckon you've blown it. And just how much do you stand to win for that lot?"

"Not quite ten grand. £9,600 I think it worked out as."

"Goes without saying that it won't happen, Sim, although the first three might have given you a run for your money. Anyway, we should still be talking about cricket in August and isn't it your round?"

"You're not going to believe this, but I left my wallet at Mum and Dad's".

"Not to worry," he said, "I'll sub you."

"Tell you what," I said, thinking of Grandpa Pal, "I'll cut you in my bet 50-50 in return for an evening's refreshment."

"Not a bloody chance," he said. "Oh, well go on then," he conceded indulgently. "It'd certainly help me out right now. You'd like me throw in a bag of fish and chips on the way home by any chance?"

"That would seal the deal."

Michael, determined to make up for a poor showing at school, had just finished the first year of a management sciences degree as a mature student. He and his wife Alison were struggling on her wage, and they had a baby on the way. Tom Summerbell hadn't been adequately impressed by his son's new resolve to offer a financial helping hand.

City went top of the table in early November. The bet was not discussed again until the spring, when City had begun to do what City do so well, finishing the job on that most miraculous, Heaven-sent of Saturdays, May 14, 1983 with a 1-0 defeat against Luton. A week later, FA Cup Final morning, I hedged our bet with £2,000 on Brighton to win the trophy. After United won the mid-week replay, I presented Michael with a cheque for £3,800.

Following in the family tradition, I went down on bended knee and promised Mum that I would wager no more. I might have missed out on Grandpa Pal's manual dexterity but I'd inherited some of his spirit – though not too much. And unlike him, I knew how to quit while I was ahead.

# CHAPTER SIX

## Fancy meeting you again

It's not just these lost girls who have destroyed my peace of mind. My ex-wife, Helen Oldfield, figures as prominently as Wendy Thomas, though for different reasons. I treated her horribly. There's no point in shilly-shallying about this.

Helen was also a blast from the past, someone from my youth. I knew her in the 1970s, when we were teenagers, but I never saw her at all throughout my 20s. During the Margaret Thatcher years when I was getting to grips with my original job, teaching in a school, I rarely gave her a second thought.

When Greg Hammond and I went to Hereford University, Helen, who was still at school, visited a couple of times. During the second term, Hammond went home on Valentine's Day weekend. Helen was expecting an engagement ring; he'd gone to dump her.

"She's always liked you, you know," Greg said later when I was rueing my celibacy, by which he knew I meant virginity. "And you'd be on a cert," he added, reading my mind. "After that silly business with Wendy Whatsername, you need to get back on your horse, Rocket Boy. Though I'm not so sure you've ever been on it to be honest."

I didn't like being reminded about Yuri, Wendy Thomas, or my lack of experience with girls, and I didn't call Helen. She was too highly strung for my taste.

So, what suddenly made her a more interesting prospect in later years? Well, Helen and I met by chance, in the Piece Hall at Halifax. That's the place where Albert Finney had his funny turn as Sir in The Dresser. It was 1988. I was 30, she was 29.

"Er, Helen Oldfield, I do believe..."

"Simon Waiters, you do believe correctly. Fancy meeting you again."

I was flattered that she remembered me straight off, no deviation or hesitation.

"The Mappa Mundi Bar, Hereford University," she added.

"Sorry?"

"That's the last occasion we met for any length of time. I was visiting Greg Hammond and when I arrived you were in the bar talking about an Indian friend."

"Oh, right," I said. "Rupesh Ruia, from primary school. Nice lad, we're still just about in touch, he's a university lecturer these days."

"No, not Rupesh. It was Bishen, I think. Bishen Patel."

Now that was a name I'd never wanted to hear again.

"Wow, Bishen Patel, fancy remembering him," I said, trying not to flap. "Greg always said you had a fantastic memory. He thought you should have been his official biographer."

Helen got a first-class honours degree. I told her that Greg put it down to hard work and a phenomenal memory.

"If I remember correctly, Greg fired me without notice in 1977, but that's all ancient history of course."

I could see that she regretted saying this immediately, as though she'd never got over it.

"Er, how is Bishen? Are you still in touch?" she asked.

"Blimey, I've not really seen much of him in recent years. We still exchange Christmas cards, though."

"That's good. And I've often wondered over the years how things were with you, what a pity we only knew each other through Greg."

"Right, same here, thought about you a lot."

"So, wasn't Bishen doing economics?"

"You're showing off now, Helen. He came back to Manchester after he got his degree. He's an accountant living in Alderley Edge"

"OK," said Helen, "Children?"

"No, I'm still single."

"Right." She sounded pleased to hear this. "But I meant Bishen."

Talk about dogs with bones.

"Two," I said. I decided against offering names and sex. "Anyway, he seems to have done all right in accountancy. Economics is a good degree subject if you want to be an accountant. It's a very sound foundation for that kind of work," I heard myself saying.

"Would that be for chartered accountancy, or for cost and works?" she asked.

I wasn't sure whom she was sending up: her or me. Either way, I hadn't previously appreciated that she could be funny. We parted with a few platitudes about taking care and keeping in touch and that might have been it. However, a couple of weeks later I received a postcard from Crete, signed Love, Helen X. This was doubly impressive, as she must have made some inquiries to find my address; it seemed churlish not to call her at work and arrange to meet up. Well, trebly impressive; the ink for the X was slightly lighter than the rest of the card. She must have thought about whether to include a kiss, not been sure, then gone back and added it later with a different biro.

But I had a rival in the form of one Spiro Pavlidis. He was a courier she'd met the previous summer while on holiday and whom she'd since visited twice. Inevitably, the possibility that Helen might be unattainable (well, inevitably in the strange way my mind works at least) made her more attractive. I wouldn't go so far as to say that bells were ringing and lights were flashing, but Helen and I got on remarkably well; she was good fun and seemed much calmer. Crete and Spiro being over the hills and far away, I decided that playing the long game might bring its reward.

Helen had looked very good on our first date at an Italian restaurant, wearing a brightly coloured waistcoat, plain silk shirt and tight jeans. I found the beginnings of crow's feet around her eyes and the flicks of grey in her jet-black hair rather touching in someone I'd last seen when she was 18. Her alarmingly direct eyes were as blue as ever.

"Well, we're not wearing too badly, are we?" she said, with that unnerving knack of homing in on my thoughts. "I see you're keeping the beer belly at bay. You weren't a big drinker, were you?"

"Lucky, good metabolism."

We'd got some common ground, not least work we didn't love. And we were living in Leeds and had both spent too long in rented accommodation, sharing houses with unsuitable people, rather than making the leap into property-owning territory that most of our peers had opted for, even those without the kind of leg-up my betting triumph had given me; half of that bonanza went on my first decent car, the rest sat in the building society.

"Pity about our jobs. You told me once that you wouldn't touch teaching with a barge pole," she said.

"Did I say that? Well, I can't deny I drifted. I can hack it for now though I won't do it until I'm 60. How on earth did you end up selling insurance with your top degree?"

"I fancied a company car."

"Just that?"

"Yes, I've never admitted it to anyone before, Simon, and this'll sound amazingly naïve, but when I saw the job advertised, I didn't realise I would have to sell anything to anybody. The advertisement said representative wanted and I just thought that I had to go round in some way representing the firm, being pleasant and maybe explaining a few things about how policies work for folk who find it ever so slightly perplexing."

"The penny dropped?" I said, rather charmed by this anecdote.

"Yes, I got lucky with a couple of pension deals from customers who thought they might as well get it from me as anyone else. I decided to give it a proper go and I wasn't too bad at it. I can hitch my skirt up a little if I'm struggling to persuade a customer, though I always say to myself: 'You shouldn't be doing this, Helen'."

I'd forgotten her way of referring to herself by name. The image of the raised skirt gave me a definite twinge.

We mined a rich seam of entertainment on our nights out in Headingley. There was a 1930s pub with a cavernous single room and a raised stage ideal for entertainment. One of our dates was on talent night. This was pre-karaoke when people did their best accompanied by a piano. As we sat through a disastrous line-up of tone-deaf wannabes, we were joined by a thin, pointy-faced man with comb-over hair, a glittery jacket and purple bow-tie.

"Not so good tonight. Some of the younger 'uns don't always respect the integrity of the song, do they?"

"A bit mixed, the standard, perhaps," I said diplomatically. "You doing a turn yourself?"

"Yup, topping the bill tonight, I am. People call me Fred, by the way, though my stage name's Steve Highway. Like the college-boy footballer from Liverpool without the 'e'."

"Pleased to meet you, Fred. I'm Simon, this is Helen."

"Hello, Fred. D'you perform elsewhere, then, as Steve Highway?" Helen said, in that friendly, open manner of hers.

Fred took a shine.

"No I only sing here, Helen. These are my people, this is my manor."

Fred's turn came round. "It's our very own Stevie Haitch," the compère shouted above the mayhem.

Steve Highway, a man at the peak of his powers on home turf, belted out Yesterday, Solitaire and My Way, in a version poised somewhere between the interpretations by Frank Sinatra and Sid Vicious. He had a nice line in outstretched arms while his left knee established a life of its own, bending inward towards his right leg. Steve was on the verge of tears as, eyes closing and right arm slowly lifting towards the ceiling with his index finger pointing the way to Heaven, he brought My Way to a cheer-laden conclusion with a valedictory: "My name is High-way".

"What do you think then?" he asked, joining us again and breathing heavily through a beer towel, like a boxer in between rounds.

"You seem to go down very well, Fred," I ventured.

"You did an excellent Solitaire," said Helen. "Very dramatic."

"Thanks, Helen. Good number, that," said Fred.

"Good night, Leeds," the compère was saying. "And if you come next Wednesday, don't forget it's Elvis Presley night."

# CHAPTER SEVEN

## Trevor's story

If there's one pillock I can't stand in this nick, it isn't a warder (even Speak, the vicious one of those screws who look like twins). It's not the governor. It's not one of the horrible Jack the Lads who comes here full of himself from a young offenders' gaff and needs knocking into shape. I'm talking about Mr Touchy Feely, Simpering Simon, that git who takes us for English.

I'd always wanted to get on Education. So, I pretended I couldn't read properly to bypass the waiting list. I enjoyed being in the class for a couple of months. Then Simon Waiters takes over. Credit to him, it was smart to suss me out and I shouldn't have fallen into his trap. But I'm a reasonable man, that's not why I hate his guts.

No, it's all the sensitive stuff that pisses me off. He even manages to look sorry for me. I can do without his fucking sympathy. It's okay for him, he doesn't live here. He does his session in the nick and then he's out of here. What's the point of stirring up all our emotions?

However, it seems that I have got Simon wrong. I still hate him, but my idea that he goes home to a cosy life has been blown away. I knew he was divorced, that's true enough. But I'd imagined his single life to be a good one. Come and go as you please, free to stay in the pub as long as you want and chase the ladies.

No! Because of something I saw in a local rag recently, I now know that Simpering Sim is a man on the verge of a breakdown. I read the paper mainly for the court cases to see if anyone I know is in there. So it was lucky that I saw this item in a gossipy diary column.

*Mystery surrounds the identity of the man who livened up Writers' Tales, a low-key Sunday afternoon fringe event at the North Yorkshire Arts Festival. Our arts correspondent Christine Cunningham noticed that a middle-aged man, a couple of seats from her, became increasingly agitated as he listened to the ramblings of three scribes. But it was the words of wisdom offered by detective fiction writer Greg Hammond that caused the greatest distress.*

*Chris says: "The chap looked a bit the worse for wear when he came in. Then he harangued Greg Hammond when Hammond said something dismissive to a member of the audience.*

*"The bloke stormed out – or at least he tried to. The funniest moment was when he was struggling to get out of the back of the tent, where there was no proper exit. Greg Hammond put his index finger to his lips, calling for silence in the audience, and we all watched the man squeeze through the smallest of gaps. When he'd vanished, Hammond put on a northern accent and said: 'What the chuffing heck was that all about? Now as I was saying when I was so rudely interrupted...' Not the most original line, but it brought the house down. There must have been some history there."*

*We've got a lot of time for Greg Hammond. After all he's one of ours, a fellow journalist. He went overboard on Sunday plugging his forthcoming book, Even the Worm, but who can blame him? And it's not every writer who puts us humble hacks in a decent light. It's great that in his stories about husband and wife team Tom Fox and Sophie Finder he casts journalists as the good guys.*

*However, as honest scribes, we know there are two sides to every story. So if the marquee limbo dancer, whoever he may be, wants to contact us, we'll be happy to give his version of the events that led to this unseemly contretemps.*

No names, no pack drill. If Simon hadn't mentioned his connection with Greg Hammond I'd have been none the wiser.

But he did, and we could have fun here, a few mind games with Simon 'the loser' Waiters. He's in a state. Well, tough shit. He's thinking why am I, a lonely divorced nobody, teaching scrotes like Frankie the Professor, while Greg Hammond is an acclaimed writer? But it goes deeper, you know. He's a man who has lost any sense of perspective and the problem is women. He has fucked up big style in the past and now knows that there's no going back.

I warmed up with Claire Daniels. That's not her real name, as they sometimes say in the papers, and not the real story. The look on his face after he'd read it was a peach. Yeah, I'm on the right lines all right.

Simon expressed interest in his usual patronising way. "Er, yes, fine. Nicely expressed, some interesting ideas. I'll take it home, have a closer look at it and make a few observations," he said to me. I hope the bastard wept.

Simon's a sentimental sort. Some of his stupid ideas beggar belief. We were talking about television ads recently. The Professor said that he liked the old tea ads with the chimpanzees. Simon said that some people considered those adverts demeaning to the animals. Did you ever hear such a daft idea? So Frankie the Professor asks Simon if he's a vegetarian.

"I'm not, actually," Simon replies. I might have made up the 'actually' bit on this occasion. He often says that, though, and it's bleeding annoying.

Anyway, Frankie says: "If you're not a vegetarian, Guv, what are you on about?"

That shut him up. It didn't make much sense if you thought about it, well any sense at all really. But Frankie got a round of applause and took a bow.

You've always got to seek out the weak spot, and Simon's is the women from his past. I'll put him through the fucking wringer over the ones that got away. I've got a few of my own to call on.

As I said to him: "That's just a starter for ten. There's plenty more where that came from."

And, indeed, he's going to get them.

How about Elaine Foster, Simon? Would you like to know why that one hit the rocks before I'd worked out how to steer the boat?

But some history, first. Before SS came along there was a great teacher called Bernadette. You could have a bit of a laugh with her and she didn't work you too hard. She'd tell you off if you were talking or looking out of the window, fair play, but you don't mind that with a lass.

I've spent all my life being pushed around by blokes, from teachers and my dad to policemen, lawyers and probation officers. It was a breath of fresh air to have Bernadette calling the shots. Especially when she wore a tight skirt a few inches above the knee.

Those were the days; English on Mondays, current affairs on Thursdays and, if we were lucky, a film that we'd discuss afterwards on a Friday.

Then what happens? Bernadette announces that she's got a bun in the oven. The next thing you know she's handing in her notice. She's telling us very sweetly that she's sorry she won't be seeing us again. She's going to be a full-time mum.

And then? You guessed it. Simon arrives. I'd seen him around because he takes the GCSE group. He comes in and starts trying to get us to read novels. There's one he's excited about, to do with a bloke in Yorkshire who gets his girlfriend pregnant. "Been there, what's the big deal about that, Guv?" the Professor said.

"Well, you've certainly been there, Frankie," said SS, who once got us to write a piece on coincidences we'd experienced. "Let's call it Who'd 'a Thowt It?" he'd said. The Prof's piece began: "Just before I went into my last nick I got this lass up the duff. When I got out, the same thing happened with another girl."

Like I said, Simon worked out both me, and the reading business, pretty quickly. We came to an agreement, helped by me standing rather closer to him than he was comfortable with.

I decided I might as well do some writing. Essays were always my strongest point at school, when I could be bothered, that was. I wrote a piece about how it's my ambition to go to Graceland. I did another about Elvis as a soldier and as a film actor and how he combined them in GI Blues.

What Simon said then was downright, bleeding unforgiveable.

"Can't you write about something else?"

Worse than that, he said that he couldn't understand what was so great about Elvis. Who is he to knock the greatest figure in the history of music? What are they doing allowing someone to teach when they think like that. What sort of an example does it set to kiddies? I wanted to knock him for six. But that would have been me out of Education, and into the kitchens or gardens.

Instead I counted to ten and said as calmly as possible: "Such as?"

"How about yourself?" he says.

"Why would you want to read about me?" I say.

"We've all got a story or two to tell," he says.

So this was when he revealed that he used to be mates with Greg Hammond. That being before Hammond hit the big time and Waiters became a bigger loser than some inmates here.

I knew who Greg Hammond was because there are some Fox and Finder books in the prison library, and I've seen a couple of the TV episodes. When I later saw the clipping from the York paper, I was able to put two and two together. So I spent the Sunday before the next class devising some totally made-up crap about a Claire Daniels in a library.

Now then, what sort of a story might we concoct for Elaine Foster, I wondered; someone beyond my reach, someone too posh for the likes of me. A solicitor, maybe – perhaps even one who had defended me in court.

So this is what I will tell Simpering Sim. Elaine Foster made a pass at me after a chance meeting in a pub and offered me a lift home. I couldn't believe that someone as intelligent and well-educated as her could possibly take a shine to me. Somehow I re-interpreted the kiss in my mind as a display of sympathy. I made no move myself and got straight out of the car. Didn't even looking back to see her driving off, I'll tell him.

I'll sign off with: "I never saw her again." You might get a second chance in the movies. But not in real life, you know, the doors are more likely to shut for ever.

Mind you, I do have one true story. That involved a girl called Kim. Annabel Barnes, shall we say, for Simon's benefit....

I asked her to go to the pictures with me and she said, weirdly: "When I go to the cinema I want to see all the film."

"Well we could go and see Terry and June, if it's still on, and maybe have a quick drink afterwards."

I'd enjoyed the repeats on television and noticed it was on at the new multiplex cinema. I'd seen a few of these film spin-offs on TV. Are You Being Served? wasn't up to much but The Likely Lads and Porridge had been all right.

"Okay," she says.

I met her outside the cinema. When I asked for two tickets to Terry and June, the woman behind the counter laughed like a drain. I realised my mistake when the certificate thing appeared on screen. We were watching Henry and June, it was an 18 and there was a lot of sex. The film was mainly about people in Paris between the wars. Some of them were writers, including one called Henry. There was no sign of Terry Scott or June Whitfield. I kept my hands to myself, because one of my mates had told me what Kim meant about watching all the film. After about half an hour she said she'd seen enough and walked out. I chased after her and tried to put a comforting arm round her shoulders.

"What a horrible film," she says. "What a nasty thing to take someone to, on a first date."

"I'm sorry, Kim, I really thought it was Terry and June, you know, an old TV situation comedy."

"You don't expect me to believe that, do you?"

"It's God's truth. It won't happen again, I promise you."

But, of course, that was the daftest thing that I could possibly have said.

"You bet it won't..."

Will Simon manage to work out that, bar Kim, these are only stories? Well, the clues are there. Ideally, he'll get there in his own time, and this will just make him feel even worse. He'll understand that I really am a man with a grievance. Then he might like to reflect on what it's like having a convicted armed robber on your case – and soon to be on the outside.

Because that's what I am. I'm a hard man, a convicted armed robber. I've got the press clippings to prove it and Simon has seen them.

# CHAPTER EIGHT

## The Shi'ite Methodist

Mum and Dad still live in the 1930s semi I was brought up in, close to the Methodist church. I'd been christened C of E but you couldn't beat the convenience of a Sunday school on the doorstep. "You'd be a Muslim if it had been a mosque," Melanie Cohen had told me.

I've no real complaints about my parents; Mum was perhaps over-protective but then I was an only child. I know, thanks to an old diary I found, that my dad never wanted to have kids. In the circumstances, as someone who had his arm twisted, he's done his best. And better to be too hands-off than too hands-on in the wrong kind of way. As I've said, Michael Summerbell's old man was a right bastard.

My parents felt they had missed out on education. They left school at 15 and were both hairdressers, although Dad spent 20 years as a bank clerk after his shop in inner-city Manchester was demolished to 'make way' for a road-widening scheme. That was the 1960s for you, the days of full employment. I don't imagine that modern-day counting houses provide shelter for refugee barbers, even less those who sympathise with the Communist Party of Great Britain.

Mum and Dad liked to put cultural opportunities my way. Theatre trips were a feature of my young life, as were the seminars that my parents liked to conduct on the way home. Confrontation not being my game, I always tried to put a brave face on it. We went to the Library Theatre in Manchester and the Forum in Wythenshawe, but more often than not it was to the South Manchester Thespians for whom Mum's younger brother, Andrew, was the star performer.

"What d'you think of Oscar Wilde, then?" said Mum, convinced that The Importance of Being Earnest had provided me, at the age of 14, with a life-affirming moment.

"I thought Uncle Andrew was pretty good as usual and Auntie Laura did her prompting very well. It's funny how she joined the Thespians, she always said she didn't like theatre. D'you think it's got anything to do with Andrew fancying the girl who played Cecily? He looked pretty keen on her to me."

"That was just good acting," said Mum, keen to hurry the conversation along. "What did you think of the play?"

"Some of it was a little queer. I didn't understand why we never got to meet Bunbury."

"It's always good to hear some of the wonderful insights youth can give us," Dad said. "There was no Bunbury, Simon. He was an imaginary character, created by Algernon so he could make himself scarce, especially if Lady Bracknell was in town."

"That's what we're supposed to think. But I believe that it might have been some kind of a double bluff by the writer."

"Really? How do you mean, precisely? Perhaps Oscar Wilde was planning on using him in a sequel?"

I didn't have a clue what I meant, and determined to pay more attention at the next Thespians' production, She Stoops to Conquer, in which Uncle Andrew was playing Marlow. This was to be his first Evening Comet 'Oscar' award for best male lead in an amateur production. It was a favourite play of Dad's.

"The *text*," said Dad, "is one of the things my old Army pal Archie Macash passed on to me. Do you by any chance remember me talking of Archie?"

"Now lives in France and never played football for Brechin City," I said, recalling a story I'd heard a few years earlier about this chap.

"Spot on, Simon, your mum's always telling me what a good memory you've got."

I found Dad's old copy of She Stoops to Conquer; it was signed "To Harold from your devoted Army pal, Archie." I read it twice before we went to the Thespians; there was to be no repeat of my radical interpretation of The Importance of Being Earnest, and subsequent mocking by the Professor of Sarcasm. As I read, I sympathised with Marlow and his difficulties over well-bred women and so did Michael who came to the show with us.

"I can see why that Marlow acted like he did, Mr Waiters," he said as we stood at the bus stop later.

"Why's that, Michael?"

"I always think my chances are better with girls who aren't too fancy. No one posh is going to want to go out with me, are they?"

"I don't believe that for a moment, Michael," said my mum gallantly.

"Well my mother does. She reckons that if my behaviour doesn't improve, no nice girls will want to go out with me. The thing is, though, I don't really want to go out with nice girls."

"Yes well…" started my mum.

"Uncle Andrew was great again but perhaps he was slightly old for the part," I said. "He's – what – 30-ish?"

"That's hardly ancient, but you might be right, Simon," said Mum, grateful for the intervention. "In amateur dramatics, they don't always have good actors who are exactly the right age."

"On the other hand, he's young at heart, Uncle Andrew. And I bet he was pleased that Miss Hardcastle was the same girl who played Cecily in the other one."

"Just clever acting, Simon," reiterated Mum.

So I learned two things from my early trips to the theatre; don't go for any women who are too posh, or excessively attractive, and always have an imaginary friend up your sleeve. A Bunbury of my own might be handy one day; say, in the unlikely event that I got a chance to stay overnight with a girl. I could claim that I was with another male friend. It was a few years before I did anything about it and it would have been wise not to share the idea with Greg Hammond.

# CHAPTER NINE

## Dad's friend the bank manager

To that tricky question 'when you were happiest in your life?' – you know, push coming to shove, a gun put to your head and all that – I'd have to say in the barbers' shop, with Dad plying his trade on a Saturday afternoon and the radio tuned to Sports Report. To put a date on it you could do worse than 1966-67; I was nine when United were in the process, as Michael Summerbell had predicted the day I met him, of becoming league champions again.

Mum worked part-time and did a Saturday shift with a local hairdresser. I sometimes spent the day with her. However, I preferred the all-male camaraderie of Hair Today, featuring jokes I didn't understand but which must surely be hilarious. Dad had me doing a few tiny tasks, such as sweeping up and bringing favoured customers a cup of Maxwell House while I kept an ear cocked to the radio for the news from Old Trafford that Denis Law had once again "sealed two points for the Reds".

Dad was quite a character in the shop, jokey with the children, expansive with the adults. He wasn't hugely skilled at his actual trade and I noticed that Mum only used the word salon when talking about her place of work. Dad was a two-note barber; those notes were the trim and the short back and sides, the trim being marginally less severe. Certificates next to his mirror suggested that Harold Albert Waiters had gained hairdressing Gold Medal Diplomes d'honneur from Zurich and Geneva. I suspected that this might be a joke.

I was captivated by a picture on the salon wall: a man and woman, shoulder to shoulder, short hair swept back behind the ears and held in place by Go-Gel. Both had high cheekbones and chiselled features. Both had their merits, although there was no doubt in my mind that the girl who looked like a boy was more appealing than the boy who looked like a girl. It was an early sign of how my tastes would develop. I was always going to be the sort of bloke who thought the principal boy, as long as she was girl-shaped, looked more attractive than Cinderella.

I was in the shop on the morning that Robert, the man who became Dad's favourite customer, walked in. A diminutive, slightly plump chap with a pretty wife who also made a brief appearance, he turned out to be a bank manager.

"Well, well, so that's your lad is it? Rocket Boy, wasn't it? Marvellous photograph," he said when he noticed the framed shot of Gagarin and me next to the 'Cum Laude' certificates from Switzerland. "I remember that picture from the Comet. I took my twins David and Robin to see him. Perhaps you should have called the shop Yuri's."

"Well, it's not in my gift because I don't actually own the place, Sir," said Dad. "I just have a chair here."

"You have a chair? I suppose we could call you the professor," he said, and Dad laughed. I took this to be another indecipherable adult joke.

This emboldened Dad to say that he had a clever Army mate, Archie, whom he often referred to as 'Prof', before adding casually: "He lives in France, you know."

"I rather fancy a house in Filey where we take our holidays," the bank manager replied.

The two of them were soon on first-name terms. Robert took his daughter every other week to watch City. When he heard that I was keen on United, but had not yet seen them play, I was invited to the derby match at Maine Road. The girl, Lois, was a couple years older than me and a little stand-offish. Nevertheless, she shook hands with me graciously at the end of the match, a 1-1 draw.

"So you're both keen Blues, then?" Mum had said to Robert that lunchtime when she took me to the bus stop to meet them.

"Well to tell the truth I wasn't really that excited about football, nodding acquaintance you could say, although I enjoy it now. I got off lightly with the boys who aren't fussed at all. I'm glad Lois chose the Blues because it's so easy to get there on the bus from us. When all's said and done City and United are both Manchester teams."

Lois snorted.

"Could be Harold speaking, Robert, you're right," said Mum, even though she'd become United through and through once I made my choice.

I found it hard to believe that Robert was a bank manager. Surely they all drove motor cars with GB stickers on the back so people knew that they took their holidays abroad? And weren't they supposed to be stuffy and correct? Possibly slightly sinister, too, to judge from a television commercial in which a bank manager had stepped out of a couple's wardrobe while they were discussing their financial difficulties.

I thought that hairdressing might be the career for me and floated the idea to Mum.

"I'll start as an apprentice in a big salon in town," I said.

"You'll do no such thing."

"But me dad cuts 'air."

"That's my dad and hair with an aitch, and we didn't have your educational advantages. You'll be going to grammar school when you pass the exam and becoming a proper professional person, in a bank like Robert, or even teaching."

"I'm not that smart," I complained.

"Look," said Mum, "Miss Dean can't argue with the fact that you are the brightest lad in the class, along with Gregory."

I wasn't sure whether the distasteful note in Mum's voice was directed at Miss Dean, Greg Hammond or both.

All things must pass, and my Saturday childhood idyll was no exception. I think an increasingly fashion-conscious 1960s clientele were already beginning to take their heads elsewhere when we learned of the corporation's highway-widening plans. That spelled the end of the road for the presciently-named Hair Today.

However, the family crisis was short-lived. Dad told Robert about his dilemma. Robert pointed out that a local bank had a notice on the counter, offering people with a good standard of education the opportunity to apply for a job.

"I haven't got my School Certificate, or anything like that," protested Dad.

"No, they only mean you've got to be literate, numerate and to be smartly turned out, Harold. You're good with customers and you seem to be able to add up any old set of numbers in your head. You would be absolutely fine working as a cashier."

"You think so, Robert?"

"Of course. I'd be more than happy to do you a reference. Just one favour I'd ask."

"Yes, I'm really grateful."

"Don't mention your sympathy for the Communist Party."

Dad kept his side of the bargain right through to the end of the 1970s when, in curious circumstances, he was to lose his faith in the dictatorship of the proletariat. Mum was happy with our small rise up the social scale, although we were no better off, and even more so with my acceptance of a future among the middle-classes.

# CHAPTER TEN

## Yuri Gagarin and the over-cooked vegetables

On my first day at primary school the head teacher had announced to the class that I was "the little boy who once met the most famous man in the world". That set a pattern for the years to come. Just when I thought my encounter with Yuri was leaving the common memory bank, someone would bring up the cosmonaut again.

The sadistic Miss Dean wasn't averse to doing so when she was having a go at me. Miss Dean had favourites, "my little saints" she called them, and I was not in that number.

Miss Dean liked to force-feed kids during school dinner when they didn't like their disgusting, stewed vegetables. That was the way things still worked in the 1960s. In fact, it was only a few years earlier that my school had stopped forcing left-handers to use their right.

If I were writing a kiddies' book about me, I'd be inclined to start it something like this: "My name is Simon Jonathan Waiters. I support Manchester United in football, Lancashire in cricket and I like reading. My favourite sportsmen are Denis Law and Harry Pilling, my least favourite teacher is Miss Dean and my least favourite food is swede."

One lunch-time, I was subjected simultaneously to the worst possible person and vegetable. After hiding some swede in a handkerchief, I'd swirled the rest around my plate trying to make it look like less, but only succeeding in making it look like more.

Miss Dean, on dinner duty, homed in on me like an inter-continental ballistic missile. "Giving your swede a miss today, are we, Simon Waiters?"

"I've tried my best with it. It's ever so slightly overcooked for me, Miss Dean."

"Hear that children? Ever so slightly overcooked for my refined palate, Miss Dean, he says," said Miss Dean, doing a silly voice. "There are little boys and girls in Africa who are starving, and you won't eat your nutritious swede."

"I think you've used that tired line about starving Africans before, Miss Dean, whether I eat my swede or not will sadly make no difference to them one way or the other. Get a new scriptwriter. Besides, any nutrition was boiled out of this shit years ago."

No, I didn't actually say that, I was only nine years old.

"Well, say something, boy. Am I going to have to make you eat it?"

The silence continued, as my ears turned red. Greg Hammond, loving this, explained helpfully: "There's some in his hankie, too, Miss". My friend Michael, no doubt thinking "there but for the Grace of God", opened his mouth to protest on my behalf. Miss Dean's hand went up with the decisiveness of a traffic cop on top of her game.

"Whoa! This has nothing to do with you, Michael Summerbell."

"It's nothing to do with Greg Hammond what's in his snot rag, either," said Michael, earning a smack for his spectacular heroism.

"Do you think Yuri Gagarin was as picky about his food when he opened his Tupperware box in outer space, boys and girls?"

Michael remained defiantly silent. The other kids, seeing the injustice of the Miss Dean's assault, switched their loyalty; Hammond alone agreed with Miss Dean's speculation about the in-flight catering.

But she was too focused on me to suspect any slight. "Rocket Boy here is entirely responsible for his own decision to make life unpleasant for himself. Right, here's the fork, here's the swede – open your mouth, it's on the way, Little Space Man."

I only told my mum this story after I'd left primary school. A little later, Mum met Miss Dean, now Mrs Bolton and with a baby in tow.

"I was very tempted to say 'does your little boy like swede?'" said Mum.

"Why didn't you? Why are we all so bloody polite?"

When Yuri Gagarin died in 1968, a letter to the Manchester Evening Comet from Mr Harold Waiters said: "People should remember that, because of scientists and cosmonauts like Yuri, the Russians have always led the way in the space race and will continue to do so." I'd left the sadistic Miss Dean behind but my new teacher, Mr Warboys, was no better. "Hands up anyone whose father is a communist," he asked the class, holding up his copy of the Comet to give us all a clue.

A few weeks later, the USSR cropped up in a children's television programme about people from other lands. We watched it with Mr Warboys during our winding-down Friday afternoon slot. The country looked pretty horrible and Joseph Stalin did not emerge with much credit, even though his excesses were toned down for the young audience. Mr Warboys eyed me malevolently as the child-friendly version of the purges was revealed on the 405 lines, 21-inch Bush TV. For the first time in my life, I took an interest in my father's politics.

"Why are you a communist, Dad?"

"Well," he told me, "Communism is the best system of government. By that I mean it is the best way to run a country. Everyone who lives in the Soviet Union gets a fair share of the country's wealth and the health care, schools and universities are the best in the world."

"It's just that we saw this programme at school about Russia on TV and it didn't look very nice," I said.

"How do you mean, not nice, son?"

"It all seemed very grey."

"Of course it was grey, unless Old Oak Primary has got colour television before the rest of us."

"I meant grey like gloomy and sad. And this Stalin looks like he was a bad man."

"Well, you can't make an omelette without breaking eggs."

"What?"

"Work it out, you're a bright lad."

I paused to think about it.

"Yes, I suppose so."

"Listen, Simon, before Lenin and the communists took over ... um, you know Lenin, do you?"

"Yes, he was the one who started to change things. It was in the programme."

"Before Lenin, Russia was a backward country and most people were starving. Now it's a World Superpower and leader in the Space Race."

"But the communists don't seem to treat people well, and they can't say what they like. Mr Warboys said that you can get on a soap box in Piccadilly Gardens and say that you think Harold Wilson's as daft as a brush, and nobody will take any notice. But if you stand in Red Square and say the same thing about their Prime Minister ..."

"You mean their General Secretary, Leonid Brezhnev..."

"Okay, this Mr Brezhnev. If you said he was useless you would get thrown in a camp and left to rot."

"Why would anyone want to criticise Mr Brezhnev?" asked Dad.

"But if they did," I persisted.

"Mr Warboys is just spouting rubbish you see on our TVs and read in our papers. In fact, the Russians decided eventually that Stalin could be criticised, despite all his great work. Yes, even Stalin, our big friend in the war, don't forget. They decided that he had broken one egg too many and now everyone's allowed to say that. It's free speech in Russia, within bounds, same as here."

"So when did you become a communist?" I asked.

"It was at the end of the war, guided you might say by the wisdom of my friend Archie Macash. We met at an army camp in Scotland, near Brechin."

"Brechin? Wow! Brechin City are bottom of the Scottish League with East Stirlingshire," I said.

"Yes, I dare say."

"How were they doing in those days?"

"Brechin City were outstanding, Simon, on a par with Celtic and Rangers."

"Really?" I said.

"Yes, but anyone could see they'd just reached their peak and would start to struggle during the next two decades."

"Perhaps they'll have a comeback one day," I said.

"Well, it's a big city club as you can tell from the name so that's possible," said Dad.

"What was your friend called again?"

"Archie Macash."

"And did he watch Brechin City?"

"He played for them, son. Just part-time, like."

"What position?"

"Left winger."

"Did you go to watch him play?"

"No, Simon, I was too busy with the war. I mainly read books in my spare time. Now haven't you got a good one from the library?"

I went off in search of my Jennings. I could always tell when Dad had had enough of me. But I returned to the subject of Dad and Archie later that day.

"Archie didn't really play for Brechin City did he, Dad? I've looked it up and there are no league tables during the war."

"No, he was what you call an intellectual and he wanted to go to university after the war."

"And did he do that, go to university I mean?"

An exciting thought occurred.

"Perhaps he became a spy for Russia."

"I don't think he'd have done anything like that," said Dad. "Anyway, he ended up living in France. He runs a small museum somewhere near Toulouse."

"Maybe we could go and visit him and his family one day," I suggested, although foreign travel had never been remotely on our agenda.

"One day, perhaps," said Dad, "although he lives on his own."

"Isn't that a bit lonely?"

"It's not easy to explain," said Dad, "but he's not exactly like other chaps and I don't think he would have had girlfriends or got married."

"Did Archie like being in the war?"

"Not much, and some men weren't very nice to him because he wasn't like the rest of us. He was posh and he flapped his hands a lot like Gary in your mum's salon."

"Other soldiers bullied him?" I asked, shocked that such things didn't stop when you got away from school.

"Yes, Simon, you could say that. There was me and another man, a Private David Hellier, who used to look out for Archie. We would try to protect him, you could say. A sergeant called Metcalfe was especially nasty."

"Well I think that Archie Macash must have been very grateful to you and this Hellier," I said. I was beginning to feel proud of my dad.

"I think he was," said Dad. "And it worked both ways because he taught David and me a few things. Archie read novels and plays as well, and passed them on to us. He always treated us as equals, even though he was so clever, and of course he taught us about politics and explained how the world would become a better place after the war when more countries became like the Soviet Union."

"And you're still in touch?"

"Yes, we send each other 'comradely' greetings every Christmas, and I sometimes get a postcard from his holidays in the communist countries like Czechoslovakia and Hungary."

"The ones that are good at football?" I said.

"Maybe, but I don't think that would have affected Archie's choice of destination," Dad laughed.

"This bullying, Dad, it's something people still do when they are grown up?" I asked, keen to make sure I'd understood correctly.

"Of course. I mean, Miss Dean and Mr Warboys are bullies, aren't they, son?"

"Yes. And does that mean they also bully people when they are not at school and they are with other grown-ups?"

"It's very likely, Simon."

Unfortunately, such characters were not unheard of among the teachers when I went to the big kids' school. For them, the lunar landing was timed perfectly. I arrived at the grammar in 1969, two months after Neil Armstrong stepped on to the Moon's surface and said: "A small step for man, a giant step for mankind."

The Comet brought out a special supplement, covering the space race from 1957, when the Russians sent Laika the dog into orbit, to Armstrong. Manchester was twinned with Leningrad (that's why Yuri Gagarin came to us in the first place) in the USSR. My dad was thrilled that the Russian part in space exploration wasn't being forgotten by the Comet.

"This is much more impressive than anything you'll see in the national newspapers. As far as that London is concerned, it's all about the Yanks. But this is great isn't it, Simon? " he said waving the paper at me.

"Yes," I agreed for a quiet life.

The famous picture had been recycled in the Comet: "1961: Yuri and Simon - The Pioneers!" This was, inevitably, seen by a couple of the teachers at the grammar. "You'll never be an astronaut without good science and maths, Rocket Boy," the physics teacher said more than once when it turned out that my academic strengths, such as they were, lay elsewhere.

My maths teacher, Stack, doubled up as head of PE. For both activities, he wore a ghastly purple tracksuit made of some strange, shiny material, thereby telling you everything you needed to know about where his limited expertise and real interests lay.

One foul, wet Mancunian afternoon Stack put his head in my face after I'd been downed by a hefty tackle in rugby and said: "Not such a pretty kid now, are you, Rocket Boy?"

But, unfortunately, Stack was right; my angelic looks went forever around puberty. That old chestnut: "He'll be real lady killer" was no longer heard among the family. A great-aunt did once bravely try to suggest that I looked like a young Robert Redford in some swish new pullover I'd got for Christmas, but the silence that greeted the idea said it all.

At some point in my teens, when everything your parents do is a source of embarrassment, my mum won a pie-baking competition which was held on a Manchester Evening Comet stall at an ideal homes' exhibition. It was bad enough that my mum, who's never been a person to blow her own trumpet, was misquoted as saying: "I spend a lot of time doing my own home-baking and therefore thought I must have a great chance of winning if I entered," making her sound both boring and conceited at the same time. But then it continued – you guessed it – with the piece of information that made "housewife Joyce Waiters, aged 41", really fascinating to Comet readers: "Her son, Simon…etc…Yuri Gagarin…etc…Rocket Boy etc…"

When I was 20, I was fined by Stockport magistrates for doing 42 in a 30 mile-limit area. I wasn't a boy racer, I just thought that I'd been driving through a 40 mph zone. Some eagle-eyed journalist must have noticed me on the charge sheet, because there I was on page three: Rocket Boy fined for speeding. Hard to resist, that one, I suppose, though I wish they'd at least had the decency to put inverted commas around my nickname.

You might wonder why everyone knew who I was. Well, as I've said it's a very rare surname and a framed picture of Yuri and me stood on the wall (and for all I know still does) close to the Evening Comet's reception desk, together with other great moments in Manchester history, such as Barbarolli conducting the Hallé, and Matt Busby and Bobby Charlton holding the European Cup in 1968.

The Comet was still on my tail in 1989, the year Helen and I got married. I was with Michael Summerbell in Manchester when a reporter hove into view, doing one of those 'vox-pops'. The question of the day was: "Should United sack Alex Ferguson?"

As United were near the bottom of the table, this was a subject that Michael and I had pondered at length. I've still got the press cutting somewhere but I don't need to look it up to tell you what it said, more or less word for word.

*Rocket Boy Simon Waiters is in no doubt – Ferguson must go. The little lad who captured Comet readers' hearts when he was pictured with first-man-in-space Yuri Gagarin as a three-year-old, has been a staunch Red since primary school days.*

*Simon, now 31, says: "There's no doubt about it, he's been given long enough. He's not been able to build on the early success, when he got us to the runners-up spot. Maybe the job's too big for him compared with Aberdeen, and he would have done better coming to England to a smaller club with lower expectations, like City."*

*But his friend, Michael Summerbell, also 31, disagreed. "I still think Alex is the best we've had for the job since Matt Busby. He'll turn it round, Rome wasn't built in a day, and Fergie's not the sort of bloke who looks to the short-term. Okay, if there's no improvement before the season is out then perhaps the directors should review the situation. But certainly not before then."*

# CHAPTER ELEVEN

## Where did my friends go?

I went to Manchester by train, to see Mum and Dad, a couple of days after reading Trevor Smith's essay. I used to choose my seat on the basis of who looked the least likely to start talking into a mobile phone, but that battle has been lost; we non-cell users are a rare breed now.

As I sat down, I smiled at the young woman with a small child sitting opposite me, as if to say: "I'm your travelling companion for the next hour and a half so I'm just saying I'm here". When she put a protective arm around the kid, I dug my Guardian out of my bag with excessive ceremony; in other words: 'Don't worry about it, you'll hardly notice me'.

I couldn't read. I'd developed a constant rat-a-tat in my head, like a woodpecker tapping away endlessly, spelling out the names of the lost non-loves in my life. If it's anything like this for Trevor, he must be going through hell, I thought, and locked up into the bargain to give him even more time to dwell on it all. For his Claire Daniels read my Lesley Linnell, the 1974 prototype.

But which of his girls would be my Anna Florenski?

"Oh for fuck's sake," I thought that I only thought to myself. "Les, Les, Lesley."

I stared out of the window for my favourite section of the journey, the mix of hilly rural and industrial landscape between Huddersfield and Stalybridge. When we entered a tunnel, the woman and child moved along to another seat, and a couple of teenagers smirked. So now I am off my trolley, it seems. I swear to myself in train carriages, in front of little kids. I'm a nutter. It's official!

When I'm feeling down, I sometimes think about the people I'll leave behind if any Great Architect decides that I've done enough damage for one lifetime and puts out an early call for me to report to HQ.

So who is there in my life? Well, there's Mum and Dad, naturally, Michael and Alison Summerbell, Auntie Laura and her post-Uncle Andrew chap Tony Jessop. And Bishen Patel. No, only joking about him, he's caused far too much bother. A few years ago I might have added Maurice Whittle, my best friend at university, but he's gone now, to all intents and purposes. Like Rupesh Ruia, pretty much Christmas cards. Not a big list for someone who has been on this Earth for more than 40 years.

I considered talking to Dad about my malaise but decided against it. He hadn't addressed his growing deafness which made communication on anything other than a rudimentary level hard work, and his constant search for key words would have led him to who knows what strange conclusion about my state of mind. We walked down to the newsagents' together. I wasn't saying much; I knew Dad had even more difficulty picking up words outdoors.

We'd always been remarkably similar, physically. Dad never had to look suspiciously at a milkman. We'd got the same build – 'like Fred Astaire' he used to say of himself – and he, with a teetotaller's head start, had managed to stay that way. A glance at Dad told me what I might be like in 36 years' time, if I looked after myself. And it went deeper than that; we'd both needed reading glasses at 40, so I figured that I could expect to keep my hair but go deaf at 70.

"Quiet, Simon," he said, as we walked past the Methodist Church where I used to go with Greg Hammond. I wasn't sure if he meant the day or me.

My old church was a nondescript, squat building that had gone up at the same time as the estate. The notice board announced proudly that on Thursday there would be a mega-zone, which must have meant something to someone. Minister: L Linnell, I read in smaller print. Did the Methodists think use of full names would lead to a dangerous personality cult?

"I see the flock's got a new shepherd, Dad."

"Sorry?"

"New minister," I said, pointing to the board to help him catch my drift. "Not seen that name before."

"Oh yes. It's a lady minister, too, Simon. Or used to be."

"Well, make your mind up, Dad. Man or Woman?"

"That's right," Dad said, as he often did when he hadn't heard.

Lady ministers. Why did my dad have to talk about ladies, as if the 20th century had never happened? And why did I have to get so worked up about something that had never previously bothered me? My father had no objection to women being ordained, or having decent jobs, even if they were still ladies to him. He called Afro-Caribbean people 'coloured' but he didn't dislike them, which was more important than whether his terminology was correct.

"So what's the L stand for, Dad? Is it Lesley Linnell?"

"Yes, but I was wondering how she spells it and if she's ever changed it."

"Why would she change the spelling of her name?" I asked.

"That's right."

I decided this line of enquiry might work better indoors when we weren't competing with traffic.

I allowed myself to speculate on whether it was the Rev Lesley Linnell. This also ended that day's futile attempts to think about something other than Trevor Smith's handiwork and its implications.

It was, after all, possible that my Lesley Linnell had gone into the Church. We'd met at a weekend Methodist church conference in North Wales when I was 16. She sat at the same table for supper with Greg Hammond and me. In such situations, my boys-only education usually let me down. Greg's left-leaning parents hadn't put him through any grammar-entrance exams. He went to a mixed

61

comprehensive and wasn't terrified of girls. He was also, if I'm going to be honest, better looking. I was average height, light-to-medium build, in fact nothing to give anyone doing an identikit picture after a crime much to work with. Looks-wise, as I've said, I'd peaked as a toddler and therefore never achieved the heart-breaker status predicted by the Manchester Evening Comet when I met Yuri Gagarin. My most distinguishing, if that's the right word, feature was the dull-brown, greasy hair I washed every other night to keep it in hand. At 16, Greg had just reached the magic six-foot mark. He wore his thick blond hair well below his ears, because his folks had a more relaxed attitude to these things than mine did. He was considered handsome verging on film-star, although my mum thought that his eyes were too close together and saw this as an indication of deceitful character.

"I can have sex legally now, Simon," he'd said to me on his 16th birthday, and I suspected he'd be off the mark pretty soon. Or perhaps that was his way of saying he'd already had it illegally. At the time, I thought the idea that any girl might one day consider going to bed, or even going out with me on a regular basis, utterly fanciful.

Despite all this, Lesley Linnell preferred me to Greg and I managed to talk to her in tolerably coherent sentences. There was no point in contemplating going out with her, however, because her dad was a doctor, putting her out of my league. And she was already doing A-levels. I didn't know much about girls but I understood that they didn't date boys who were younger than them.

"She might not be as old as you think, Simon. Fast stream or some such. She uses too much make-up – heavy on the blusher and even more so on the lip gloss," said Greg.

These weren't terms with which I was familiar but I liked the overall effect on Lesley; at that age I preferred girls to have a look that verged on what my mum would have called tarty.

"Actually, I think that she might be over-compensating," explained Greg.

"She might be what?"

Greg sighed to indicate his frustration that everything had to be spelled out to me.

"You know, over-compensating for the fact that, despite a pleasing figure, she looks androgynous."

"I think the word you're looking for is gamine."

"There's no accounting for tastes. Her voice is like a bloke too."

"She sounds husky, sexy even. She does look older," I added, trying to find reasons she wouldn't fancy me rather than approaching the issues from the more positive end.

"I'll make some inquiries for you," said Greg.

On the Sunday afternoon we had a football match. Greg claimed to have a pulled muscle, so that he could stand on the touchline and chat up another girl he'd got his eye on. At one point I saw him standing with Lesley, who, until half-time, shouted words of encouragement to me.

"Sorry, Simon, I don't think she's interested in going out with boys," Greg reported back later. "She doesn't want the commitment of a long-term relationship at the moment."

Well, that was something else I understood, even at 16. If a girl said she didn't want the commitment of a long-term relationship at the moment, there wasn't much point going back to her six months later to ask if she'd changed her mind.

"Did you say I fancied her?" I asked for form's sake.

"No. But I did get a few facts and asked her about when she was born, in fact I tried to dig out the exact month and everything. I really tried on your behalf."

"What'd she say?"

"She just said, 'Sorry, I don't play that game' and walked off. Don't understand what she meant by that, Sim. Anyway, she's probably a bit good for you, she'd only break your heart, so you're probably well out of it."

While Dad told me a story about the old neighbourhood, I kept replaying that conversation, or rather the Greg Hammond version. What were Greg and Lesley on about? Perhaps Hammond had played some kind of low trick, on top of undermining my confidence, which went without saying. It wouldn't have been the first time he'd given the impression of looking after my interests while doing the opposite.

That weekend marked Hammond's farewell to the Methodists, a couple of years before I also decided to throw in the religious towel. When the coach arrived back in Manchester Hammond announced that he had become a Marxist, a political stance incompatible with belief in God.

When we were all going our separate ways, Lesley ignored me. I put it down to some unfathomable difference between men and women, a code which I had failed to crack and probably never would. It meant that I could never be a success with girls. I was doomed to score idiotic own goals at crucial moments and, as no one would ever be able to explain what had gone wrong, these mistakes would be repeated until doomsday. This truth was etched indelibly on my mind. I thought about Lesley Linnell every day for about six months, and every other day for the next six. Gradually the memory faded to an occasional flickering image. I squeezed Lesley into a box, in a dusty corner of my head. She would lift the top very occasionally. "Did I have a big 21st birthday party? Am I married now? Have I got children?" she would ask, before slipping away once more.

Now, almost 30 years on, she had emerged with the force of a Jack-in-a Box. And the thing about a Jack-in-a-Box is that you can only put it back yourself.

Apart from the deafness, Dad was in good form, still taking Mum on holiday to warmer climes and employing the DIY skills that had mysteriously passed me by. I was admiring the recent decorating job in the living room, nifty for someone in his 70s, when Mum returned to the room with a cafetière of fresh coffee. It was good to have elderly parents living in a nice cosy semi, rather than a crumbling nursing home smelling of cabbage, boiled fish and urine.

I examined the framed photograph of me with gown, mortarboard and rolled-up degree certificate, Hereford 1979. I was half-smiling, but almost ruefully. On many visits here I'd speculated idly about what was going through my head at the moment that picture was taken. Maybe even then I was thinking of Wendy Thomas, and how she might have transformed my life.

"One girl at a time, one girl at a time. Let's concentrate on the Rev Les Linnell," I thought.

"Who's the new minister, Mum? Dad mentioned somebody."

"Lesley Linnell. From London but local originally, I think, and lovely with the children. And George is equally nice."

"George?"

"Lesley's special friend. They've won over everybody, even the old ones in the congregation."

What problem might the old ones have? Minister living over the brush, maybe; I always like the way that Mum doesn't consider herself an old one.

"Not married, then? Lesley and George, I mean?"

"Hardly, don't be a caution," she laughed.

"Perhaps they're just good friends, then."

"If you like," said Mum gently, as if I was ten years old again.

"Sorry, I've got you. George is gay, right? Slow off the mark there, Mum."

She laughed in the fetching way that must have brought admirers by the dozen in her youth. Once considered very pretty, Mum was now, with her white hair and kind, wrinkled face, like any other old woman; funny how age removes beauty and plainness. I sometimes wondered when they were younger whether she looked at Dad, and thought: "How the hell did I end up with him?" Those diary entries I came across from 1957 were very cryptic although they usually involved what she called her 'chuntering about Harold'. Occasionally, and most often on a Saturday, Mum had written C. About a year before I was born, this becomes: "No C, no bloody explanation." Michael Summerbell told me that C stood for condom, and therefore what No C was all about: my dad's reluctance to launch or even discuss Project Simon, and his unenthusiastic engagement after reluctantly removing the obstacle to creation of a new life.

I was about to pursue my line of enquiry about Lesley when Dad, who had lost the thread and was gazing out over the back lawn, put in a request for bourbons.

"We're very modern in the Methodists now, aren't we, Harold? And you know where to find them."

I'd stepped into a parallel universe where different fashions of discourse applied. I didn't know what anyone was talking about, apart from the biscuits. Dad scurried off to the kitchen to forage.

"Let's go on the patio as it's so grand out," he said when he returned with the tin.

The garden, Dad's pride and joy, had been a wilderness when my parents bought the house. He'd tamed it gradually over the years, with a short break in the mid 60s when I brought mates round to play football, until we were old enough to go to the park.

"Can't beat the month of May in England," I said.

"Lesley Linnell back on the scene. Won't do any harm to look her up," I thought.

# CHAPTER TWELVE

## My night as Elvis

There are so many Elvises around, you have to stake your claim early. I became the Meanwood Elvis; there was already a Headingley Elvis.

I'll never know what persuaded me to dress up like him for the tribute night on one of my dates with Helen Oldfield. My performing days hadn't stretched beyond a concert with the primary school recorder group when, as the only boy in the band, I had to stand in the middle. I'd mastered just four notes, so I could only play with one hand and was forced to mime my way through Yellow Submarine and a couple of tunes from old musicals. Retrospective humiliation; it only occurred to me later that the audience would have worked out my tactics and been nudging themselves as they watched "the cute boy who was pretending to play". Yes, aged 10, I was still cute. Still, I reckoned I could come out of retirement for one last gig. I could sing in tune and Helen, being an Elvis fan, might like it.

"Greetings, Simon. Hello again, Helen," said Fred, a non-Elvis, greeting us like long-lost friends when we returned to the Shoulder of Mutton for the King Tribute Night.

"You're not singing tonight then, Fred?"

"I'm just a compère, give someone else a chance to take the limelight. To tell the truth, I'd be uncomfortable in a performing capacity. It's the Elvis thing, I'm sure you understand."

I didn't but Helen said: "No one can really get him right, can they?"

"That's just it." Fred looked at her admiringly.

"You don't mind everyone else having a try though?" I asked.

"Not at all, not at all," Fred reassured us. "So long as it's done with integrity and out of love for the King, that's what counts."

Fred and Helen pondered this; I had a couple of pints for Dutch courage.

"And now," said Fred, when my turn came round, "it gives me great pleasure to introduce a personal friend of mine, making his debut here at the Shoulder. It's Simon Waiters, the Meanwood Elvis. He's singing The Wonder of You for all of us, but I'm sure there will be one person above all others in his heart, a very lovely lady called Helen, as he gives us his own interpretation of this special song."

Faced with that ultimatum I had little choice, shamelessly directing my imploring arms to Helen. She liked it, and so did Fred.

"Well, ladies and gentlemen, what a performance! I shouldn't be at all surprised if we hear an announcement before long about church bells."

The audience, sentimental after a surfeit of Elvises, applauded generously. You couldn't go so far as to describe my reception as rapturous, but I'd acquitted myself better than in my one-handed recorder playing days.

"I was proud of you," said Helen, as we sat in her Ford Sierra in the Shoulder of Mutton car park. "I had my doubts, but you pulled it off…"

"Thanks, Helen."

"…just about. Now promise me one thing."

"What's that?"

"Quit while you're ahead."

"I think I can safely agree to that, I don't think I'm cut out for a career in show business."

She leaned over, kissed me on the lips and smiled mysteriously.

"Penny for them," I said.

"Well, I was just thinking to myself while you were serenading me: 'I wonder what Spiro would have made of all this, Helen.' I'm not so sure he's equipped for Elvis nights in Yorkshire pubs."

I didn't think that necessarily counted against Spiro, who for all I know would have gone down a storm at a Demis Roussos tribute night in Crete. Nevertheless, a couple of months after our chance meeting in Halifax, my performance as the Meanwood Elvis had finally made me number one with Helen Oldfield.

I'd become fond of Helen in a low-key kind of way. We had a similar sense of humour which revealed itself in all sorts of odd ways. We would have fun with people's faces. A favourite game was Cross Betweens, watching out for anyone who was like the love child of two famous people. A couple of minutes' companionable silence in a pub would be followed by: "Michael Portillo and Madonna" or "John Major and Barbara Windsor."

Helen was good at this because she knew a lot of actors' names. She'd suddenly produce a Cross Between Joanna David and Danny Webb, people who turned up regularly in TV dramas but most of us couldn't put a name to. Then she'd say: "You know, Sonya from War and Peace and the guy who always plays white-collar villains and bent coppers." And, sure enough, Danny Webb would be on the box a few weeks later, as a detective inspector taking a back-hander from a drugs dealer.

Odd couples was one we liked, where you had to come up with unlikely male and female partners, such as Linford and Agatha Christie, or George and Kate Bush. Another favourite was Dream or Reality. I'd tell her something bizarre first thing in the morning such as: "In South Korea, you can only operate as a masseuse if you are blind" and she'd have to work out whether it was true, or if I'd just dreamed it.

I was never too concerned about Helen's split loyalties, especially when she said that Spiro was nothing remarkable in the looks department. I also considered that, if Helen was playing both home and away fixtures, the door remained open for me to have a few little adventures. I had not reckoned on the stakes being upped so suddenly. A few weeks after my Elvis triumph, Helen announced that Spiro was no longer part of the equation. He'd taken it well and wished us all the best for the future; I did think he might have put up more of a fight.

"So where do we go from here?" asked Helen, although it was not really meant as a question.

I weighed up my options. This wasn't the great love of my life but I would be 31 in a couple of months' time and she was 30; it didn't look like the big one was going to show for either of us. Maybe it was time to settle for something less than perfection. Helen was bright, nice looking, loyal and calmer than in my student days when her treatment by Greg must have made her unhappy. Plenty of blokes have settled for less.

"Where do we go from here? I suppose we tell Fred that his prediction was spot-on. Church bells or register office job, I'm easy either way."

"Register office will do nicely."

Elvis Presley had made his first major intervention in my life.

# CHAPTER THIRTEEN

## Russia's famous love machines

Historians will inform you that late 1979 was the high tide of the Soviet Union with its invasion of Afghanistan. It was also the year I went there, and a watershed in my friendship with Greg Hammond.

My dad was excited about our trip.

"I've told Archie all about it."

"Your commie friend in France?" I remembered. "I hope you didn't suggest that I was a fellow traveller."

"Not exactly."

"What do you mean, not exactly?"

"Well, I told him that you were sceptical but would probably come round to our way of thinking."

"We'll see," I said.

I'd been an imperceptibly left-wing liberal since I could first vote, thanks to Mum's timely interventions, and saw no reason to shift my stance.

"Actually, I did express one or two reservations to Archie," Dad said, deciding to come clean.

"Reservations? About my going?"

"No, about communism".

"Wonder how he'll take that."

"Nothing too serious, Simon. And I pointed out that, with Thatcher looking like a lame duck PM, it was a good moment for the Labour

Party to bring in a real socialist, like Tony Benn. Sonny Jim Callaghan can't cling on for ever."

"I'd go for Denis Healey myself," I said.

"Well you would. But I also told Archie that I've been wondering recently if the Scandinavians are closer to getting the balance right. Maybe you do need some forms of private enterprise, just so long as there are plenty of checks in place and vital services and the like are run by the government."

"Steady on, Dad, you'll be telling me you're a social democrat next."

I'd been about to start at teacher training college in Manchester when Greg Hammond said: "Let's go to Russia for a week some time before Christmas."

Hammond was a trainee reporter on a weekly newspaper in Stockport and, boy, was he full of himself.

"It's not a bad job, rather bland. Not sure journalism is for me long term. Keep me going for a few years until I'm ready to announce my arrival on the world stage as a writer of detective fiction."

He'd pronounced himself too smart for university life a couple of years earlier; this sort of thing was beginning to get on my nerves but at least you had to give him credit for acting on his beliefs. Hammond wasn't a guy to hang around once he'd made a decision.

"One thing I'd like, however, is one great journalistic 'scoop'; you know, something that people would forever associate with me. Like Woodward, Bernstein and Watergate," he added modestly. "Exposing some kind of scandal, as Fox and Finder are going to do but for real, of course." He was almost talking to himself now as he wrote the story.

"Who or what is Fox and Finder?"

We were on the plane to Moscow. Hammond's tongue had been loosened by a couple of drinks when he told me for the first time about his two made-up characters; a more healthy idea than my Bunbury because they were going to be used in a kosher enterprise, a series of books. Tom Fox and Sophie Finder were amateur sleuths

72

who worked on a local newspaper and always got to the truth before the cops. It didn't sound like pie in the sky, either; he seemed to know what he was talking about. In other words, an idea doesn't have to be a crap one just because it is Greg Hammond coming out with it.

Ideologically speaking, Hammond was still hard left. "I have shifted my stance," he admitted, "I'm rather more in sympathy now with Trotsky's concept of permanent revolution."

"We'd better keep that one from the Politburo."

Hammond had wanted to visit the Soviet Union since his conversion to Marxism at the end of his Methodist days and, Russian history having been one of my big things at university, I was happy to tag along. I did point out, while he was banging on about exploitation of the workers in Britain, that he didn't mind taking advantage of young Muscovite kids by packing two new pairs of Levis to sell at an inflated price. Neither was I delighted when, during the trip, he'd produced from his wallet the Manchester Evening Comet photo of me with Yuri Gagarin. "My friend as little boy (for some reason putting on a Russian accent as he pointed at me then placing his right hand about two feet off the ground, to make sure they'd got the message that it was an old picture) when he was very famous in England," he said, hoping that by association with me his Levis would command a higher price.

Our fellow travellers to Moscow and Leningrad were a mixed bunch. We were all pretty much joined at the hip as a party, not really willing or able to do much under our own steam. Hammond found common ground with the more politically committed travellers – there was one old chap who'd fought against the Nationalists in the Spanish Civil War – while others were just idly curious about the country which many people in those days thought might nuke us to extinction at any moment. I'd read a book by a former British Army General in which, during World War Three, the Russians dropped an H-bomb on Birmingham; I don't suppose it made him very popular with estate agents in the Midlands.

There was a bloke called Alan Tipping in our party. The name stuck because of our guide Natalya's heavy-handed roll call at Moscow airport. At first I thought Natalya was a bossy Russian version of Miss Dean and Mr Warboys. Later, I appreciated that she was nervous; couriers who mislaid tourists in the old Soviet Union would not have received the Order of Lenin.

There was much hilarity when she ran through our names alphabetically.

"Mr Tipping?"

"Yes."

"Mr Waiters."

"Yes. Tipping always welcomed."

Alan got really worked up while we were being shown around the Lenin Museum.

"Lenin decided that when the right moment arrived, Soviets – councils of workers, soldiers and peasants – should be the instruments of total revolution," said Natalya, emotionally.

"Gosh, sounds like a hot potato, this Lenin," said Alan.

"I've heard it all now," said Hammond later. "The most important political figure of the 20th century described as a hot potato. Maybe you could set it as one of your history essays: "Discuss, in depth, this culinary analogy and its importance in the establishment of the USSR.""

"Well, we're not all as sophisticated as you are, Greg," I pointed out.

"Even so, how can you visit the Soviet Union and not know who Lenin is?"

"Alan might be having us on. Haven't you noticed that he's actually braver than any of us? He wanders off alone, despite Natalya's warning against doing so," I pointed out. "He knows some Russian, too."

"Really?" said Hammond. "There must be a straightforward explanation." He appeared to give this some brief consideration but was interrupted by the arrival at the hotel bar of two pretty Australians, together with us the youngest members of a mainly middle-aged and elderly party. You could usually rely on girls to take his mind off the matter in hand.

The following evening the four of us decided to skip the grim hotel meal (I'd got in trouble with the waiter over my caviar when the old swede-spreading-round-the-plate-trick failed) and seek out a restaurant. We battled through the sort of weather that had made Russia such a tough gig for Napoleon and Hitler before finding a massive, two-tiered barn of a place which looked like an old circus venue. In the circular, higher section, diners overlooked an arena where a big band played Russian folk melodies with a few American show tunes woven in cunningly. I spied Alan Tipping chatting comfortably with a wild Russian who could have been a young Rasputin. I invited them both to join us, as much to irritate Hammond as anything else.

"You seemed to be getting on well with your Russian there, Alan," I said.

"No, it was just pidgin stuff," he said. "Ivan here's English is better than my Russian."

"Russia's famous love machine is fluent in English?" I asked.

The Aussie girls and, more reluctantly, Hammond, laughed. Alan's lack of knowledge of 1970s Euro-disco hits let him down, and Ivan was equally mystified but happy to be the centre of attention.

"I like you, Simon," he said.

"Er, talk us through the menu, Alan," I said. "No need to be modest."

Alan obliged, pretending to make heavy weather. Ivan approved his choices and reiterated his approval of me. Alan went into unnecessary detail about his dull Civil Service job and his Russian night class, and things took a turn for the worse when the bills arrived.

"I like you, Simon," Ivan said, picking up his tab, "but for this I no money."

"Tough," said Hammond.

An angry exchange between the two Russians (Alan shrugged to us as if to say "don't understand a word") ended with Ivan throwing his chair at the waiter. Christ, I didn't think that things worked this way in the USSR.

"You – no money, no coat," the waiter said in English.

We had a whip round, the only thing we could do in the circumstances, and a coated Ivan waved us off cheerfully as if this happened to him every night, which maybe it did.

"I like you all, but I like you special, Simon."

It had been a great evening, even if Hammond, Foxing and Findering and generally getting too full of himself with his latest conquest, was stretching my patience ever more. Shortly after we returned, Hammond got a job on the Bolton Evening News. He moved away and our ties were loosened, although the final showdown was a few years down the line.

I'd expected a hero's welcome from Dad when I flew in from Leningrad; red bunting, and hammer and sickle flags draped around the garden gate at the very least. But he wasn't even in the house to greet me. As I stood talking to Mum, Dad waved from the bottom of garden but he didn't down tools immediately, pump his fists and come rushing to the kitchen.

"We've had a nasty shock," said my mum, "a letter from that Archie Macash. What a horrible little man, I feel as if he's walked in here and defecated in our hallway."

"Blimey, Mum, that's putting it strongly. So, Archie wasn't hugely impressed by my visit to his Motherland?"

"I don't think he even mentioned that. And Harold had written him such a nice note. Your dad really was upset, close to tears I would say and you know that's not really like Harold at all."

"What the hell did he say? I'm not so sure whether I want to read that or not," I said.

"I got the impression that he did want you to have a look," said Mum. "You know your dad, though; he'll do it in his own time when he's good and ready."

I shared some of my traveller's tales with Mum: enigmatic Alan Tipping, freeloading Young Rasputin and the brawl in the restaurant.

"I suppose that's the sort of thing that's likely to happen when you hang around with Gregory Hammond," she said. "He could have got you both arrested over that jean-selling business."

You're probably wondering why I'd hooked up with Hammond in the first place. You can blame, indirectly at least, Michael Summerbell's redneck father who had no time for "the coloureds".

Once Michael was established as a regular rainy-day passenger in Mrs Ruia's Ford Zodiac he became my best friend. He'd given up on his dad's view of dark-skinned immigrants; Michael was also sweet on Rupesh Ruia's younger sister, Nadia, which probably helped. In fact none of Michael's old man's opinions or commands ever made much impression on him. It was something that I, with my feeble line-of-least-resistance policy on just about everything, admired.

Michael slouched his way through comprehensive school, before taking a string of jobs from trainee hairdresser to supermarket shelf stacker. His dad, a self-made director of a small engineering company, had offered increasingly desperate financial rewards for academic success. Michael was on £100, a tidy sum in 1974, to get five or more O-levels. He managed two and his dad was not amused when he said: "Where's me £40 then?"

But, here's the rub, I only heard of this later. Michael slipped off the radar for a few years in my teens. A couple of Asian families had moved into the neighbourhood.

They became friends of the Ruias, so Tom Summerbell decided that "they were taking over" and that it was time to head for sweet Cheshire-Derbyshire border country; I doubt that Michael's timid mother was consulted much about this move. Our contact was therefore intermittent for a few years during which Greg Hammond, previously a marginal figure, became the main lad I hung around with.

Michael re-emerged suddenly in Manchester when we were 21, just after I finished university. He heard that I was back at home and got in touch. He remained on the chunky side, but he had slimmed down and his head was more in proportion. He'd sorted out his teeth and, though he still looked pleased with himself, it was more contentment than conceit. He was working in a gentleman's outfitters and living in a flat with his girlfriend, Alison, a secretary.

I was deeply, deeply impressed; I thought you only left home at that age to go to university; otherwise you went from living with your mum and dad to living with your wife. I always felt Michael was ahead of the game; marrying Alison at 23, two nice kids within a few years, buying his council house in the 1980s. By then he'd done A-levels at night school and gone on to UMIST to do a management sciences degree. Turned out he'd inherited some of his father's entrepreneurial skills. He went on to do well for himself in the promotional gifts business, although too late for his old man's approval. Tom Summerbell had a fatal heart attack at 50 and never saw Michael begin to fulfil his promise. Michael's lads were turning out to be bright sparks, too.

Actually, Mum could have been reading my Soviet-week thoughts about Hammond. It occurred to me more than once that it would be good to resume my friendship with my old mate and get to know Alison better.

# CHAPTER FOURTEEN

## Nevertheless

Does anyone ever really, the way you read in the papers, pinch themselves to make sure that they are wide awake? Well, I've just learned, they must do. I've been doing it all morning. What it confirms, as they say on the National Lottery, is that the woman who rang me just before I left for the prison really was Wendy Thomas.

The voice, slightly breathless, did not sound familiar.

"Is that Simon Waiters? My name is Wendy Carr."

"*The* Wendy?" I said, because I'd been thinking about her the other day.

"Well that's highly flattering but rather unlikely," she laughed, composing herself. "We've not met for 20 years, it was at university in Hereford."

"How strange, you sound just like another Wendy who was a teaching colleague at my first school," I improvised. Had I still been pals with Greg Hammond, I'd have assumed that he'd paid some woman to play a hilarious practical joke on me.

"Wendy from university days," I said. "Weren't you – just let me think now – weren't you Wendy Thomas?"

"I was! I heard your name on the radio, on Sound of the Sixties. Nevertheless, by The Election, was it?"

"The Eclection."

"Oh yes, what a lovely tune. You do remember me, then?

"Of course I do. Would you like to meet up, Wendy?" I said, pronouncing her name with relish.

"That would be lovely, too. We, er I'm, in Scarborough, and I come over to York on my own now and then."

She gave no more information other than that she lived in a district between Scarborough and Filey. She gave me her mobile number and said that was the way to contact her. "Not the landline", she emphasised.

Why the subterfuge? I guessed that I would find out soon enough when we met up.

I was sharing this news with Michael Summerbell when I drove over to see him the following day.

"I remember that name," he said. "Remind me what went wrong."

"Who said anything went wrong?"

"You didn't have to."

I also told him about Trevor Smith, and the way he was messing around with my head.

"He's just the messenger, isn't he?"

"Is he?"

"Of course. Or maybe catalyst is the word I'm looking for. If it hadn't been him, someone or something else would have set you off. We've all got baggage. Mostly it's tucked away then, suddenly, it's in your face and you've got to deal with it. I reckon you're going through a midlife crisis, Simon. It can happen to anyone."

"Even you?"

"Sure, I went through a phase of getting mad with myself for wasting my time as a kid and having so much catching up to do. And I never got the chance to play the field like you 'cos I settled down so early."

"Nobody played the field like me, or if they did I feel sorry for them."

"Maybe, but you know what I mean."

"So you've had the odd regret about that?"

"Very briefly, but I got it out of my system. You've got to admit that we're cosmetically differentiated, Mrs Summerbell and I. I'm on a good number."

This was true enough; Alison looked better now than when she was a 19-year-old secretarial student. She was also one of life's great listeners which was a nice characteristic, although it did mean that you could never get away with anything; she committed everything you told her to memory.

"Wouldn't you be better exploring some fresh avenues?" she said, when she realised that I was on the trail of Wendy Thomas. I thought it best not to mention Lesley Linnell as my long shot. "What do we know about this girl? Did she mention a husband? Perhaps he's got a history of violence and will come after you."

"Great, you're certainly covering all the angles there, Alison."

"Tread carefully, my dear," she said. "You know who I've always thought might have been a good one for you?"

"A good one. Go on, astonish me."

"Melanie Cohen."

"You are joking? I didn't think you'd ever met her. It was a couple of years before your time."

"I didn't. I just liked the sound of her, the way you talked about her once when you were in your cups. She must have had something about her and I reckoned she was very smitten with you."

'In your cups', 'very smitten'; Alison was full of old-fashioned expressions like that.

"I've heard it all now. Melanie Cohen was always having a go at me. She was politically correct in the days before anyone had come up with the term. For a while I thought she was a lesbian, though I found out later I'd been given duff information."

"I'm not sure what political correctness and being or not being a lesbian have got to do with one another, but I'm guessing the informant was Greg Hammond," said Alison.

"True," I conceded. "Melanie was scary, she messed it up between Gill Todd and me. She was very against all sorts of things."

81

"Poverty, military dictatorships?" suggested Alison.

"Those I suppose, but trivial things, too. The Miss World Contest, the Black and White Minstrels." I didn't mention that she lost her rag over some unwise words of mine in an Indian restaurant. "I mean, we didn't worry much about those things then, did we?"

"Well, maybe we bloody well should have done. Just because Melanie was politically correct on some things doesn't mean she was always wrong. Anyway, you were well out of it with that Gill Todd."

"Bloody hell, Michael. She's pitiless your lass, isn't she?"

"She's hard but fair," Michael allowed.

This was true enough. Alison had come up with a few choice words when she heard about my betrayal of Helen.

"Well maybe I've got the wrong end of the stick, but I can only go on what you said to me," she told me now.

As I've said, there are the lost girls who rake up thoughts of what might have been. Then there are the Melanie Cohens of this world, Gill Todd's sidekick, whose legacy is harder to pin down. During that brief but golden era with Gill, Melanie was always in my face, asking endless questions and challenging my view of the world.

Gill was never ready when I went round, she'd be upstairs, emerging from a shower or talking to someone on the phone. This would give Melanie her chance to corner me. One night I was telling her about a film I'd seen on television, The Watermelon Man.

"It was weird. This bigoted white guy turns into a black man overnight," I said.

"What happens?"

"In the end, he faces up to remaining black forever."

"You mean he just has to accept his lot," snorted Melanie. "Get a job clearing tables or, if he's lucky, as a school janitor."

There was more to the film than that, I thought later; I'd missed a chunk because someone rang in the middle. I lost the thread, but he appeared to have turned into a campaigner for black people's rights. Melanie always made me nervous and I either failed to express myself properly or started conversations I couldn't see through.

She was almost beautiful and had a wonderfully husky voice, but she was determined not to be admired for that, or for her dark eyes, perfect white teeth and olive skin. Her thick black hair looked as though it had been fashioned with garden shears and she wore dungarees which didn't do her any favours. She had a curious soft spot for Gary Glitter, a fact she trotted out habitually as if to refute the charge that she had no sense of humour.

One evening, she challenged me about the way that Gill had asked me out, something considered forward for women in those days, rather than waiting for me to take the initiative.

"What would you have said if it had been me doing the asking, Simon?"

"I'd have said I was washing my hair."

This throwaway quip made her furious. My tendency to rely on facetiousness when the conversation got beyond me, into politics for example, would inevitably rebound. Determined to improve my political education, she suggested one evening that we might go to a Communist Party meeting together. "The guest speaker's subject is Finland and the Soviet Union, a peaceful coexistence," she said temptingly.

"I'm meeting a pal that night," I said quickly, while wondering who Gill was nattering to on the phone in the other room.

"What a pity," Melanie said, a little crestfallen. "Anyone I know?"

"Old friend from Rusholme, Bishen Patel," I said, thinking Melanie might be dazzled to learn that one of my friends was not white. Although why the need to impress her, who knows?

"Right," she said. "He could come along as well."

"Not quite his thing, traditional family," I said.

"Okay," she said, admitting defeat.

It was hard to think of a woman less likely to appeal to Greg Hammond. However, big-hearted me was in love and I was determined that everyone else should be. With a bit less generosity I might have been spared the humiliation that followed.

# CHAPTER FIFTEEN

## Shakespeare and other buggers

There's no point in having this on hold any longer, I might as well get it over with. This is how I loved and lost Gill Todd...

My primary school sweetheart had come back into my life while I was working at a dairy during the summer of 1977. I was humping around the crates of empty milk bottles brought in during the morning by the roundsmen. I'd been reading Zen and the Art of Motorcycle Maintenance which was all the rage then, so I was thinking about that and what it was supposed to be about, then trying to empty my head of anything much, to make time move on more quickly, when I became aware of a voice calling me.

"Hey. You."

The young lass standing a few feet below me loading her milk crates onto the ramp was wearing tight, faded blue jeans, a small waist-length denim jacket and a Stranglers' Rattus Norvegicus t-shirt. She'd got a roll-up cigarette tucked behind her right ear, visible because her wavy blonde hair was cropped so closely. She looked like a boyish Roman emperor, a point emphasised by her aquiline nose, which she rubbed a couple of times, as if faintly conscious of it.

"Hey, you. Can you give us a hand with this lot, I'm running late."

"Sure," I said jumping down from the ramp.

"One of the guys told me you're Simon Waiters."

"That's right."

"The Simon Waiters?"

"There aren't many of us around."

"You haven't changed at all, Pet."

"Since?"

"1966…Oi'm still a tomboy," she said, to help me along.

"Tomboy?"

"Oi'd of played for the football team if oi'd of been a boy."

"Blimey, Gill Todd."

"He got there in the end," she said, as if to an audience.

"Last time I saw you, you bowled me out in the playground at Old Oak. I was under par, chicken pox on the way. Er, not that I'm making excuses, it was a good delivery. In fact the previous couple of balls…."

"Okay, okay," she interrupted, "oi was pretty quick for a seven-year-old, though oi don't suppose oi'd've made anything more than a useful medium pacer."

"You seem to be the only milk lady here. How do you manage that?"

"Woman," she corrected. "I applied like anyone else."

"Er, right, woman. How long have you been doing it?"

"Long enough. You a college boy?"

"Yeah, Hereford. I'm doing History and English."

"What's English involve? A girlie course, isn't it?" she said, slamming down a couple of crates on the ramp with unnecessary force. I'd thought about Gill often enough down the years. She looked fantastic, and she hadn't lost her feisty edge.

"It's literature mainly," I said, trying to pitch my explanation at an understandable level for a milk woman, without being patronising. "From modern writers like James Joyce and T S Eliot, to old writers like Chaucer and Shakespeare."

"Who was that other bugger?" she said, "The Oirish one who thought he was better than Shakespeare?"

"What did he write? Plays, poems or novels?"

"Why do you assume oi'm talking about a man? Could be a woman. Oi mean it isn't as it happens, but it could of been. Think he moight of written plays."

I was stumped for words for a few seconds.

"Alroyt, Simon. Just a merry jest, you can take me out for a drink this weekend if you loyk."

"Shaw," I said.

"Good, where?" she asked.

"No, I meant it must be George Bernard Shaw. The Irishman."

"So, you don't want to go out with me?"

"Well, yeah, sure. I mean, course I do."

Greg Hammond, working nights in a biscuit factory to pay off the debts to his marijuana dealer, had some advice.

"Take it from me, Simon, all this radical feminist malarkey is a front. Give her a good time somewhere nice, gallons of Babycham, pay for everything. If you treat her like a lady, you'll get your reward."

I thought a fancy wine bar, in the centre of town near Albert Square, might do the trick.

"It's Hoyde's or Boddington's for me."

"We won't get that in a wine bar," I said.

"Precisely."

"You one of those real ale people?"

"What if oi am?"

"No that's fine, it's not as if I was planning on plying you with, er, the genuine champagne perry."

"Foin. There's a good Hoyde's pub in Portland Street."

We met in a small, neat bar that was unlike any I'd entered with Greg Hammond or Maurice Whittle. Gill was looking impressive in a plain white t-shirt and tight, bottle-green crushed velvet trousers.

"Yes, love?" said the middle-aged barmaid; she seemed pleased to see us.

Space was at a premium but working men, office types and an elderly couple shared it comfortably. I assumed that Gill would want a pint and I asked for two bitters. The beer pump was a kind of cylindrical glass dispenser, in which the ale swished from side to side as the barmaid flicked a handle one way then the other. I dipped in tentatively and it didn't taste anywhere near as revolting as I'd expected.

Gill made no comment on receiving a pint but a faint smile told me that I'd made the right call.

"Not so bad is it?" she said, suddenly minus the Hampshire twang. "Perhaps we'll be able to educate your palate after all."

I raised my eyebrows. "I lost the accent years ago," she said. "Well before I came back here to university."

"So you're doing the milk round as a holiday job? Why didn't you tell me?"

"I'm a wind-up merchant, I suppose. You figured that I looked the part so I thought I'd string you along a bit."

"So what are you doing, then? At university, I mean."

"What would you expect an unreliable narrator like me to be interested in?"

"English?"

"The girlie subject. Right."

"Oh."

"You sound disappointed."

"Why should I be?"

"Yes you are, college boy," she said, giving me a playful nudge. "Oi suppose that you'd of felt more secure with an innocent dairy maid."

She was right; she'd stooped to conquer. Gill now started talking about Eng Lit in a manner that made her sound like a candidate for a first-class degree. She had a better job with the dairy than me and she was independent enough to have stayed in Manchester for the vacation instead of going back to her mum and dad in Portsmouth. I wasn't in the same league. Why couldn't she just have been a milk woman?

"Looks like we're both keen on old writers and new writers," she said, "but oi can always pretend to be a dairy maid if that's the way you prefer me."

So, I made the first of those visits to the terraced house in Moss Side where Gill was never ready, and it was always Melanie Cohen who answered the door.

Gill set about widening my horizons. She introduced me to decent beer and European films ("Get a grip, what's so bloody hard about a few subtitles?"), two things I still thank her for. And on the night of our second date, she offered me a useful practical lesson, too.

I'm not wild about descriptions of sex in books or films. In an ideal world, the door shuts and we cut to the couple sharing a post-coital cigarette. However, I can hardly gloss over such an epic moment with Gill.

"It's only fair to let you know...," she said.

"You're not a virgin?"

"Not exactly what I was about to say. I always expect – nay I insist, Simon – on an orgasm."

This was alarming. Looking at the walls, while playing for time with my response, I saw nothing to soothe. I had been in a couple of girls' bedrooms before without making much progress; they were home to cuddly toys, pictures of David Cassidy and The Osmonds, and Desiderata posters. But this was grown-up stuff. Karl Marx looked down sternly, and Germaine Greer and Susan Sontag delivered less than cordial messages to any male readers – quite a few I was now beginning to appreciate – who had ventured into Gill's lair. The only representatives of the music world, The Slits, gave me a fuck-off sign. I wondered if Melanie might be standing behind the door, tut-tutting hypocritically in the light of her own legions of lovers, and making notes on a clipboard.

"Only joshing again, Simon," Gill said, "special exemption for first-timers."

Under the sheets I decided that a list might be a good delaying tactic, and set about trying to name United's team in the 1968 European Cup Final: Stepney, Brennan, Dunne, Stiles, Foulkes, Crerand, Best, Kidd, Charlton, Sadler...what a pity that Denis Law, my all-time football hero, missed out because of injury. Anyway, who played outside left? He was the man of the match, for Christ's sake.

I'd hit the spot; Gill let out a sudden cry of ecstasy.

"Johnny Aston," I said, unable to hang out any longer.

Gill lit the roll-up she'd had ready on her bedside table.

"Beginner's luck," she said, taking her first drag.

I invited Gill round to meet my parents. She wasn't a big hit with Mum who went so far as to suggest later than she was a "bit of a clever clogs". Gill's observation that I was "a grumpy little bear" first thing in the morning had been catastrophic, once the penny dropped.

"I rather think you should spare us those details," she said sniffily while Dad, not a man for confrontation, played around with the contents of his wallet.

Uncle Andrew saved the day by turning up in his latest motor, Hazel. He was more enthusiastic about Gill than Mum had been, and I basked in a glow of pride when he complimented me on my tastes via a surreptitious wink and thumbs up. Gill, learning of my uncle's trade, suggested that property was theft, but Andrew was too enamoured with her to take offence.

"How's the Stag, Andrew?" said Mum.

"Great on a good day, not the most reliable motor I've had, certainly takes some handling."

"Bit like you then, Andrew," said Dad, keen to keep the exchanges light.

"Wow, you've got a Triumph Stag," said Gill.

"You've no objection to nice motors, then?" said Andrew.

"Oi can't help myself, once a tomboy, oi'll always be a tomboy, I suppose."

"I should take you for a spin in her sometime."

"Her?" said Gill, indignantly. "And are you one of these people who gives cars female names as well?"

Just as well that Melanie's not here, too, I thought.

"Oh no, of course not," said Andrew hastily.

"That would be very childish," agreed Dad.

"Hi Hi Hazel," I said.

"He calls the car Hi Hi Hazel?" said Gill.

"No, no, I was just trying to remember the names of two old Troggs' obscurities. Hi Hi Hazel, and, er, Night of the Long Grass."

"You really have got a butterfly mind, Simon," said Gill.

Mum was vexed by Gill; it was all right for her to say I'd got a butterfly mind, not for some girl who'd taken my innocence when she had only known me for two weeks. Uncle Andrew, pondering a contribution to the debate about my shortcomings, thought better of it, maybe because I'd let him off the hook about Hazel.

"Good girl that, no harm in fillies who speak their mind," he said to me as we left after lunch.

I was sure that I was in love, although I did fret over whether she felt the same. For the first time in months, I was able to put Wendy Thomas and the Hereford Easter Ball incident finally into a little section of my brain marked unpleasant memories, with the lid slammed down like the old Hartley's Jam advertisement where all the flavour's being sealed in.

Melanie was tricky, though. For all her talk of a woman's right to assert herself, she had a quaintly old-fashioned disapproval of my overnight stays.

"Perhaps she'd be up Greg's street," I said to Gill, who had told me that Melanie, despite protestations that she didn't need a man "to make her complete", was looking for love.

In late August, Gill's dairy days were coming to an end. She was going to Italy for a couple of weeks with Melanie. We piled into Hammond's mum's Mini and made a foursome at an Indian restaurant in Rusholme. In those days the Manchester curry mile wasn't so well developed. Some of the joints were unrefined although none the worse for that, especially if you were on a student grant. We went into a basic mop-it-up-with-chapattis place where you could take your own booze.

The funny thing about one of the lousiest evenings of my life was that, for the first half hour or so, I was getting on well with Melanie. I started on the right foot when we walked in and Greg Hammond commented on the appalling Bengali pop music, which featured one of those dreadful female singers with high-pitched voices and no bass notes.

"There's one good thing to be said for it," I said.

"Nothing springs to mind," said Melanie.

"It isn't Elvis bleeding Presley."

"You've got a point," she agreed.

"Give me your mate Gary Glitter, he's naff but he's funny," I said.

Elvis had died a few weeks earlier, an event which didn't move me one way or the other. That summer you couldn't get away from his music and the endless tributes.

I told Melanie that jazz was my thing. She said that her dad had some 78 recordings of Jelly Roll Morton playing with the Red Hot Peppers. I was excited about the prospect of hearing and actually handling them, when the subject arose during the main course of what we would do after university.

"I'm going to be a professor," said Gill. "Probably in the US. Better money there for academics."

"You're going to need a first just for starters," said Hammond.

"That shouldn't be a problem, I'm one of only three or four potential firsts in the department and the others are no great shakes. I've already identified some areas worth exploring for my MA."

"Time shifts and memory in the novels of Muriel Spark," I said, like an eager puppy.

Greg sneered but didn't make the expected observation about the futility of academic life; someone with Gill's formidable intellect would have a few killing responses at her disposal.

"What about you, Simon?" said Melanie.

"I'm not sure. I always said I'd never teach but I've been thinking that I might give it go."

"Kiddies beware," said Hammond, putting a spoonful of raita on to a poppadom.

"I think you've got to be more committed than that, I had too many teachers who'd just drifted into it," said Gill.

"That doesn't follow," said Melanie. "I bet a lot of people who go in full of high ideals about something they've always wanted to do are no good when they're faced with the reality of the classroom."

She looked at me almost fondly and added: "I think Simon would be a very good teacher indeed."

"So, what are you going to do then, Melanie?" said Hammond quickly, words of praise for me a virus that had to be eradicated before it ran riot.

I braced myself for a diatribe about feeding the world and saving the whale but all she said was: "I've thought about social work but I'm not sure if it's really for me."

"You'll probably think about it a bit more, then decide you'd rather make piles of money," said Gill.

There was an uncomfortable silence while we dipped into our meals. I almost asked Gill to explain herself, then decided that I didn't want to fall out with her. Melanie looked at me as if expecting that I would spring to her defence. I hesitated, assuming that Gill surely didn't mean what it sounded as though she meant, then remained silent.

Hammond said: "You do all realise that the best arts graduates go into the publishing business, the second best go into journalism and the rest go into school teaching?"

"You'll be a school teacher, then," said Gill.

"I'll be going into publishing via journalism. I'll start on a local newspaper," said Greg.

"My apologies," said Gill. "You're obviously going to be a second-rate graduate, rather than a third-rate one."

"Who said anything about being any sort of graduate?" said Greg.

"Don't be so pessimistic, you'll probably get a pass degree," said Gill.

"I wouldn't bank on it," said Melanie.

I was beginning to feel sorry for Hammond: it wasn't nice being picked on by both women.

"This rogan josh is good," I said.

Gill winked as if to reassure me that she was just having a little fun, that she hadn't expected our attempts at playing cupid between Greg and Melanie to be successful, and that it didn't really matter.

However, that wasn't the real cause of my growing unease. As I looked around at the other tables, I hoped in vain that Greg wouldn't recall a way to cause me some embarrassment.

"Expecting to see someone you know, Sim."

As I said, in vain; here it comes.

"No." I blushed at the apparently innocuous question.

Greg's face lit up at the possibility of a little mischief. "Aren't we in Bishen Patel territory here?"

"Oh yes, Bishen, you mentioned him, didn't you, Simon?" said Melanie. "You said he was from round here."

"You call him Bill, don't you?" said Greg. "Wouldn't you be better respecting him for what he is. I've always suspected there was a bit of cultural imperialism in that friendship."

"It's his decision to call himself Bill," I protested.

Greg was pleased at my discomposure, then he looked more doubtful. Bishen Patel had become my imaginary friend, my Bunbury, and Greg was the only person who knew this because I'd unadvisedly confided in him. Perhaps he now realised that all I had to do was come clean about the Bunbury story, Gill and Melanie might even have seen the funny side to it. That's exactly what I was going to do but then I stopped myself. The trouble was, I was beginning to think Melanie wasn't so bad after all and she for all her earnestness had some kind of soft spot for me. I couldn't hurt her feelings now by saying that I'd used an imaginary friend to avoid going with her to a Communist Party meeting.

Greg watched me suffering then, deciding I wasn't going to come clean, delivered the decisive blow.

"What about the rest of the family? I don't expect that Mrs Patel calls her lad by any other name than Bishen. But then I know you've never been to his house or met his parents. I mean there's a limit to how close you want to get to our Commonwealth cousins, isn't there?"

"He's not a close friend, then," said Melanie.

"Not really," said Greg.

The heat was suddenly on me.

"Simon, isn't that rather patronising?" said Melanie sorrowfully.

"I can see why you chose to answer a question on Kipling in your end of years," said Gill. "It all fits into place, doesn't it? It's all tied up with your cosy, lower middle-class, petty bourgeois complacency."

All three of them stared at me malevolently, as if I'd wandered in from a National Front meeting. I felt the beginnings of tears pricking up in my eyes at the sheer injustice.

"This is all total fantasy," I said.

"You'd know about that, of course," said Hammond, giving me a significant look.

"So you're a Paki lover now, are you?" I asked Hammond desperately, in a bid to get away from Bill Patel. I couldn't believe I'd said that, but there it was. And my timing couldn't have been worse; in between records during a lull in the conversation at every other table. A couple of diners looked in our direction and tried to identify the white supremacist.

"Rich coming from you, that," I said.

"Are you accusing me of being a racialist?" said Greg. "That's a very, very serious allegation."

"No, course not. Sorry."

Melanie, suddenly pals with Greg, looked at him sympathetically.

"Why don't you just call me a Yid to my face, while you're at it, Simon?"

"I'd never say anything like that. It was just a slip of the tongue."

Gill looked at me as if she'd been conned into dating the English department's lavatory cleaner. If I'd been more sophisticated I could have got out of this hole, I thought later; I was being ironic, I was using the term 'Paki' to make a point, I might have said, about Greg. He certainly was a racialist, as we used to say in those days. He routinely referred to black people as touched with the tar brush. Not an expression you hear much these days. Instead I got flustered, as I always did when faced with outbreaks of hostility. I should have gone on the offensive but wasn't sure enough of my ground. And yes, I can see now that I should have targeted Gill's jugular. Wasn't there a whiff of anti-Semitism in something she'd just said? Come to think of it (as, once again, I did hours later as I tossed and turned in bed) hadn't she described me as "looking like a little Jew boy" because my school cap was too small? As I lay in turmoil, a few hours later, the best excuse of all for skipping her abject Finnish-Soviet love-in hit me between the eyes. "No thanks, Melanie, my dad reckons he's a communist, so I can get all that at home as I've been doing all my life."

"His generation knows all about fascism," says Melanie. "That doesn't mean he's got to be a communist," says I. "If indeed that's what he really is," adds I. "You are one patronising shit if you can't respect the integrity of your father's viewpoint," replies Melanie.

Hang on, you're thinking. I never told her about my dad's communism, so she couldn't have said that. True; and if it's mad to mull pointlessly over things that should not have been said, how much more imbecilic to imagine how an argument which never took place might have panned out, basing it on the prejudices you hold against your adversary.

In the Rusholme restaurant, Melanie, on the verge of tears, had looked more vulnerable than I'd seen her before. A walking-out and banging of chairs and doors seemed to be on the cards, and that's what we got after she'd wolfed down a few, final forkfuls of vegetarian bhuna.

"I've had enough of listening to this. You're all as bad as one another. I'll make my own way home," said Melanie, putting her contribution to the bill on the table and leaving us to sort it out.

"I'd better go after her," said Gill, leaving an unfinished veggie korma and no money.

"I'll phone you," I said.

"If you like."

I gestured hands-up to the waiter, to let him know that we weren't all doing a runner. There was a strange look on Greg Hammond's face now. It was one of exhilaration that he'd persuaded the others to join in the attack, combined with shock, as if he realised that even he had gone too far.

"Shit, I'm really sorry about that, Sim," he said eventually. "I didn't really mean to land you in it that much. But look at it this way, you're well out of it."

"How can you say that?" I asked, incredulous but looking for something to cling on to.

"Look at those histrionics, and Gill rushing out to make friends again. They're obviously an item aren't they? They're lesbians."

"Rubbish, where's your evidence?"

"They're just the types aren't they?"

"I'm sure that Melanie would have something to say about such pigeon-holing."

"Just look at them. They've both got bog-brush hair…"

"Gill's is stylish," I protested.

"If you like choir boys," said Greg. "Thing is that they've both got feminist agendas and they are both vegetarians. The whole thing is an aggressive statement. And don't you think it's odd that you share a house with someone and then go on holiday together?"

"Not particularly," I said.

"Come on, look at them. A) One of them tries to look as much like a boy as she can, even if, okay, she's shaped like a woman, as you seem, thank goodness, to have found out."

"And B)?"

"The other tries to conceal the fact that she's potentially top totty by not shaving that down above her lip. I bet she's got hairy legs."

"A few stray hairs, maybe. Some people might like that."

"And," added Greg, "she is violently anti-men."

"Then again, she's anti a lot of things. Just because she doesn't like men much doesn't mean she doesn't want to go to bed with one."

"You think so? You might be right," Greg said, suddenly thoughtful. "What you planning on doing with your dosh from the dairy?"

This sudden change in the conversation was a fairly typical Greg Hammond tactic, thrown in while he was still winning an argument. There was plenty of stuff I should have shoved in his face, but I was weary and defeated and just wanted to go home.

I paid the bill and included a generous tip.

"Good night," I said to the waiter, as cheerfully as possible, before following Hammond out of the door.

The waiter ignored me and tilted his head in the direction of the most outraged table, confirming that I was the red neck.

I was 19 years old and had been on a learning curve in all sorts of ways. I was beginning to understand that life and love contained all sorts of grey areas of which I'd previously been oblivious. That not everybody was entirely straight or gay, for example.

A hard-drinking dairy worker called John Brown kept manhandling me and another student. John Brown was married with two teenagers but he clearly got a kick out of us. Except that it wasn't obvious to me, it had to be pointed out by the other victim, a drama student in his mid 20s called Kevin Moody.

"He's got a foot in both camps, that John Brown," said Kevin.

"Sorry?"

"Do I have to spell it out, Simon? He likes it both ways, with the boys and with the girls. "The term," he added as if talking to a 12-year-old, "is bisexual".

Well, maybe that was the right way to talk to me because, believe it or not, I had never heard the term bisexual.

"But that can't be right, Kev. He's a really rough bloke and there's all that talk about giving the whisky some stick on a Saturday night."

Kevin was taking advantage of a break in the conveyor belt which fed crates of dirty bottles into a washing plant. "The trouble is this, Simon," he said, lighting a roll-up while doing a look-out for the foreman, "People like you, members of the bourgeoisie, think that everyone is one thing or the other. Straight or gay. Or queer, to put it in terms you might understand."

"Aren't they?" I said, ignoring at least two tacit insults in an attempt to get at the truth.

"Of course they're not, the sexual percentages are as varied as the weather, and it's just pot luck how your combination comes up."

"What's your combination?"

"Bi, with a slight preference towards men," he added. "Not, it goes without saying, that I welcome John Brown's advances."

I took a half step away from him. Kevin made no comment, other than blowing out a plume of smoke with a gesture of mild irritation.

"I guess I'll have a few more flings with men and women, then maybe I'll settle down, run a provincial theatre company. Wife and two bairns would be nice some time," he said. "Long as she looks boyish, like that lass that's just gone off to Italy."

He winked at me, maybe to indicate that he knew the nature of my relationship with Gill, wet his index finger and thumb, put out the roll-up and stuck it behind his ear as the foreman came around the corner.

"So John Brown," I reminded him, as the belt started up again. "You're saying he's a bit of both."

"You don't have to be an upper middle-class university-educated aesthete to be gay."

"But it helps," I said, without knowing what I really meant.

"Well, in a way, you're right, Simon, it does help, yes. You don't need me to tell you that John Brown's a guy from the wrong side of the tracks. A council estate in Wythenshawe isn't the sort of milieu in which sexual ambiguity is encouraged. He would have been forced down the straight road, even if he could only just manage it. How old d'you think he is?"

"Fifty?" I guessed.

"Maybe slightly younger, he's had a hard life. I'll wager he doesn't have sex that often with his wife these days. But if he could take you and me behind the bottling plant I bet he'd give us a really good going over."

He nodded, almost to himself, pleased at the succinct way he'd summarised John Brown's dilemma. I still had a lot to learn. I was surrounded by people who were light years smarter than I would ever be. Kevin Moody was so together that he'd got both his future sex life and his career planned. If John Brown, from a Wythenshawe council estate, was such a strange and complex pot of sexual emotions, the chances were that Gill Todd and Melanie Cohen could serve up something equally savoury.

Greg could be right after all. Maybe Gill and Melanie were bisexual. They would right now be discussing stream of consciousness, interior monologue, the difference between intertextuality and plagiarism, and socio-linguistical exclusion, or whatever sociologists talk about, over cappuccinos in the Piazza Navona in Rome.

I had rung Gill, to apologise for saying Paki, and to test the lie of the land. She said she didn't want to meet up again because she was now an item with an older and wiser man. I was less upset than I expected to be; I'd got out of my depth. Over the next few years, my early twenties, I applied this lesson religiously, never swimming too far. You could have brains or good looks in your women, I figured, not both. I saw a film on television recently in which a character died and had to defend the life he had led in Judgment City. He said your women should be just good looking enough to fancy them, but no more. Anything else is trouble; a man after my own heart.

Perhaps Gill Todd decided to spend the next couple of summers in Portsmouth. Anyway, she vanished for the second time, and I never saw her again, well, not in the flesh anyway. The same is true of Melanie, although I had discovered her whereabouts when the York Minster bells were announcing the arrival of the new millennium.

Greg Hammond didn't return to Hereford. His debts all paid, he went from the biscuit factory to that job as a trainee newspaper reporter on the Stockport Express. To judge from the sardonic smile on his face when the four of us discussed post-university life, he had already got that one lined up.

Mum wrote to me early the following term to say that she'd seen Hammond down our street "linked together with a striking girl, dark but not native, maybe Jewish or Greek".

It wasn't the worst development that autumn, although I was only to learn of a greater betrayal later. Mum's over-protective instincts had reasserted themselves; she'd told me about Hammond and Melanie, and left out an even more unpalatable truth.

My final sighting of Gill Todd was on TV the following December. She was captaining Manchester on University Challenge and the Evening Comet ran a small story about the side, "headed admirably by 20-year-old Gillian Todd from Portsmouth". In view of my track record with the Comet, I wouldn't have been surprised to read: "Gill Todd was previously best known as the girl with whom Rocket Boy Simon Waiters lost his virginity."

Manchester University won a couple of rounds before going out against an Oxford college. Gill made a big impression on a critic in one of the posh Sundays. I've still got the clipping. You know me well enough by now to appreciate that I always keep things which create opportunities for future torment.

*…Move over Joan Bakewell, there is a new, undisputed holder of the title, Thinking Man's Top TV Totty.*

*She is Todd, the Eng Lit student from Portsmouth who captains Manchester University's team. In a girls' boarding school, the perky Todd would make a perfect head pupil, subject of truly awesome crushes among all the first-years. Captain of hockey and lacrosse, decisive but not bossy, ever so slightly flirtatious but still the girl-next-door, she's the type of lass who would have the junior school tots queueing up outside the prefects' room after morning prayers to run errands and get those little jobs done for her.*

*Once again last week we saw dreamboat Todd marshalling the Manchester team with the precision of Rommel and the charisma of Jack Welch. Quicker on the draw than her three half-awake team mates, she beat the even more dozy Hull side almost single-handed. The shell-shocked quartet from the Land of Green Ginger will by the tide Of Humber be licking their wounds Till the conversion of the Jews.*

*Occasionally, Todd pulled the trigger too soon. Bamber Gascoigne did a double-take worthy of Jimmy Finlayson when she suggested that "The face that launched a thousand ships" came from The Tempest. "So, you're only human after all," said love-sick Bamber as our gal from Pompey looked fetchingly all at sea.*

*Perhaps Bamber, like adoring middle-aged men and moping 11-year-old-girls everywhere, is rooting for Manchester to go all the way to next year's final. I'm going on the record now to say that we will be hearing much more about Todd. One day, you can bet your bottom dollar that Granada TV will dig out archive clips from her University Challenge days.*

*As a natural leader, she might fancy going into politics. But my message is this: "Don't do it, Toddy. You're too good for Westminster. Go off to America, get an English chair at Harvard or Yale, save Shakespeare from the structuralists, cultural materialists and New Historicists. Or do TV – when it comes to photogenic, you'd give Doris Day a run for her money. BBC economics editor maybe. We all promise to sit up straight and listen carefully when you're explaining stagflation and the misery index."*

*Of course, if any of us at the back of the class are caught talking out of turn, we'll take our punishment manfully… Here will I dwell, for Heaven be in these lips. And all is dross that is not Toddy…*

Well, it's hardly illegal for a middle-aged journalist to moon over a 20-year-old girl like Gill. My dad was highly impressed by one of my better-endowed girlfriends and his eyes once went out on stalks, like they do in the cartoons, when she pulled off her top and allowed him a clearer picture of what lay behind her skimpy t-shirt. But would a newspaper editor let through a column like that one these days? I'm not so sure.

"We all know what a little minx that one turned out to be," said my mum when she'd read that piece. "You were well out of it, you take my word for that, Simon."

By then, thanks to Greg Hammond's tireless efforts to keep me fully informed, I had to agree.

# CHAPTER SIXTEEN

## Jesus on the modern campus

Well, while I'm hitting myself over the head about Gill, you might as well hear about how I loved and lost Wendy Thomas without loving her in the first place.

Indirectly, I can blame my mum, although I would have no doubt managed a different self-inflicted disaster if I hadn't heeded her absurd suggestion.

"Will you be joining a few societies?" Mum said to me a couple of days before I left for my first term at Hereford. "It's a good way to get to know a few people outside your course and hall of residence."

As I've said, neither Mum nor Dad had received much education, let alone gone to university. So where she picked up this idea, which she spoke of with some authority, I couldn't say.

"I might." It wasn't something to which I'd given much thought.

"You could do a lot worse than join the Christian Union."

"Why would I want to do that?"

"It might be a good place to meet a few nice girls. It doesn't matter if you're not very religious any more. Who knows, you might rediscover your beliefs."

I could have pointed out that I felt indifferent about my religious faith. Neither was I convinced that "nice girls" were what I was looking for at that stage of my life as a wet-behind-the-ears 18-year-old. A few sluts might be nice.

"I'll think about it…"

I also pondered what Greg Hammond would say, and I wasn't disappointed.

"The Christian Union? I thought our church days were over."

"Well, I just happened to be passing their stall and I saw this dead pretty girl helping out."

"So she's probably a spoken-for second year if she's that involved already."

Hammond always worked these things out before I did.

"Maybe."

"Even if you get anywhere, you might be in for a long wait before you hit the jackpot, you know what these religious types are like. Still, what you never had, you never miss."

"They've got a debate tomorrow night. 'Is there a place for Jesus on the modern campus?'"

"Well, I hope she's there, that Jesus is there and that you all have a bloody good time. I'll be enjoying a few pints of Worthington E and negotiating for some nice Moroccan gear."

After two hours of debate the Christian Union agreed that there was a place for Jesus on the modern campus. I had nothing to contribute on the subject and neither had Wendy Thomas, but she must have remembered me from the previous day because I managed to get a smile from her across the crowded room. I collared her in the Christian Union coffee bar later.

"Worried which way the vote was going to go at one stage."

She laughed at this, a good start.

"It was a challenging debate," she said.

"Er, I'm Simon, by the way."

"Hello. I'm Wendy."

"Are you a second year, if you're already involved with the society?" I asked.

"No, I've just started. I know one of the members, Elliot over there, from home in Bristol."

An earnest-looking bearded youth returned her wave.

"He's a friend from school days. He told me that Hereford was a nice place to come and it's good to know someone from home, don't you think?"

I thought about Greg Hammond, hiding from Jesus somewhere on campus in a haze of marijuana smoke, and wasn't so sure.

Elliot, a skinny chap with a pale blue t-shirt, cheap jeans and a beard that looked as if he had thrown it up, came over. This growth put a few years on him, it was hard to believe that he was not yet 20. He put an arm around Wendy and there was something passive-aggressive about the gesture, if that's the right expression; hands off, she's mine, even though they weren't as far as I could gather, an item.

"I think the Lord has overseen a good evening's work. Would this be a recruit for our army?"

"I'm a floating voter at the moment, Elliot," I said, settling for agnosticism.

"No room for them in the Lord's house," said Elliot, smiling despite the tough love. "But I'm sure we'll win him over, hey, Wends."

Wendy smiled sweetly.

"Christ, man, she is utterly gorgeous and so gentle natured," I told Greg Hammond the following day.

"You realise that your chances of bedding her are zero?"

"What I feel for Wendy goes beyond that."

"Just as well. Christian Union, theology student, it doesn't get much worse. For what it's worth, you'd be better off chasing that Yvonne Unger from your tutorial group. She, I guarantee, would be a fucking cert."

Yvonne Unger was a tall, dark late 20s divorcée, viewed by all the teenaged undergraduates as an exotic presence.

"Well, far be it from me to put you off, if you're still determined to try your luck with Wendy."

"You bet I am," I said, although the seeds of doubt had been planted.

I bided my time with Wendy Thomas at university. She was full of encouraging smiles, but I figured that might have more to do with her being touched by the spirit of Jesus than by any affection for me, and Elliot Carr was often in the frame. I was always good at convincing myself girls weren't interested, often in the face of substantial evidence to the contrary.

I might have struck on a few occasions; serendipitous meetings on the student bus heading for the campus, or as we came out of classes in adjacent lecture theatres, and in the coffee bar. Over a tasteless frothy coffee in a polystyrene cup she mentioned an ex-boyfriend and then added former boyfriend, in case I hadn't got the message first time.

Greg Hammond mocked my indecision over a lunch-time pint of lager in the Mappa Mundi Bar. It was my first of the day, his third. Hammond rolled a cigarette and I noticed that his fingertips were yellow, something that had taken Uncle Andrew, with his daily pack of Three Castles, years to achieve. Hammond had given up on American Studies and said he was putting out a few feelers about jobs on newspapers. He'd been mugging up on journalism and was sharing his learning as if he were the first person to have discovered these truths.

"You know, Simon, one of the golden rules in interviewing is not to ask more than one question at a time."

"You don't say."

"You'll only get one answer, or the wrong one."

"Is that so?"

"It is."

"Well, here's a single question for you," I said. "Why should going into journalism and having a degree be mutually exclusive?"

"Why wait? Who needs a degree?"

"Time's on your aside. Plenty of folk find one useful."

"Did Dickens have one, did Shakespeare have one? Did James Joyce have one?"

"No, no and yes," I said.

There was an Easter Ball in Radford House, the most traditional of Hereford's female halls of residence. It was common practice for some of the hall's more reclusive or unattractive residents to advertise, often in pairs, for male escorts. "English undergrads Victoria and Bethany want two presentable young beaux to accompany them to the social event of the term," was a typical request on a notice board that year in the union building.

A few days before the ball, I met Wendy, rigged out in a tight, silky maroon blouse and the trademark ankle-length skirt, under which, I guessed, were legs that she was hiding because they were nothing to write home about.

"Are you going to the Radford Ball, Simon?"

"Perhaps. Not so sure it's my cup of tea," I said.

"It's probably worth going to once, just for the experience," said Wendy. "Although finding someone to take you can be challenging."

She stood there looking coy, and twiddling with the ends of her golden locks. She was stuck in a groove with that word. Why did she always have to say things were challenging, whether she was trying to fathom contradictory evidence in the Gospels or to make a choice on the cafeteria's lunchtime menu? Somehow, I allowed the moment to slip by. Wendy disengaged her fingers from her curls and, after a few more pleasantries, we went our separate ways.

Fuck fuck fuck. There will be other opportunities, I reasoned, although how many does a man need? I made a half resolution to go round that night to her hall of residence, only to find that option had been removed. Greg Hammond said he'd fixed up for us to take Victoria and Bethany to the ball.

"What have you done that for?" I protested.

"You're not taking anyone else are you?"

I had to admit that I wasn't.

"Well, be a laugh then, won't it? Be nice to do a couple of ugly girls a favour. They'll miss out if we don't take them."

"You're all heart, Greg."

A few nights later, Victoria, a tiny egg-shaped girl, suddenly grabbed me tightly as the DJ switched from something danceable at arm's length to Love and Affection by Joan Armatrading. Bang on the chorus, as I was shuffling along and looking down on Victoria's dandruff, Wendy glided past. She was dancing with Elliot, who gave me the evil eye. Wendy's smile was not ironic but any notion that I might ever take her out just died of embarrassment.

During the final term of my first year I was sheepish whenever I met Wendy, although her angelic smile remained intact. Yvonne Unger, who used to call me Bebop Boy, was no longer available and girls didn't feature in my life at all until the reunion with Gill Todd that summer at the dairy. That enabled me finally to compartmentalise Wendy although, like Lesley Linnell, she had retained the capacity over the years to leap out at me from nowhere.

But now, in my darkest hour, Wendy really was back in my life.

# CHAPTER SEVENTEEN

## The end of history

Dad produced the offending letter from Archie Macash when, as Mum predicted, he was good and ready. He held it at arm's length, by the corner between thumb and index finger, as if it really had been dropped in shit and left for us in the hallway by Archie.

"This is unbelievable, son, the letter I sent him was mainly full of family news with a few harmless political observations that could have been lifted from the leader in your Guardian. I've never admitted that I work in a bank, so that can't be the problem."

The bile coming off these pages from Archie Macash was laid on so thick that I struggled at first to get any kind of handle on what I was reading. The words fascist and fascism leapt out of the notepaper as if they had been written in the blood of slaughtered partisans.

"Never really seen you as a fascist, Dad," I said.

"I've hated fascism all my life," said Dad. "I was happy to sign up during the war, even if I wasn't much use as a soldier. Hitler, Mussolini. That was fascism. Jim Callaghan, even Margaret Thatcher, say what you like about them, no one could call them fascists."

"I guess that Archie Macash would," I said. "If you're one in his eyes, I'm sure they are. Perhaps I need time to absorb all this."

Dad left me to it, heading once again to the bottom of the garden even though, in late December, I wasn't sure what he could find to do down there.

"I am not impressed with your new, bleeding heart liberal act, Waiters," wrote Archie. "In South Africa during the 1960s, liberals like you were no better than dyed-in-the-wool Afrikaaners. They were too cowardly to take up the armed struggle, so they organised an all-white party for themselves, to remain within the bounds of the law. Only the communists, people in the mould of David Hellier and me, those who made up the dominant faction of the ANC, had the guts to break the law and organise a multi-racial movement which might change things.

"It was always David who looked out for me when those evil bastards like Metcalfe were on the prowl. You just tagged along for the ride, in your patronising middle-class way, while you waited for the opportunity to get home to what really counted in your world – your ambition to pander to the glossy lifestyle needs of the south Manchester bourgeoisie. You were never really one of us, were you? I'm glad that David's faithfulness to his communist roots has helped to keep him a decent human being, even if you have been his anti-communist Doppelganger…

"I'm coming to England for a few days soon. I don't want to run away from you. We could meet up, and I could explain more about your fascism. It's an ethical duty to tell fascists how much you hate them…"

And so it went on into areas where Dad was largely blameless, such as T S Eliot's anti-Semitism and Christianity's creation of imperialism, resulting in millions of deaths. "The gas chambers would never have been built without nearly 2,000 years of Christian anti-Judaism," wrote Archie, before adding in a moment of rare generosity: "I'm not saying that all Christians are fascists."

"Well then," said Dad later, "what did you make all of all that?"

"We've already established that your anti-fascist credentials are fine, and I think we can safely agree that Hair Today didn't pander to the glossy lifestyle needs of the south Manchester bourgeoisie. In a nutshell, the bloke is just bonkers."

"I know that," said Dad, "but it doesn't somehow make it much easier to take. He's probably got worse over the years, too much time on his own to dwell on his weird view of the world. You know what hurts me the most?"

"The idea that you weren't really his friend?" I guessed.

"That's right. Me and this Hellier were equally on his side. If anything, Archie took a greater shine to me. He used to follow me round, like a faithful pet."

"The love that dare not speak its name, perhaps Dad?"

"You might be right, Simon," said Dad. "You mum says just ignore any further communications. It's pointless to engage with him."

"Well, she's right, Dad."

"I'm bloody well done with the lot of them. Bloody communists, they can go and hang themselves as far as I'm concerned."

"Well, the Soviet variety, at any rate," I said.

"And now they're in bloody Afghanistan, that's going to end in tears."

"I think that Afghanistan's one place that might be improved by the communists," I said. I wasn't sure whether I believed that or not, but I was determined to soften the blow.

"This is a horrible thing to say, Simon, but it makes me think the bloke might have deserved to be bullied in the Army."

"That would be writing history backwards, Dad. You and this Hellier definitely did the right thing."

"Thanks, you're probably right there, son."

"You once clarified something for me about bullies," I said to him, "when we were talking about my horrible teachers. I hadn't realised until then that grown-ups were as bad as children. For what it's worth, I think that Archie Macash is the classic victim who turned into a bully. There are plenty of them around, including some who are running what Mum calls the 'more fierce' countries."

"Aye, true enough again. Not much more we can really say on the subject, is there? Time for more tidying up perhaps," he said.

I watched Dad walking disconsolately towards the garden shed which once marked the kick-off spot for my childhood football games with Michael and Rupesh.

This was the day I understood Dad's loss of faith in an idea that had been an important part of his life; I felt sorry for him and even, in an odd way, closer to him than at any time since the World Cup final, when he consoled me about Gill Todd. His communism had survived the tanks rolling into Budapest in 1956 and into Prague 12 years later. Now, giving up finally on the Comrades, it was not because of military interventions condemned throughout the western world, or because of the words of dissident writers and scientists, or because of the gulags; it was because a lonely, spurned little ideologue had chosen this moment to take a petty revenge.

# CHAPTER EIGHTEEN

## An equable relationship

Wendy Carr, as she was now called, was wearing well. She could have passed for mid-30s, no question. Time was when that would have sounded ancient to me. But everything is relative and everything is related to age. If a five-year-old wants to marry her dad, that's cute; if a 15-year-old wants to marry her dad you've got problems.

Taking a more critical look, it struck me that Wendy was like the pantomime princess in a village show where they couldn't persuade anyone young enough to play the role. The long blonde hair (her best feature once, but not necessarily something that looks so great on a 42-year-old woman) and porcelain complexion were as I remembered her. The frilly top, too girlie for my taste, remained a favourite.

There were a few variations of the "well, here we are, then" and "how lovely to see you" variety while she sipped her coffee and braced herself to say whatever it was she wanted to say. She also mentioned that she'd heard my name on the radio in connection with Nevertheless, ("lovely record, by the way, Simon") and got my number from my mum (here we go again, only Waiters in the telephone book) after finding that I wasn't listed.

"I remembered your red and white scarf and that you supported Manchester United, that's why I tried the Manchester directory," she said.

"Good thinking," I said. As she probably knew nothing about football, I didn't bother complicating the issue by pointing out that following United didn't always involve coming from Manchester.

"Yes, The Eclection, Nevertheless, that was a lovely record," she said.

I hoped we weren't going to go around the houses for too long, before she came to the point.

"Very nice," I agreed. "On Elektra, they had a good reputation."

"Elliot didn't like it at all," she said.

"We can't all go for the same things."

"He was actually very rude about it," said Wendy. "Unnecessarily so, I thought."

"What did he say?"

"Well I said to him, isn't that a lovely song?"

"He took a different view?"

"'If you like that sort of thing', he said to me. So I said, 'What sort of thing's that?' I was, you know, taking care to sound curious rather than argumentative, that's very important with Elliot."

"So what did you say to that?"

"He said it was a juvenile tune, sentimental twaddle, that sort of thing."

"Does he always talk to you like that?" I asked.

"When he's nursing his usual Saturday morning hangover he does tend to be more critical and likely to find fault. Then your best bet is to make a concession. 'Well, I suppose it is a period piece and sounds dated now, you're right there. But I remember it from when I was a little girl,' I improvised. So, it's a harmless nostalgia for me. And for Simon Waiters, too, from the sound of things,' I said. That got his antenna going. 'Who's this Simon Waiters?' he said suspiciously, 'sounds familiar.' I reassured him that you were the chap who asked Brian Matthew to play the record, you know like he read it out, Simon Waiters of York."

Wendy paused to take a breath from her rather plodding narrative, and I needed a second or two also to absorb all this information before she re-launched herself.

"'Well,' he said to me, 'I thought your taste was bad enough but this Simon Waiters of York sounds like a man who hasn't moved on in 30 years, if that's his idea of decent music, Barrie.'"

"Barry?"

"As in Peter Pan. That's his pet name for me. Things are usually okay when he calls me Barrie."

"How could anyone ever accuse me of not moving on?" I said.

"Moving on is one of Elliot's favourite expressions. As in moving on after he's settled the argument with an arm lock or a painful nudge in the ribs."

We were suddenly moving into the darker territory which might account for her looking me up, I thought.

"God, I'm really sorry, Wendy. Life must be exhausting having to watch your Ps and Qs all the time. One slip of the tongue and it's trouble. What do your friends make of it?"

"They have not got the first fucking clue," she said, surprising me with the out-of-the-blue expletive. "Our friends think we are fine. 'You and Elliot are so equable together, Wendy. You're an example to us all! Why can't some of us be more like you two', they'll say. If any of our friends, well Elliot's friends really, because mine have mysteriously disappeared, paid attention to what was going on they might have a different perspective. I don't argue with him. I've learned my lesson, it just isn't worth it."

"That must make it hard for you to be a sparkling conversationalist at dinner parties."

"I bet you think I sound like a complete and utter drip. Actually, some folk find me amusing with my harmless quips on inconsequential subjects. When it comes to actual debate, I might state a contrary view to Elliot's but I'll withdraw eventually, as if I've seen the error of my stance when confronted by his giant intellect."

114

"Like someone who taps his nose at an auction during the early exchanges then ducks out when the bidding goes too high," I suggest.

"Sort of, yes. It's funny to see Elliot tensing up before the little lady backs down and allows that she has probably got the wrong end of the stick all along."

"How's it come to this, Wendy? Lack of confidence, maybe, low self-esteem?"

"You think I've never asked myself all those questions? Who else would have had me? That's another favourite."

"That's preposterously hard on yourself," I said.

"I was shy, no question, and that deterred many men who assumed I was stand-offish. One or two of the more predatory types probably realised that I was unlikely to, how shall I put this, reward them with intercourse at an early stage of the relationship."

"We're not all like that," I said.

Well, at least not all of the time.

"True. Now and then, at university for example, a boy might persevere a little longer than the rest. Like Simon Waiters of York, maybe."

"Er, yes," I gulped. I could feel my ears going red. "Is that why you contacted me?"

"Well, you always struck me as having a sympathetic ear. I've got very isolated. I need help," she blurted out suddenly. "He's made my life a misery and it's got to change. The thing is, he's a bully and I've had enough. But I'm terrified of leaving, he'll just come after us."

"Us?"

"I mean me and Tina."

"Tina?"

"My sister. Sorry, haven't mentioned her yet, have I?"

"Is he violent?" I said, sticking to Elliot. "I mean, does he knock you about?"

"Not any more. He doesn't have to," she said. "He's a control freak. He runs the show, he decides what I'll do, what I'll wear, when and if we'll go out, who our friends are."

115

"Surely you've got to get out of there," I said. "Is there anyone else to think about here?"

"Anyone else?"

"Have you got any kids, Wendy?" I hadn't wanted to bring up that one directly in case it was a sensitive subject, but she was the one asking for help here and I needed to establish a few facts.

"We've got a son, Nicholas, in his first year at university."

"What's his subject?"

"Well, he applied for law."

"Oh dear. Like father like son, hey?"

"Actually, nothing like, you'll be pleased to hear. He stuck it out for a fortnight and switched to philosophy."

"I bet his dad liked that."

Wendy looked down at her cup, took a deep breath and then asked: "Have you got time for lunch? My treat."

# CHAPTER NINETEEN

## We speak of famous Belgians

"There's Adolphus Sax, of course."

"You can't count him," said Greg Hammond.

"Why not?"

"You couldn't exactly say that he was famous, could you?"

"I would have thought that inventing a musical instrument on which the 20th century's greatest music has been played was pretty damn good," I said. "If you've got no Adolphus Sax, there's no Charlie Parker, no Sonny Rollins, no Gerry Mulligan, no Stan…"

"All right then, I take your point," said Hammond grumpily.

Sooner or later, everyone has a conversation about famous Belgians; take it from me, there are more than you might think.

Greg Hammond and I were in the Mappa Mundi Bar at Hereford University, the most austere drinking establishment I have ever used. The bare plaster walls, so shabby they might have passed for distressed ten years later, were adorned only by tatty posters for a Sex Pistols' gig and an Anti-Nazi League rally. The juke box, belting out Girl of My Best Friend by Elvis and If You Leave Me Now by Chicago, was the only fixture in the bar, other than the Formica tables and stools which were screwed to the floor, for the same reason that the glasses were plastic.

The bar manager, a heavily-tattooed bodybuilder, dispensed pints of lager and fizzy bitter with a gracelessness that suggested his t-shirt should have said 'I hate students', rather than 'I love Newcastle Brown'.

Although Hammond and I had both applied to Hereford we didn't have much to do with one another when we got there, unless it suited him. Looking back, I think he cold-shouldered me when he got in with the Hereford smart set. This is something that has only begun to anger me recently, though the fact that it has only recently made me angry is what really makes me angry. That night in Hereford, I suspected he had invited me along for moral support. It was January 1977, a couple of weeks into our second term. Helen was arriving for the weekend and Greg wasn't enthusiastic.

"She'll be pleased to see you, she's always liked you best of all my pals," he said. In all fairness that was probably true although Greg Hammond didn't have too many friends.

The choice of venue, and Hammond's decision to meet her here rather than making the effort to pick her up at Hereford station, suggested to me that Helen's days were numbered. While we awaited her arrival we spoke of famous Belgians.

"My favourite painter is Belgian, though I used to think he was French," I said.

"Yes, yes, Rene Magritte. I wondered when you'd get round to him."

"Actually, I was thinking of Paul Delvaux. Must be in his 80s now."

"Oh, right, yeah."

I guessed that Greg had never heard of Paul Delvaux, and to suggest he was really famous was pushing it. However, Greg wasn't a man to admit to ignorance about anything.

"Okay, I'll allow you that one," he said magnanimously as Helen walked into the bar.

"Hello, you two," she said, like someone in a radio play reminding us how many people were present. She was an attractive girl, rather Irish-looking with her jet-black hair and bright blue eyes which always seemed to be trying to suss you out. She stood there, in her student uniform of jeans, floppy pullover and duffel coat, looking harassed as she awaited some sign of affection.

"Journey okay?" said Hammond without getting up.

"Yes, fine, Greggy. It was raining in Manchester and the train started late. I said to myself: 'You could be in for a long journey, Helen' but it caught up."

"Here's a quid. Get the drinks in while you're on your feet, hey love? One lager, one Newci Brown bottle and yours."

Helen padded cautiously across the sticky floor to the bar. She nodded in the direction of the juke box and said something to the bar manager, perhaps to do with Elvis who had come around again, and he managed to smile.

"She's a friendly lass, your Helen," I said.

"I dare say. How's your Bunbury getting along? He's a Paki, isn't he?"

"His parents are from Bombay and he's a British citizen," I said. "He was born here."

"I do beg your pardon. If it's possible to be racialist about a person who doesn't exist, that is."

I'd revived my Bunbury plan during the first few weeks at Hereford. I seemed unlikely to need him now I was away from home but he had come to mind when Oscar Wilde turned up on the Victorian literature course. I read The Importance of Being Earnest and felt homesick as I thought about one of Uncle Andrew's finest hours, with Auntie Laura prompting and keeping an anxious eye out for any excessive chemistry between Algernon and Cecily Cardew.

"I decided to call him Bishen Patel," I said.

"So what's he do? Let's have some details. Favourite colour, star sign, best country visited, who he'd most like to meet."

"He's an economics student at university in London right now. He's going to do accountancy, I should imagine."

"Is that a G&T you're drinking?" said Hammond, as Helen placed three glasses on the table.

"Just the T, actually," said Helen. "I'm feeling rather queasy."

119

"Does that mean there's some change?" said Hammond.

"A few coppers. Would you like me to count it out for you now?"

"Okay, just kidding," said Hammond, who wasn't.

"So, who's doing accountancy?" said Helen, never someone to forget where the conversation had got to before an unwanted interruption.

"Just some guy I know in London," I said. "Don't think it's anyone you've ever met, Helen."

"He was visiting last week. He's called Bishen Patel," said Hammond, "although his mates call him Bill."

I looked daggers at Hammond but, perhaps peeved by his defeat over the Belgians, he was determined to score a few points somehow.

"Very bright indeed, is our Bill. What was it at A-level? Top grades in double maths and history, your classic combination for economics. And you know, he's an absolutely lovely guy, too. Because A) there's no side to him and second, he's really modest. He said this to me last week – and remember, I'd only just met him. He said: 'What do I know? I'm just a Mancunian Paki who's had a bit of education'."

"That's terrible, Greggy."

"Sorry, love. I'm not with you," said Hammond.

"He really should have more respect for himself than to talk like that. Will you be seeing him again soon, Simon?"

"I should have thought so, he's only a couple of miles up the road in Rusholme," said Hammond grinning unpleasantly. "His parents have got a corner shop on Wilmslow Road."

"Er, yes, Helen, we'll meet up for a drink before Christmas."

"Well, if you ever hear him talking like that again, you must tell him off good and proper. He sounds like a credit to himself and his family, making something of his life, and he shouldn't be saying such demeaning things."

I thought that 'making something of his life' was patronising but, not wanting to be involved in a war on two fronts, decided to let it go.

"Right, I'll do that," I said.

There was an awkward silence, during which I tried to avoid looking at Hammond's face. The moment passed when I might have told Helen that there was no Bill Patel.

"Oh dear, Helen, you're getting on your high horse again. Still I think it's a fair point I'm making. You do promise to say something to him, Simon, if it happens again."

"Of course, you can always rely on me."

"Good. I'll be checking up on you next time we meet." She smiled, to make it clear she was just teasing.

But it was to be 11 years before Helen and I met again. And she never forgot Bill Patel.

# CHAPTER TWENTY

## Faces in the crowd

My second year at Hereford University was, I decided, going to be a time for fresh starts, new avenues. Things would be different; for the second time in my life, I'd had to recover from the loss of Gill Todd. I shed a few tears, albeit behind closed doors this time and not into the security of my dad's smoky cardigan.

On balance, I wasn't too sad that Greg Hammond was no longer around to beckon me for drinking sessions when his more hip mates were not available.

"I'll drop you a line and let you know what's going down," he said over a farewell pint at the end of September.

Within a few weeks, Hammond was as good as his word. A letter arrived, first-class to boot, marked on the flap: "contains epic photograph". The contents – he wrote about shorthand classes, first front-page story at the Stockport Express and relationship with Melanie Cohen ("We're going nowhere, pants of steel,") – made no reference to the grainy black and white picture clipped from my nemesis, the Manchester Evening Comet.

I was oddly pleased to hear that Greg's sexual overtures to Melanie had been unsuccessful. But that brief bubble of delight burst when I examined the Comet pic more closely. The paper ran an "Is your face worth a tenner?" prize. Once a week they would print a picture of the crowd at a football match and circle a spectator's head.

*"There wasn't much to cheer at Maine Road on Saturday, as City went down 2-0 to Wolves. But at least one supporter in the Platt Lane End will be able to afford a smile now. If you recognise yourself as our chosen Blue, contact the Evening Comet office to claim your £10 prize. (Winner at Burnden Park, Bolton v Mansfield Town: The Rev James Henderson of Rochdale)."*

I didn't recognise this week's fortunate fan and Hammond couldn't have been referring to the lucky vicar whose name was unfamiliar. But then my eyes were drawn to the happy couple on the edge of the picture, ringed in pencil by Greg. It was Uncle Andrew and Gill Todd, having a good laugh despite City's drab performance.

The bastard, I thought. That's the last time I'd have anything to do with the rake. So that was Gill's "older and wiser" new beau. Older, yes.

The post of girlfriend remained vacant until the following year, as I once again felt the need to lick my wounds. But I found a new college mate almost immediately. I wasn't desperately keen on any of the lads in the house that I lived in now, so Maurice Whittle, from one of my tutorial groups, stepped effortlessly into the breach.

A footballer once observed that after the hard-case Scottish manager had quit and been replaced by an easy-going foreigner, it was like stepping out of Colditz and into Butlin's; I had similar feelings about the changing of the guard courtesy of the revolving door that despatched Hammond and delivered Whittle. Life was suddenly calmer. There had never been a dull moment when Hammond was around. I used to take the view that it was occasionally a rough ride but the journey compensated. Or at least, it did most of the time, when I found myself at the best parties or tagging along with Hammond if he was reviewing a concert or a play for the student magazine, Cock and Bull. Now and then I had my doubts. Hammond would often let you down at the last minute because he'd got a better offer, and he was not a nice drunk. He often started scoring points or putting you down when he'd had a beer too many. I also had a silly habit of falling for his regular line of manipulation: "Have you got anything on tonight?" After which you'd say no and then find yourself making up a foursome with a couple of snotty girls or doing him some sort of favour which was slightly off.

You never got anything like that with Maurice, as nice, gentle and straightforward a boy (man hardly seems the appropriate word at the time for either of us) as you could have wished to meet. If Maurice said he'd be there at eight o'clock, you could set your watch by it. At times he was almost pathetically compliant with your wishes and you really had to stop yourself from exploiting his good nature. It's all very well being one of those people who will "do anything for you" but there's got to be a modicum of discrimination about who you apply that maxim to. Maurice had some self-knowledge and understood that he was "not exactly rock 'n roll". He used to send himself up something rotten; he was to self-deprecation what I became later to self-loathing.

Maurice was a short, slim guy with mousey hair and a weak growth, which he was constantly licking, above his lips. The moustache, like Maurice, was never quite the finished product and he always felt like an unformed character, a work in progress, someone who had never adapted to college or decided what he wanted out of life; he went home every other weekend to Yorkshire and used to talk about the number of weeks left in the term as if university were no more than an extension of his school days.

He invited me to join him one weekend in the Pennine market town that he came from and whose praises he was forever singing. His parents were friendly towards me up to a point, as if trying to work me out, and whether I might be a bad influence on Maurice. This was a strange new role for someone who was more often a polite favourite with the parents of my handful of friends. My other main memory of life Chez Whittle was enjoying the rough and tumble of being in a large family, something I'd only experienced previously with Rupesh Ruia; Hammond and Michael Summerbell, like me, were only children.

Maurice introduced me proudly to his folks as if he'd arrived in a pith helmet with a magnificent find from his explorations of Africa. He had a younger brother, Fergus, doing A-levels and twin sisters at the O-level stage. Bernadette and Maria were sporty, extrovert types, verging on the precocious, and they were as fascinated by me as if I had been a tribal chieftain shipped from Chad. "Gosh, so you're the famous Simon Waiters," Maria said.

On the Saturday afternoon, we watched the fabulous Whittle sisters playing for the school's hockey team. Some of the talent on display was an eye-opener, although Maurice was less stirred than I was by the sight of those perfectly-formed 16 and (in some cases let's be honest) 15-year-olds gliding around the field.

Maurice did like sport but he had no skills in that direction. He took a masochistic pleasure from telling me that he had never discovered any real talent for anything. "I've always been the runt of the family," he'd say.

I wasn't keen on the friends we met in his local pub. They gave the impression that they thought Maurice's decision to go to university rather than getting a job was a sign of weakness and he seemed inclined to believe them. "Well, who in their right mind would want to employ me?" he'd say. "Although I suppose I'll have to get a job one day, probably some kind of accountant as I'm good with numbers and careful with money."

He'd drag me to the Catholic Society's monthly disco, despite my protestations that it wasn't my kind of thing and that chatting up girls on the dance floor wasn't playing to my strengths.

"Those two over there look interesting," he'd say, but always after we'd just been to the bar and had a full pint of beer in our hands. We'd never quite make it on to the dance floor and I was quite happy to leave it that way.

He did once get collared to go on a blind date during Rag Week. He asked me if I had any "good chat-up lines" that he could use.

"Just be yourself, Maurice, you're a nice guy. To thine own self be true."

"What about jokes?"

"What about them?"

"Should I try a joke or two?"

"Well, as long as they are brief, clean and you don't fluff your lines, maybe. Could be if it's related to something you're talking about. Anecdotes or off-the cuff quips sometimes go down well. Girls like blokes with a sense of humour, and you've got one of those."

God, it was like trying to explain to an alien life-form how to pass himself off as a member of the human race.

"Thanks, Sim, I wish I had your self-confidence when it comes to dealing with the girls."

Well, that just goes to show that everything in life really is relative.

# CHAPTER TWENTY-ONE

## The enervating classroom

Wendy Carr's sister lived in West Yorkshire. Tina was constantly telling her that the spare bedroom was always available.

"It strikes me, Wendy," I said when she first recounted her grim story, "that what you need most of all is a van, and pen and paper."

"I know this sounds pathetic, but I can't drive."

"Elliot took you out a couple of times but wasn't very encouraging when you found it difficult."

"How do you know that?"

"Just a guess."

"You are smart, aren't you? I'm glad I contacted you."

"I can also drive a van."

"What do I need pen and paper for?"

"To leave Elliot a goodbye note."

Who'd have thought it? My number one lost girl; getting her started on a new life really was that simple. And young Nicholas, the real catalyst, would be delighted too. Because he wasn't a chip off the old block, as Wendy had explained to me proudly; he was the very reason she'd started to review her life.

"Nicholas is the only one we've got, and I think that was largely down to Elliot deciding enough was enough," she told me.

"He sure sounds like a wrong 'un, Elliot I mean," I said.

I awaited a backlash from Wendy: 'He does have some good qualities, you've never met him.' People can be strange like that – you know, it's all right for me to say such and such, but not for you. However, Wendy had just mulled over my observation in silence.

"So Nicholas dropped his legal studies, you said?"

"Yes, two weeks into the course."

"Was that wise?"

"Nicholas thought so. Elliot doesn't want to have anything to do with him right now and the feeling is mutual. I'm thrilled."

"Seriously?"

"In his teens he was quiet, almost timid and afraid of his dad. But I think that he'd planned this for some time."

"So it kind of dislodged something with you?"

"Too right. I thought that if my son was smart enough to bide his time then pull a stroke like that, I really ought to take a look at myself."

"Have you discussed this with anyone else?" I said. "Other than Tina?" The question I really wanted to ask, naturally, was: "Why me?" It had to be more than a vague memory of my having had a sympathetic ear, as she put it, all those years ago.

"Tricky," she said, "most of my real friends have gone off the radar. Driven away by Elliot, I suppose. All *our* friends are actually *his* friends as I said."

"It's sometimes useful to get an outsider's view," I said. "Although it sounds as though Tina has got him sussed."

"She's always disliked Elliot, in fact she tried to warn me off him, and we fell out for a while because of that." She paused. "I've got some running-away money, you know," she added. She made it sound like a Victorian novel; some chap with a top hat, scarf and gloves holding a ladder steady and trying not to look up her nightgown as she stepped unsteadily on to the top rungs from the bedroom window.

"But the thing is," she said, "I've always been worried that he'll come after me."

"Somehow I don't think he will. I reckon it's now or never, Wendy."

"But he's a solicitor," she said.

"What's that got to do with the price of fish?"

"He knows the law, he'll take me to the cleaners," she said.

Easier, I thought, to reassure her about cash than an impending threat of violence.

"No he won't," I said. "You're entitled to half of everything at least, I would have thought. Probably more, for all I know. I used to share a house in Headingley with the son of a solicitor who specialised in divorce work. He told me that there were a lot of north Leeds wives who thought that the sun shone out of his mother's legal bum…and an equal number of north Leeds husbands who didn't."

She laughed out loud at this and clapped her hands, like a child.

"You were always very funny, I remember," she said.

I didn't think it was a particularly amusing observation, but that's neither here nor there.

So that's how I came to be White Van Man, driving Wendy to her sister's house.

"You'll like Tina," Wendy assured me as we turned into her street in Halifax, one of those small terraced jobs where the door leads straight from the pavement into the front room, "but I should warn you that she's very direct. It can be somewhat challenging for anyone meeting her for the first time."

In my experience, direct usually means rude so I prepared to fight my corner. I was helping Wendy; I'd nothing to reproach myself for.

Tina was a former teacher who had given it up to be a full-time artist. I'd decided that she must be an altogether different breed from her older sister and I wasn't wrong. She looked like a street fighter, with her plain white t-shirt, puce-dyed crew cut, ring through the nose and that peculiar fashion (or perhaps non-fashion) statement the slashed jeans. With Wendy still majoring on her blonde hair it struck me that both sisters were presenting themselves in an age-inappropriate manner.

Tina probably thought that all men were shit – Elliot Carr hadn't done us any favours – and I shook hands firmly to show I wasn't afraid; she'd be examining me minutely for signs of ulterior motives. I hoped Wendy wouldn't say something fatuous about my coming to the rescue of a damsel in distress.

There was no coherent style to the front room although the throws and rugs gave it a vaguely bohemian vibe, as did some interesting, mildly surrealist paintings.

"Simon's my knight in shining armour, Tina," she called from the stairs.

Tina raised her eyebrows.

"Well, a man with a hired van and a free day," I corrected hastily.

"I understand that we're both refugees from the world of school teaching," said Tina.

"Yes, I gave it my best shot but it wore me down in the end," I said. "I lasted the course better than some of my contemporaries from teacher training. Even enjoyed it for a while."

"Me too."

"I pulled out all the stops, well most of them. I produced plays, refereed football and did some tennis coaching, although I drew the line at taking the little bastards on skiing trips."

"So why did you get out?"

"It all got too tough at some point. Or maybe I had less stomach for a constant battle of attrition with the lower streams. You didn't get any respect as you got older and you could never take your feet off the disciplinary gas. I had a career criminal's son in my class. He called me a dickhead one day and I decided that I'd had enough, just like that."

"Ironic in view of where you ended up," she said. "I guess I just ran out of steam, too. What's that word we learn in school geography about the sub-Saharan African climate …enervating?"

"It is," I confirmed although the question was evidently rhetorical.

"The job just fucks you up, every which way but loose. It's a pity the powers that be can't create some kind of 25-year-old useful-idiot robots who can do the job for a few years then be returned to workshops for recycling and reprogramming, with the latest dumbed-down curricula and knowledge of mindless popular culture, to give them the right street-cred to do the next few years until they are too old, ie over 30, to get down with the kids."

"Could be me speaking," I agreed.

I admired Tina's paintings; English surrealism, weird-round-the-edges like 1967 pop music before the horrors of prog rock, and even greater frightfulness of punk. I told her that I had a Paul Delvaux-style mural.

"That must be hard to live with."

"I'm afraid you're right. My ex-wife hated it. But your stuff is nice and restrained."

"Did you have me down as a three-in-a-bed, used condoms, fluorescent light strips coated in tar sort of a girl?"

"Maybe," I admitted and asked if Wendy had any artistic talent.

"No, but she's got an eye for colour and style. Her place in Scarborough's very classy. If you ever want some help with internal decor, she's your woman."

A thought occurred to her.

"They'll have to sell up of now course, unless Elliot can buy her out for an arm and a leg. We'll find a good divorce lawyer to make sure that everything's divvied up properly."

"What about Elliot?"

"What about him?"

"Is he going to make life difficult when he sees the farewell note?"

"No, that nasty control freak is just a coward at heart."

"Does he still do religion?" I asked, remembering Elliot's warning about my slim chances of getting into the Kingdom of Heaven.

"No, that all went by the board eons ago, it was just another manifestation of his control freakery," said Tina.

"It sounds, though, as if your nephew's worked him out."

"Yes, I used to worry about the effect on Nicholas of witnessing Wendy constantly being put down. Elliot was very careful not to be handy with his fists when he was around. And he also made sure never to mark Wendy anywhere immediately visible. But more often it was the threat of violence if she didn't toe the line. Did Wendy ever tell you that when our parents retired they moved up here to be nearer to her? It was Mum's decision, she began to get an inkling of what was going on, but she never shared it with Dad who would have gone apeshit…which brings us to you, Simon."

"Hardly," I protested.

"No, you look like a thoroughly reasonable guy, I even remembering Wendy talking about you when she came home at Christmas from Hereford. You know, 'Have you got a boyfriend yet? 'No, but there's someone nice'." My heart sank again over further evidence of the price I'd paid for my timidity.

"But do bear in mind, Simon," she said smiling sweetly, "that my boyfriend works in concrete. If you give her a bad time in any shape or form, he'll take great pleasure in breaking both your legs."

"Before burying me in his favourite industrial product?"

"Only for a second offence. He's a fair-minded man."

"I'm sure he is, and you'll have no need for any action so drastic," I said.

# CHAPTER TWENTY-TWO

## The single life

I've no memory of time ever dragging when I was a teenager. Sundays had most potential for boredom, but I could usually find someone to hang about with, even if it was only Greg Hammond.

I was happy to spend the afternoon with a book. If I'd not yet done my homework, they didn't have to be absolute page-turners either. Anything moderately passable could be interesting compared doing my physics or chemistry. The point is, I suppose, that if I was on my own it was because that was my choice. Believe me, that's not the same as being a 42-year-old single guy. It starts out okay, a lie-in and an hour over the paper with coffee and toast. Then what? The pub and a couple of pints while talking to whichever loner in the same boat happens to be propping up the bar. After that, home at three in the afternoon and a general feeling of lethargy.

I suppose it's a day when being a DIY fanatic helps but that's never been my bag. I always put the car through a wash at the garage, the back yard is paved and low maintenance, and Kath, my cleaner, comes in once a week to tidy up and do a pile of ironing. Kath sometimes leaves me a note or two, which I glance at then stuff in a stainless-steel wine bucket which I never use. 'Tap in bathroom dripping', 'curtain track in front room coming down', 'damp under window in dining room cupboard'.

Occasionally, I am forced to act, calling out one of the army of tradesmen whom Helen marshalled effectively both here and in Leeds. Although she upped sticks more than four years ago one or two still ask after her. "Nice girl, I thought," they will add, with a hint of reproach in their voice.

After she left, I verged on living wild, but pulled myself back from total annihilation when I tired of near squalor. The turning point came when my hand hovered over a Pot Noodle in the supermarket. I had to try harder. Now, everything is shipshape, if a little run down, and I cook a proper meal twice a week just to prove to myself that I still know how it's done. I'm also well turned out, as a rule, if only to increase my chances with the ladies. As Maurice Whittle, my old Hereford mate, used to say: "You've got to think about the girls," an observation that was curious on two fronts. First, Maurice never did, and second, he used those words, presumably by way of reassurance, shortly after making what I can only describe as a possible semi pass at me, involving our legs touching briefly while I was introducing him to Errol Garner's Concert by the Sea album.

My mural, in the style of famous Belgian Paul Delvaux, is the only feature of note in a house lacking in character, the nearest I've ever come to imposing my personality, whatever that means. But I do have a classy Bang and Olufsen music system. Since the marquee debacle, I've banned myself from licensed premises before eight in the evening, and on Sundays I've been working my way through the vinyl collection, mainly jazz, especially bebop, with a smattering of classical, blues and a few pop and rock essentials such The Beatles, Stones and Bob Dylan.

The other Sunday development aimed at keeping me on the straight and narrow is jogging. This is a depressing by-product of my age. Football for the over 40s is undignified, apart from Stanley Matthews and a few goalkeepers, and I can no longer find anyone to play tennis with. The local club which welcomed Helen and me turned cool when I became a single member. People often take sides when a couple split up and nobody was very inclined to back me.

What else is there? Swimming? That's just an embarrassment. I can stay afloat forever but I move so slowly that lifeguards are poised constantly to dive in to save me. I don't understand the physics of swimming. Why can a seven-year-old go faster than me when I would annihilate him at any other sport, even rugby or lacrosse? So, it has to be jogging. At 20 minutes, the run doesn't kill me. I don't have to go anywhere to do it and three times a week is only an hour out of my life. The view is not up to much, so you need to find something to pass the time of day and lists aren't bad. I once managed to get round on near auto-pilot by working out every film I'd seen that year and all the football grounds I'd ever been to, division by division. But lists can lead into dangerous territory, such as former girlfriends or, in my case, non-girlfriends. And when I reached Anna Florenski today I got stuck in a loop.

Now that really was an odd case. Anna Florenski was a dark-haired girl with Polish parents, who looked more Mediterranean than central European. She was a vague acquaintance but when I bumped into her in a bookshop in Leeds and it turned out that she was going to a party near me the following Saturday, she was keen to invite me. "You really should come along," she said.

Anna was doing a Comparative Literature MA at Leeds University. Her looks-brains combo surely put her in a higher division than mine but I went anyway deciding, for once, that fortune might favour the brave.

I had never mixed in student circles in Leeds. The girl who opened the door looked at me blankly when I said I was a friend of Anna's but she let me in anyway. However, Anna wouldn't allow me into her world. She spent the evening drinking orange juice and talking about God knows what to a closed circle of Polish-speaking chums. She barely acknowledged my presence and whenever I approached she just spoke louder, in Polish.

I tried to convince myself that my main crime was not being from Poland but realised that there must have been more to it than that. And if a woman turned against me with such brutal finality, I needed to know the cause so that it didn't happen again. But I've never worked it out.

There were parallels here with at least one of Trevor's stories and he's still nipping away at me. He came into the class yesterday nursing a black eye, which he says he picked up bumping into a cupboard handle while thinking about a girl called Irene. I didn't think he would encounter many cupboards in HMP Archway but let that pass.

"That's a new one on me. Was this before or after Gillian Hay?"

"The black eye?"

"No, Irene."

"After."

"So you're giving me all this stuff in the order it happened?"

"That's right. Thought I might as well make use of the experience in an article for you."

Articles, he's calling them now.

# CHAPTER TWENTY-THREE

## It couldn't have worked out

"Is that the Rev Linnell speaking?"

"Yes, this is Lesley."

"I was wondering whether you would be conducting the service this week at Southlands, or whether you'd be at St Peter's."

"Really? Why would you want to know that? Are you checking out the quality of my performance for a good gig guide?"

"Er no, ha ha, I just wanted to have a word with you about something after the service."

"Do I know you?"

"Possibly. My name's Simon Waiters, I used to live in the area."

"Well, I'll be at St Peter's on Sunday, Simon, 11am prompt. Is it something personal you want to discuss, or would it be more of a theological issue that concerns you?" she said.

"Personal, I suppose. St Peter's on Sunday. Thanks very much for that. I'll see you then."

That hadn't gone as well as I'd hoped. The Rev Lesley Linnell sounded as if she thought I was loopy. The Southlands minister always had charge of two churches. I wanted to know when I could catch Lesley at St Peter's, rather than the church on my parents' doorstep.

It was a baking hot day, ridiculously so once again for the beginning of May, and I'd got a bit of a sweat on when I arrived at St Peter's. I approached the tall-spired nineteenth century building, flashy by nonconformist standards. The interior of an old church would be agreeably cool.

I stood outside, baffled by the lack of a proper ecclesiastical entrance. "Church?" said a woman arriving with her daughter.

"Yes."

"Flats now," she said with impressive economy, pointing to the modern single storey building, not much more than a portable hut, which was the new place of worship.

It felt fine to be embraced again by a no-frills Methodist church. Everything was as I remembered it on a smaller scale than Southlands: the cheap, felt-like aisle carpet, the plain pulpit and the board giving the morning hymn numbers. The turn-out was good. If the Church was struggling these days, St Peter's seemed to be holding its own better than most. Perhaps the charisma of the Rev Lesley Linnell was bringing in all these young families. Suddenly I realised that, while I'd been daydreaming, Lesley had appeared, and was gazing down magisterially from the pulpit. Looking, perhaps, for the man who'd made the strange telephone call?

"Welcome, everybody. I'd just like to say that it is good to see a few fresh faces here today. The odd old face, too. Perhaps you will all join me now in our first hymn, number 307, page 128 in your books."

The Rev Lesley Linnell led the singing in a lusty contralto, or was it closer to a tenor? Lesley's eyes were everywhere, a nod to a mum here, a wink for a child there. The teenaged organist finished hymn 307 with a jazzy flourish and Lesley smiled indulgently while preparing to address us. What form would the sermon take? Would it be child-friendly, or would we get the heavy stuff?

Lesley was very trim but significantly different now and I worked out in what way pretty quickly. I would not be plighting my troth any time soon.

"Phew, it's a warm day out there today, isn't it children?" Lesley began. "My garden gets so hot that I'm thinking of going to Death Valley to cool down this summer. Doubtless many of you will be planning your holidays right now and I'd like to talk briefly, before you go off to your Sunday school classes, about holidays – why we need them and what we can learn from them. I'm sure that Jesus would understand the need to get away, and that he would encourage us to come back refreshed for the next stage of life's journey.

"But before that, I'd just like to tell you an old joke I heard this morning. Two men are sitting in a café talking about horoscopes. One says: 'I'm a Pisces and we are free spirits.' The other says: 'I'm an Aries and we don't believe in star signs.'

It's a load of tosh, isn't it, astrology? Have you ever looked at the birthday column in a newspaper? There's not much evidence that everyone on that day falls into a certain personality type is there? Would one horoscope fit them all? Would Our Lord allow our fates to be decreed by the position of Neptune in relation to Saturn? Seems unlikely. And where's the free will God gave us if everything is written in the stars? Sorry, I can hear you saying, 'Give us a break, Lesley, get off your hobby-horse'. Well, I won't labour the point, so let's return to the subject of holidays…."

Later, the kiddies trotted off to Sunday school classes, we sang more hymns, Lesley made a few announcements about forthcoming church events, gave a more grown-up sermon about the perils of technology and our increasingly isolated lives, and we all trooped out.

I caught up with Lesley by the church door as regular parishioners were being seen off.

"Hello, Simon, I believe you wanted a word with me?"

"You remember me?"

"I remember everyone and everything. I'm not sure whether the Almighty intended it as a blessing or a curse. How is the famous Greg Hammond, by the way?"

"Blimey, what a memory…no idea, we lost touch years and years ago. I'm living in York these days."

"Lovely city, I try to get over there once a year if I can manage it. In April, when the daffodils are out near the walls ideally. Have you any family?"

"I married Greg Hammond's ex-girlfriend," I said. "No kids."

"Happy?" This was said like someone who knew what my response would be.

"For a while. Didn't work out."

"Seems to be the way of the world these days."

I couldn't bring myself to spout some disingenuous rubbish about how we had grown apart, or how Helen had not understood me.

"Yes, I had a couple of flings. I got away with it the first time but not the second. I wasn't much cop, I'm afraid," I said.

"I'm sorry about my little dig before the sermon."

"Dig?"

"Yes, about your astrological leanings back in the day. If it hadn't been for your friend Greg, I wouldn't have found out that you took that stuff seriously. When I was a teenager, I was a po-faced about things I didn't agree with."

"That's teens for you," I said.

I've never had the slightest interest in astrology. A penny was dropping.

"Still, Simon," Lesley said, "I was confused about my identity then and as you can see it's hardly likely that things would have worked out between us."

"My first crush and you go and have a sex change on me."

"About ten years ago. I'm flattered that you liked me so much and I trust you're well balanced enough to appreciate that it doesn't make you retrospectively gay. It's lovely to meet you again, and I do recognise a mid-life crisis when I see one."

He tugged at his dog collar, as if adjusting himself mentally to move on from my trivial obsessions to the spiritual nourishment of his flock. But then he had another thought.

"This might sound like a cliché but don't dismiss it: 'By all means look at the past but don't stare'. And if you've ever got any problems you'd like to talk over, you know where to find me."

"Sure."

"Don't be a stranger. God bless."

Well, what a nice woman – man, I corrected myself, as I drove a couple of miles down the road to see Michael and Alison. But I was angrier than ever with Greg Hammond. Lesley Linnell must have stood on the touchline in 1974 being Little Miss Angry about astrology. So that bastard Greg Hammond, instead of finding out if she fancied me, said: "That's interesting you should say that, because my mate was wondering what star sign you are."

# CHAPTER TWENTY-FOUR

## Different stages of life's cycle

We had a discussion today about the Royal Family during current affairs. None of the inmates had a good word and the Professor was horrified that I'd even had the gall to discuss the subject.

"They're our enemies, Guv."

"You mean enemies as in class enemies?"

"I mean as in our jailers. I mean, our *real* jailers. If it wasn't for them, we wouldn't be inside."

"How do you work that out?"

"What's the name of this nick?"

"Archway," I said.

"No, the full name, Guv, with the big letters first."

"HMP Archway."

"There you are then, Guv. Haitch Em Pee. I rest my case."

The Professor folded his arms, nodded to the rest of the class and looked supremely pleased. There was some smirking before Trevor Smith came to my rescue.

"What he means, Simon, is that if Britain became a republic, they'd have to let all us cons out, because we are detained at Her Majesty's pleasure. The right to detain us would disappear with the Royals. Of course, some of us don't think it would necessarily work out like that."

"You can fuck off for a start, Smith."

"I'm just expressing my opinion. I don't like the Royal bastards any more than you do, Prof," said Trevor. "I'd shoot them all like they did in Russia. But I don't think a republican government would necessarily open the gates and make us all free men."

"That's a pile of bollocks, Smith. You're doing me head in."

At which point, I decided that it was time to watch the video, about the history of press coverage of Royal events. This was greeted with groans and the Professor was upset because the early sections were not in colour.

"They used to make them like that, in black and white, to hide the mistakes, Guv," he told me.

"I'm surprised you've not heard that one before, Simon," Trevor said as he handed me his latest essay at the end of the class.

"About black and white covering up the mistakes?"

"No, about the Royals and the prisons."

"Where did he get it from? What's he on about?"

"It's an idea that goes round young offenders' gaffs. Some of the dafter lads who end up in full prisons never manage to shake it off."

Trevor removed his glasses, the thickest lens I'd ever seen, breathed on them and wiped them with a dirty handkerchief, using the hand with the missing finger tip. He had wispy hair, a blank canvas of a face with almost non-existent eyebrows and a terrible squint in one eye. He was about 30 if the dates are right in his memoirs but not wearing well. He didn't strike me as much of a ladies' man and, with such unprepossessing looks, I could understand why his nerve failed him at key moments. I suddenly felt sorry for him, and looked at him sympathetically.

"Have a butcher's of that, Simon. I thought these incidents could be the basis for a novel."

"Why not. Maybe try starting first with a short story."

"Hope you're not suggesting I'm not up to writing a novel," said Trevor, doing his moving up close to me trick again.

"No," I said cautiously. "It's, er, just that different creative ideas lend themselves to different formats. Your experiences could be a short story, or even a radio play, but yes, I suppose it could turn out to be a bigger project. I'll have a look at them over the weekend."

"Okay." Trevor pushed his glasses up over the bridge of his nose, Eric Morecambe style, and was happy again.

*There are some memories which are so vivid that you wonder how they got stuck. Why, for example, do I remember so clearly ordinary incidents? My dad told me he'd been in a hotel where a top football team was staying. "Most of them hardly knew how to use a knife and fork, Trevor," he says. I hated football and was always one of the last to be picked at school, so I couldn't understand what he was getting at.*

*I think he was trying to teach me a lesson. I might be no use at football but I'm intelligent. If I worked hard that would surely be more use to me in the long run, he seemed to be pointing out. But, like I say, I sussed that out years later. Why should that, and countless insignificant exchanges going back decades, stick around in my head? I can even remember where the conversation took place. It was outside our shed and my dad was showing me how to mend a puncture.*

*I have a theory. We all live our lives a number of times as the same person, getting the chance to do a few things differently on each journey on Earth, and so become better. We are all at different stages in this cycle. The people with the best memories of incidents from the past are those who are at a later stage in the cycle. They are the people who have lived their lives more often. Those with vague memories of the past are only at the beginning of the process.*

*I am cursed by the way my memories stick around. And in particular by thoughts of my lost loves, like Elaine Foster and Claire Daniels.*

Some of Trevor's tales were more believable than others. I didn't buy one about a posh solicitor and began to feel we had slipped into the realms of fiction. I also wondered if there was any significance to Trevor's choice of names for his lost girls. And that's before we even began to look at two substantial holes in Trevor's theory. If he'd come back many times, accumulating all those unwiped memories on the way, how had he learned so little that he was still bemoaning missed opportunities with women, and spending half his adult life locked up?

The other hole related to the nature of his memories. If the Trevor Smith version of Hinduism was right, he had also lived the remainder of his life many times. This should have given him a few half-remembered insights into what would happen next. But he never mentioned the future; he had no more idea of what lay ahead than anyone else.

# CHAPTER TWENTY-FIVE

## My life as a situation comedy

My cleaner Kath had been at her work again. She'd put a flyer on the dining room table, in which an estate agent was 'looking for houses in need of modernisation'.

"This arrived just after you'd gone out," she'd written in red biro on a sheet of A4 notepaper.

Maybe it was time to give her Barry a call. Kath's brother was a reliable local Mr Fixit who could turn his hand to most jobs.

I resented an estate agent thinking that my home might need modernisation, before being flogged by someone else at an obscene profit; especially as the previous owner had been a pensioner, and the building company who did it up before Helen and I moved in had stripped out all its interesting period features. However, I conceded that some TLC was needed. I took one of my occasional, critical looks at the front. The front gate was neatly propped up but the hinge was broken so you couldn't close it. The small shrubs that Helen and I planted had become 'jungly'. The outside needed painting. I made a mental note to ask Kath about the availability of Barry.

Kath, never a woman to cut corners, had done her usual good job which was important because Wendy was coming to York and could conceivably make her first visit to my place. We'd met a couple of times in the fortnight since she'd moved in with her sister. During that time Elliot had made one of two abusive telephone calls, fielded by

Tina, who used her line about her boyfriend working in ready-made concrete.

"What's that mean?" Elliot had asked.

"Work it out, Big Man," said Tina.

I wondered if there was a reminder for me, too, but I got brownie points from Tina for my self-deprecating retelling of how the Bill Patel Bunbury got me in trouble with Greg, Gill and Melanie. It was a selective narrative which omitted Helen and my loud exclamation that the now famous novelist was not a "Paki lover".

Wendy had looked at me fondly over this anecdote and I wasn't sure how to play my cards. She was attractive enough but not really, I could now see, the lost love of my life. Then again, who was I at 42 to expect the same level of hopeless infatuation that you experienced in your teens and early 20s? I'm sure I was at least as drawn to Wendy as I'd been to Helen when we met up in Halifax after all those years.

So today could well be make or break, I guessed. Wendy said she would like to see where I live after we'd spent a few hours in town. We were both grown-ups; this could be the start of a nice, but not outrageously intense relationship. Friends with benefits, as they say. Now I'd established that to my satisfaction, it was not easy to keep thoughts of sex at bay.

If this had been a television situation comedy, an Inner Voice might have been egging me on, as we sat in the window of a coffee shop and watched the world go by.

*"It's going well, don't get too carried away – but you're doing fine,"* says Inner Voice.

"Do you remember a record by Joan Armatrading called Love and Affection?" I asked Wendy.

"No. Who is Joan Armatrading?" she said.

"You don't know who Joan Armatrading is?" I asked carefully, not wanting to imply any criticism.

"Well, she must be a singer," she said, "But I don't know her. It's more Elliot's field, in fact I only heard your name on Sound of the

Sixties because he listens every week. I've never known much about pop music. It's one of Elliot's little jokes that I'm thick about it."

"Thick about pop music. I think that's rather charming," I said.

*"Nice one, Simon," says Inner Voice.*

"It's a long time since I found anything about Elliot remotely charming," she said with her new resolve.

"Gosh, no, I meant it's rather charming of you, Wendy."

She blushed fetchingly.

"Anyway," I said after another silence. "She's perhaps not so big now, but she's still around. Love and Affection was her first hit I think, not that I'm a big expert on these things myself. It was a distinctive record, and it was played at the Radford House Easter Ball."

"Yes they were fun, those Easter balls," she said.

"Are you still friends with that Greg Hammond?" she continued after a brief silence. "I do remember seeing you with him but not after the first year."

"He left in the summer and we lost touch eventually. I still see his mum and dad in Manchester when I'm visiting my parents, they're only a few streets away."

"They must be very proud of him," she said. "I really love those Fox and Finder books."

I got the impression from both Mum and Michael that Arnold and Barbara Hammond would have preferred a nice son and daughter-in-law, and a couple of grandchildren who they saw occasionally, rather than self-centred Greg, his brittle, metropolitan wife Samantha and kids called Toby and Jocasta. But saying so might make me sound bitter and twisted.

Wendy was one of those touchy-feely people who would brush your arm when making a point. Inner Voice reckoned that this all looked very promising; getting her to come back to my place proved easy and she chose to sit on the sofa with me rather than on one of the single chairs.

As I say, Kath had left everything spick and span. For my part, I'd remade the bed with clean sheets, my best linen. I still thought that it was early days for hitting the sack but I was keen to play every angle and I thought this might be the moment. Did I want a relationship with her? There is no one more dangerous to himself than a sex-starved man presented with an opportunity to break a long-term duck.

I thought about Tina and her boyfriend's menacing means of earning a living. *"No, no, no, you'll be fine…consenting adults, consenting adults".*

"You're rather beige, Simon, apart from that thing," said Wendy, homing in on the Delvaux.

"You're not keen."

"It's pretty hideous. Tina thinks that my tastes in art are conventional but, I don't know, it just sucks, somehow. Sorry, Simon, I'd paint over it."

"Sucks. That's not an expression I've heard for some time," I said. I wondered if Wendy was enjoying a sense of liberation, the opportunity to say what she liked to a bloke without worrying about whether a reprimand, at best, or a left hook, at worst, might be heading her way soon.

I smiled and prepared to move a little closer to Wendy.

The doorbell rang, and I heard the front door opening.

"Just me, Simon, are you there?" Kath called. "Left a couple of things behind."

Sometimes life really does resemble a situation comedy.

# CHAPTER TWENTY-SIX

## How about a refreshing Kia-Ora?

The Who'd 'a Thowt It, the village pub near the prison, is a 19th century building with a plain, tidy exterior. I must have passed it several hundred, even 1,000 times, without ever having much curiosity about its interior. Our attitude to public houses reflects a growing conservatism as the years go by, as well as a more limited capacity for alcohol. When we're young we want to explore them all unless someone offers a good reason why we shouldn't. When we're older we don't want to try new places unless someone offers a good reason why we should. But the Who'd 'a Thowt It, yes, worth a look.

At the prison, Vera Corbett thanked me for the suggestion that her Diane should try out an Internet chat room to find a boyfriend.

"It wasn't exactly my idea was it, Vera, though I can't remember precisely what I did say."

"Thanks, anyway, whatever it was. She seems to have met a nice lad, she's a lot more cheerful right now."

"Good, fingers crossed it works out," I said, hoping that the nice lad didn't end up strangling her at a local beauty spot.

The Bad Screw had tried unsuccessfully to wind me up with some hot news from the cells.

"You'll be missing your star pupil today, Mr Waiters."

"Who's that?" I stalled, though I knew who he had in mind.

"Your mate Trevor Smith."

No bad thing, I thought. The other inmates are usually more amenable when Trevor's not around. His enthusiasm rubs them up the wrong way.

"We'll get by. What's up with him?"

"Got to see the dentist," said the Bad Screw, implying that the problems weren't caused by wear and tear.

Thursday was the day that Trevor liked to give me the latest instalment in his life story. I didn't teach him on Friday morning and he believed that his creativity demanded a weekend's attention from the reader, so that the text could be fully absorbed and analysed. I thought, therefore, that his absence would spare me another slab of his fantasy world. I was wrong because Jamie Dickinson, a young inmate who got on with Trevor better than most, came in with an envelope.

Jamie was a former charity worker, if going round pubs on behalf of the local hospice and pocketing the proceeds counts as charity work. He was proud that Trevor had entrusted him with the latest chapter and assured me that he hadn't read it first.

Rather than addressing the envelope to me, Trevor had written: 'It's Gillian Hay!' The exclamation mark was infuriating, as if I had been in an agony of anticipation over the woman who invited him to the cinema then failed to show, "leaving me to partake of a boxette of Payne's Poppets and a refreshing Kia-Ora on my lonesome".

Trevor had got my head spinning again with thoughts of what might have been. How often had an ill-judged remark at a key moment undone everything that went before? If you never found out what that wrong word was, you couldn't adjust for next time. Each relationship with a woman was like a separate chess match; even if you did work out how you had blown it, you never got the chance to put things right because no two games were the same. Trevor might well have strayed once again into make believe, but that didn't affect the basic truth of what he was saying. His story of Gillian Hay, as he called her, reminded me of Anna Florenski. It was Anna who made me confront, at the age of 28 and a couple of years before Helen came back on the scene, the knowledge that I had never acquired any real insight into the nature of women.

But, I tried to convince myself, your star is rising. You've met an attractive woman from the past who likes you, and you're helping her to rebuild her life. A few more doors might open; go with the flow, and see how things pan out.

To an ironic cheer, Trevor, escorted by an officer, made an appearance in my class ten minutes before the bell went. He was holding his hand against his mouth and looking sorry for himself.

"Apologies if I'm a little slurred, Simon," he said to me at the end of the class. "Broken tooth that had to come out. Slightly numb from the anaesthetic."

"Oh dear," I said, then couldn't think of anything sympathetic to add. "Had a quick glance at your work," I said. "Looks interesting."

"Interesting?" snapped Trevor, as if this was damning him with faint praise.

"Well, yes, actually. There's a nice empathy."

"Empathy," echoed Trevor. "That is good."

"Yeah, I like the way you've put yourself in the shoes of the kiosk character. Woman, I mean," I said, correcting myself hastily. "Anyway, I'll give you some proper feedback on Monday."

"Right, Simon," he said. "You all right, by the way?"

Strange question; it wasn't typical practice of inmates to ask after my health.

"I'm fine, just met up with an old flame, actually."

"An old flame?" he said. "Sounds like trouble."

"Maybe. Only time will tell," I said, trying to make light of something I shouldn't have mentioned.

"Yeah," said Trevor. His smile as he left the classroom was, I thought, rather sinister.

# CHAPTER TWENTY-SEVEN

## An eternity in Castleford

Elliot had got wind that I'd been in touch with Wendy and was now involved in some way in her welfare. He'd discovered my phone number, too.

"I'd like to meet you, Waiters," he said.

"Now, why would I want to agree to that?" I said.

"You've got some explaining to do, putting ideas into Wendy's head and all."

I wasn't going to be intimidated. Nevertheless, it was with some relief that I could say honestly that Wendy and I had not slept together.

"I'll come to you," he said. "Don't worry, I'll not be knocking on your door. We can meet in the Museum Gardens. There's a dinosaur exhibition I want to see."

It was our first face-to-face since Hereford days. There must be something in the water at Scarborough; Elliot, like Wendy, hadn't been changed much by the years. Partly because he'd always been frozen in time, one of those men who was middle aged at 20. Now, in his 40s, he was about right; give it another ten years and he'd be on the young side. He was tall, angular and still thin; the vomit beard had been tamed as a sop to his legal clients. Carr looked like a man born to play Andrew Aguecheek.

I was sitting on a bench near the museum watching Mr Indigo, one of those blokes who stands around like a statue until someone gives him a few bob, when Carr came round the corner seeking a likely candidate to be me.

My Swiss finishing school hadn't prepared me for this encounter. Hand-shaking didn't seem the thing, but I got up out of politeness as he approached me, then changed my mind about the courtesies and pretended I was standing to search my pockets for change.

Carr wasn't a fashion figure. He wore shapeless dark-beige cord trousers, and a light-beige Millets anorak which obscured a medium-beige t-shirt.

"Elliot. You all right?" I said, nodding and keeping my hands trousered, eyeing his wardrobe with fascination.

"I wear a suit for work, don't I?" he said defensively.

"You look well."

"Why wouldn't I?"

"Moving on from the social niceties, what is it that you want to say to me?"

"Wendy's a very delicate girl, you know."

"I'm not so sure that's true. She seems okay to me, if a little cowed by you."

"What's that meant to mean?"

"What it's meant to mean, Elliot, is that I know all about you and she's had enough."

"You know fuck all about our marriage."

"I know what she's told me and I've no reason to believe that she's an unreliable narrator."

"That's right, dress it up in your English Literature bollocks. Have you two been to bed yet?"

"We haven't and we won't be. To my knowledge, she's not been to bed with anyone – yet."

"It's that Greg Hammond, isn't it?" he said, as if he'd had a moment of epiphany. "She's got his books and I know that you were a friend of his."

154

"Were is the operative word. There's not much chance of our paths crossing again and even if they did, I wouldn't wish Hammond on my worst enemy."

"You don't seem to like anyone very much do you, Waiters?"

"I'm not crazy about you, Elliot."

I thought he was going to take a swipe at me, but he was suddenly distracted by a big cheer from a group of kids as Mr Indigo suddenly came to life. It was a cool, late-summer day. The sky was grey but, in an attempt to blot out Mr Indigo and concentrate on the job in hand, I put my hand to my temple as if the sun was bothering me.

"You can tell that bitch Tina, that if Wendy isn't back in Scarborough by the end of the week I'll take her to the fucking cleaners."

"Why don't you just piss off and find some more common ground with your dinosaurs, Elliot," I said.

Carr, nimble on his feet, was in my face in a couple of seconds, making a fist with my jacket and pinning me against the back of the bench. He spoke very quietly.

"Look, Waiters, you want to watch your fucking back. Blokes like you are ten a penny, pathetic penis-led individuals. Your only thought is when you're next going to get de-spunked. And if the person willing to do that de-spunking is a troubled young woman like Wendy then what difference does it make? Just so long as the bog gets a regular flushing, you're happy."

"That's…that's…" I said, indicating that I'd be more willing to explain myself if he let go, "A very basic view of male sexuality, Elliot. Anyway, it takes two to tango, not that we're tangoing in any case."

I regretted the cliché immediately but Elliot's anger had peaked.

"I knew you were trouble from the first time I laid eyes on you, Waiters."

"Did you?"

"Yes I did. Making a nuisance of yourself with Wendy."

"It wasn't what it looks like. I was very shy where girls were concerned," I said. "Inexperienced northern grammar school boy."

"You expect me to believe that? And what the fuck has the northern bit got to do with anything? You are an unbelievable low-life piece of shit, and the same goes for that erstwhile chummy of yours. I hope you both rot in hell for ever and ever, in a state of eternal spontaneous combustion while digging for coal at the bottom of some god-forsaken pit on the outskirts of Castleford."

I was impressed by the content of Elliot Carr's outburst, and the lawyer-like way he'd homed in on the irrelevant adjective. But he stood there looking like a man taken aback by his own eloquence, and with nothing more to offer. He'd had his time; in the end he was all bluster. Wendy had nothing to fear from him any more.

"Well, thank you for your pertinent views," I said. "I'm sure that Wendy will be seeing you in court before long, and that you can both come to an amicable settlement."

# CHAPTER TWENTY-EIGHT

## Even the Worm (I)

"Stop sulking for a second and look at this, Simon," said Uncle Andrew, trying to hand me a piece of paper containing a childish scrawl.

It was Christmas Eve, 1977. I was standing next to the mahogany and cut-glass bar of an Edwardian pub in Stockport, a place of which Gill Todd would have approved. An appropriate thought in view of Andrew's presence; he'd been tipped off that this was where he would find me. As I hesitated over the notepaper, he thrust a pint of bitter into my hand and said: "We need to have clear-the-air talks. You can't go on ignoring me. We're family, you know, flesh and blood."

Technically, that was false. But it was the wrong moment to say so, was in any case irrelevant, and would have drawn attention to an unsavoury and best-forgotten moment in family history.

"We all know about your adventures, Andrew, why did you have to pinch my best girl when you've got the pick of the finest talent south Manchester has to offer?"

I had a tendency to start talking like him when we were together.

"And north Cheshire, old boy."

I couldn't help smiling, and knew I would weaken under the relentless Uncle Andrew charm offensive.

"I am really, really sorry about what happened, Simon, but you've got to believe me when I say that I didn't nick her from you."

"Yeah, like offering to take her for a spin in your Triumph Stag? I should have bloody well told her you called it Hazel. That would have nipped her interest in the bud, all right. Would have served you right if you'd gone for Melanie Cohen, she'd have had you castrated."

"Melanie Cohen? The ultra-feminist pal?"

"That's her."

"They were fierce madams, the pair of them," said Andrew. "The Cohen girl especially so. And both of them bloody attractive, too, in an idiosyncratic sort of way. That TV critic in the Observer certainly had the horn for Gill. But with me it was only flirting, well in the first place it was. You know I like the company of the ladies, even when I'm not romantically involved. But, look, she came on strong to me, and also made it clear it was no more than a quick tumble or two. Damn fine arrangement for all concerned."

"With the possible exception of Auntie Laura."

"True enough, old boy, you have me there. Now, hand on heart, you know there's no way I would have pinched a woman, even someone of Gill's undoubted calibre, from my nephew if – an important bit this, Simon – if she'd only had eyes for you. She said that she'd been trying to find the right moment to finish with you nicely."

"You're saying my goose had already been cooked by the time we went out for a terrible night in an Indian restaurant? Not my best moment."

"Yes, she might have mentioned that. It gave her a good get-out-of-jail card."

"Bloody hell, Andrew, going out with me couldn't have been that horrible."

"Course not, badly expressed. Sorry again, Simon."

I wondered what else Andrew knew about us.

"Most of her comments about you were good," he said, then added, determined now to be unsparingly honest, "a few not so good."

Like mentioning her orgasm on my first outing, I guessed; then pointing out that I never repeated the trick.

"As I said, just get off your high horse and have a look at this," said Andrew, "It fair brought a tear to my eye when Laura dug it out. She still remembers the day your mum gave it to us, together with a ludicrously cute picture of you with the first snowman you'd ever constructed."

I finally accepted and read his offering.

*"My uncle and aunt live in a big house at Wilmslow, in Cheshire. They are very glamoruss, and I like them very much. They give me lots of treats, and they have been very kind to me so far. Uncle Andrew looks like Roger More and Auntie Laura looks like Pechula Clarke".*

"We both loved the 'so far', Simon."

"Well, I couldn't have had you and Auntie Laura resting on your laurels."

"That's the spirit, old chap. Drink up and I'll get you another pint."

Auntie Laura had two miscarriages and I used to receive talks about things not to say before we went to Wilmslow. Uncle Andrew and Auntie Laura would make a huge fuss, sending me home with chocolates, pocket money and the occasional Corgi toy. Somewhere in my junk room there is an East African Safari VW Beetle, with a tiny tyre on the roof to make the car's front wheels turn. With the original box, safari scene and plastic rhino, all long lost, it would be worth the best part of £200. Thanks to Andrew, however, money is now the least of my concerns. I used to turn over my empty boiled-egg shells and say: "That's for Uncle Andrew." He was the tallest man I knew and I wanted to provide him with extra sustenance.

When Mum was ten, my grandparents went to a private orphanage. At the risk of making this sound like Sophie's Choice they looked at two babies with a view to taking one home. Andrew, a charmer from the off, suddenly produced an adorable gesture which secured his future. My mum and dad speculated on the nature of Uncle Andrew's natural parents, and much later on the possibility that one or both of them might have been on the stage. Acting was a talent that Andrew discovered in his mid 20s, by which time he was already on the way to becoming a successful estate agent. I'd wager that he initially joined an amateur dramatics company in a search for female talent. If acting was in his blood, so was philandering. When Auntie Laura began to lose her appealing similarity to the singer of Downtown and Don't Sleep in the Subway, Uncle Andrew cast his net far and wide, and the South Manchester Thespians was a well-stocked sea.

Auntie Laura joined the Thespians briefly, to do set painting and prompting. That wasn't enough to discourage Andrew although it was years before she finally lost patience. His divorce settlement was generous; Auntie Laura stayed in the Cheshire house, and Uncle Andrew moved into an apartment in the centre of Manchester. I'd come across him a few times on his various assignations. The most memorable occasion was in an Indian restaurant at Handforth. I was with Greg Hammond, the first time I'd seen him for more than a year. He'd put on weight; 24 was on the young side to be getting fat in the face and starting a paunch.

Hammond was telling me about his admiration for Margaret Thatcher (I wondered what happened to the Marxism, but I decided the answer would annoy me and I didn't bother asking), his posh new girlfriend, Samantha, his job on the evening paper in Bolton and his detective fiction books. He'd completed the first and had a few rejections from publishers and literary agents but was continuing undeterred with the second. I went through my usual range of emotions. I had to admire Hammond's total faith in his ability to get things done. On the other hand, I wondered, how much more can I take of someone whose favourite subject is himself, and who takes a constant delight in putting you down?

"I'm on a roll, Simon," he was saying. "The premise can't fail. The rejection notes have encouraged me to stick at it, agents and publishers don't say that kind of thing unless they mean it, and I just know I'm going to spend the rest of my life with Sam."

"You've only just met, she lives in London, and you always seem to love 'em and leave 'em in double-quick time."

"Not this time, this is the big one. We are not in Helen Oldfield stroke Melanie Cohen territory any more," he said, doing an elaborate diagonal line in the air on the stroke. "I've paid me dues with some rough 'uns. This time it's for keeps, and I've given up the fags – how's that for commitment."

He held his hand up to show me his fingers, now less yellow, if not yet entirely nicotine free.

"On due reflection, unfair on Helen, that last bit," he said. "Funny, I sometimes thought that you two might have got it together after we split up."

"Not my type, temperamentally," I said. "But a very nice girl."

Hammond took a self-satisfied swig of his lager and looked around the restaurant. Perhaps he was imagining the day staff would fall over themselves when he came in, and lovers of detective fiction would scrabble round for pieces of paper for him to sign.

"Hang on a second, doesn't that guy over there know you?" he said. "No, don't," he added as I started to turn round, "his body language suggests he doesn't want you to see him. He's looking over here in spite of himself."

"Intriguing," I said. The diversion was welcome; the next thing would have been how Hammond's decision to quit university had paved the way for his brilliant career.

"Don't think I've made too many out-and-out enemies, Greg. Describe him."

"He's got a sort of faded matinee idol look about him. Middle-aged, a tad overweight, but still with the vestiges of his good looks."

"An out-of-condition Roger Moore, maybe."

"Not a bad description."

"That'll be Uncle Andrew with one of his girls," I said.

"You could have a bit of fun here, Sim, you could really put the frighteners on him."

"I like it, Greg," I laughed. I thought for a moment that Hammond had been suggesting a spot of blackmail. I went over to say hello; Uncle Andrew looked like a man who had been confronted by the grim reaper.

"Simon, what a surprise. This is Hilary, she's an actress," he said, theatrically. "Simon is my, um…"

"Nephew," I helped out.

"Yes, nephew. My sister Joyce's lad. He's the brains of the family, university degree and now teaching."

For someone who must be practised in playing away, Uncle Andrew was extraordinarily flummoxed to be caught out.

"What are you teaching?" said Hilary, a deliciously curvy mid-thirties red head with a big smile.

"Children?" said Uncle Andrew, snapping a poppadom and putting lime pickle on it.

"That's *who* you teach, plonker. I asked Simon *what's* he's teaching."

"English and history, probably."

"Good luck and watch out for those young girls. I'd have eaten you alive when I was in the sixth form."

"I'd have dabbed the pickle on myself."

She liked that, so I decided to leave them to it while I was ahead. Maybe Hilary talked that way to all young men who looked passable in the half-light of an Indian restaurant. It was pretty clear that nothing much was going on with Uncle Andrew beyond a bhuna and a quickie back at her place.

"What d'you make of all that, then?" said Hammond, barely able to contain his excitement. "She looks like a serious piece of merchandise, that's a big bus for any man to drive. Just think, Sim, she could be your auntie one day."

"Somehow I don't think it will come to that. Interesting thought."

"Here's another. Your Uncle Andrew, he's worth a few bob isn't he?"

"Probably."

"So he could always throw a few nourishing scraps your way. Might be a good time to tap him up and get those student debts sorted."

"Suggesting, I suppose, that it would be a pity if anyone got to hear about Hilary."

"Could be the case," he said with a malicious gleam in his eye.

"I thought you were joking earlier, you are an unbelievable piece of work, Hammond."

"Cool it, it were just a whim."

"Like hell it was. You're deadly serious, aren't you?"

We finished the meal in silence. I didn't want to make a song and dance with Uncle Andrew sitting a few tables away, so I didn't tell Hammond to fuck off forever until we were out of the restaurant. There had been a few previous occasions when I should have done so, but there was a pleasing symmetry attached to the venue. It was five or six years since Hammond's biggest crime, also in an Indian.

I looked at my watch. There was still time to catch a bus. I braced myself and went on the offensive as Hammond searched his pockets for the car keys.

"Is there nothing you won't stoop to, Greg?"

"Like I said, that were just a joke, about the blackmail," he said.

"Greg, this might sound odd, but I'd rather we didn't see each other any more."

"Hey? What are you on about? We're not dating. Blokes don't normally finish with one another, or is there something you haven't told me about yourself. It might explain your occasional reticence where the ladies are concerned."

"Well, I agree that this might sound weird," I said, determined not to be diverted.

"Yes, I think you just said that."

"But I'd just rather not meet up again."

"Have you gone mental or something, Simon?"

Hammond stood there leaning on his car door, looking at me for signs that this was an oddball joke.

"I've never been saner. The bottom line is this: the last few times we've met I've come away feeling unhappy with things you've said."

"What sort of things."

"The way you reproach me for the way I conduct my life, I suppose. Taking the piss out of my inability to make decisions, for example."

"You've never been the quickest have you, Rocket Boy? Why have you never challenged me about it before, you big baby?"

"It's more than just that. If I'm going to be honest, I reckon you're so full of shit that everything you say is something I want to challenge. If we only meet up every few months, I don't want to spend the whole evening arguing."

"No, you've never been a man for confrontation."

"Well, I'm confronting you now....even the worm turns eventually," I added.

"Right, Simon," he said after a pause, as if I'd come out with something profound. "Even the worm. And it's taken a mere 20-odd years. Shoot, then."

"Hey?"

"Shoot. Tell me something unpleasant about myself, apart from the fact you've decided that I'm a potential blackmailer."

"Well, for starters," I said, shuffling uncomfortably from foot to foot but ploughing on, "there's a kind of hardness about you that I'm increasingly aware of. It's always been there but it's getting worse. It comes out of your solipsistic nature."

"Ooh, very nice."

"You can't see life from any perspective other than your own."

"I do know what solipsistic means."

"And you're just so fucking aggressive, the way you argue about anything you don't agree with. It's as if any criticism of your world view is a heinous offence."

"You're just fucking jealous, Waiters. At the end of the day, I was too smart for university, plus I'm doing something I really want to do: I'm a future best-selling writer."

"Well, I wouldn't want to be like you and you wouldn't want to be like me."

"Too bloody right. Going into a job designed for life's failures, because you don't know what else to do with yourself."

Hammond had got into the car and slammed the door. He was sitting in the driver's seat with the window down. My heart was banging away as it did only when I was really angry. He'd turned the ignition and I took a final deep breath to focus on what I was saying, to make sure that I got it right.

"Look, I take off my hat to everything you've achieved so far, and if the book thing works out good luck. But knocking around with you has always been a rocky ride that was only worth it because I thought the journey was interesting. Now I don't think it's worth it. So fuck off out of my life, I don't want to have anything more to do with you."

"If that's the way you want it, then it's bye bye, Simon," he said, winding the window up. "Bye, bye," he mouthed with an Italian style wave of the hand, as if to a small child. "Bye, bye, Rocket Boy. I hope that you get to meet Yuri again in Heaven." He pushed the car into gear and sped off out of my life.

A telephone call about six months later confirmed everyone's suspicions about Uncle Andrew. I was in my first job at a comprehensive, just about coping. Mum came into my bedroom looking distressed. I was beavering away behind a pile of exercise books.

"That was Auntie Laura on the phone."

"She's split up from Uncle Andrew," I said.

"My brother's left his wife and you didn't think you should tell me?"

"No, you've just told me, Mum. I guessed."

Living at home was taking its toll. Having meals on the table and the washing done had helped to ease me through the first couple of years in the classroom. There was no energy left for a social life, and all I could manage at the end of the day was mumbled thanks for a pork chop and two veg, and some graceless bickering over alleged verbal infelicities by Dad. At the age of 25, I was behaving like the churlish adolescent I had never been. It was time to find my own place.

"I told *you*? What are you talking about?" said Mum.

"It's obvious. You are the bearer of bad tidings. Your manner suggested that something was amiss, but nothing as traumatic as bereavement. We all know that Uncle Andrew is a bit of a womaniser.

Ergo, he's had one fling too many and either he's left Auntie Laura or vice versa."

"Is it having a degree makes you such a clever dick? Well, you'll be pleased to hear that you're right. Andrew's staying with a friend, a male one as far as I know, and Laura says that there is absolutely no going back. It's the end."

She burst into tears. She'd always had a tender relationship with her little brother, having accepted his arrival without demur when he turned up out of the blue as an eight-week old baby. I realised that facetiousness was not the order of the day; there would be enough of that from Dad.

"I'm really sorry, Mum," I said, putting my marking aside and giving her my full attention. "Maybe it's better that this happens now, while Auntie Laura's still young enough to build a new life."

"Andrew was such a lovely little boy. I wonder if it's something in his genes, to do with his blood parents being actors. That funny little gesture we talk about, your Grandpa Pal thought he was about to deliver a witty after-dinner speech."

"No, Mum, it's just to do with him being a cad," I said. "A rogue, albeit a likeable one."

After that I saw more, rather than less, of Uncle Andrew. It started when I bumped into him in a pub in Didsbury early one Friday evening, a few months after the break-up. He wasn't looking well, his face had a greyish tinge to it and I wondered whether several Three Castles cigarettes and a couple of pints of bitter on an empty stomach was a smart move.

"Things tough in the estate agency game, Andrew?"

"No difficulties at all, old boy, I wouldn't go so far as to say that it's money for old rope but things are fine. Even when the market took a dive we were still shifting houses. Perhaps I should sell up, make a tidy pile and live in Tenerife."

"Why so glum, then?"

"This bachelor life isn't all it's made out to be, coming home to an empty flat, boil-in-your-bag meals. Even when you make an effort you've got to eat it on your own."

He stared gloomily at his pint pot, then added almost to himself: "Laura seems to be doing all right, got a new chap I believe."

"Tony Jessop. She brought him round the other week. Seems a nice enough bloke, offered to give me a hand with shifting some stuff to this flat I've found in Heaton Moor. Hope you don't mind that, by the way, I'm not becoming best mates with him."

"Not at all, old boy, glad this Tony's all right. Laura deserves to be happy. Good girl, that."

"Yes."

"What was it Joni Mitchell said? 'You don't know what you've got 'til it's gone'."

Uncle Andrew nodded his head back and forth and sang the next couple of lines of the song to himself. There was a pause while we thought about the merits of Laura as wife and auntie. I was sorely tempted to ask him what happened to the fiery red-head Hilary. Not the most tactful question, I decided, but then Andrew's thoughts turned out to have been travelling the same path.

"Bit of an irony here. When you met me with the red-haired girl in the Indian restaurant I was having a crisis of conscience."

"Would the red head have been, er, Hilary?" I said, nonchalantly.

"Ever thought of going on stage yourself, Simon?"

"No."

"Probably a good thing. Come on, old boy, you've not forgotten Hilary. Your eyes were doing a merry little dance."

"Okay, bang to rights."

"As I said, crisis of conscience. I'd finally decided that I was getting past this womanising lark. Then some bastard shopped me to Laura."

"Who was it?" I said, thinking of Greg Hammond.

"A fellow thespian who'd also had his eyes on Hilary. He was a pal, or so I thought, and had once been Othello to my Iago."

"Crikey, jealousy is a terrible thing."

"My exact thoughts. I do appreciate, by the way, that you didn't spill the beans. A lot of young lads would have."

After that, we met regularly. He told me about a few girls, but they didn't seem to amount to much more than the occasional date. He was younger than the James Bond who had admitted to having just three expressions. But a few years before Roger Moore played 007 for the last time, Andrew's matinee idol looks had vanished like a melting dream. When I found a new teaching job in Leeds, Andrew put me in touch with an acquaintance in the property letting business who helped me to find a flat. Shortly after that he had his first heart attack.

# CHAPTER TWENTY-NINE

## The Misleading Dream Syndrome

I have declared 2000 my International Year of Eco-Tourism. I'm staying at home.

I can afford to go anywhere I like, but travel doesn't suit my introspective personality. Let's just consider some trips abroad and my biggest single memory.

**Albufeira, 1989, the honeymoon.** Michael Summerbell did the honours as best man, as I had for him ten years earlier. We had a great send-off, a small register office ceremony followed by a reception at a swish hotel in Harrogate. Fred from the Shoulder of Mutton in Headingley came along and did a quick turn as Steve Highway, imploring us with a specially rewritten version, Your Way, to have a happy life together. It was almost one of the best days of my life, despite a couple of dodgy flashbacks. Although I did my best to block them out there was a brief visitation from at least two lost girls, and Wendy was certainly in there.

The first seven days in Portugal were fine, though I wasn't very sold on the Algarve. I had a dream about Lesley and, curiously but not for the first time, Melanie Cohen. I was going to an England match with Rupesh Ruia. But we'd got separated and some shaven-headed supporters with white-supremacist tattoos had taken me into their fold. Melanie saw me. She didn't have to speak; those dark, reproachful eyes said it all for her. "It's not what it looks like," I shouted, but no sounds were coming out of my mouth. "You'll never change, Rocket Boy," she said sadly. "But Melanie," I tried again. "I have changed." "Too much important work on my hands to be hanging around with you and your trailer-trash mates," she said.

So there I was, on the first morning of our honeymoon, barely aware of my new wife lying next to me. I hadn't conjured up Lesley, Gill or Anna. The subject of my daydreams was Melanie Cohen, suddenly the most attractive woman in the world. "Mind you, I'm not saying I thought her unattractive in the first place, I'm just pointing out that we didn't hit it off," I muttered.

"What's that?" said Helen sleepily.

"Nothing, love, guess I was thinking out loud."

I've always been subject to sleep-induced infatuations with women. I call it the Misleading Dream Syndrome, where you wake up fancying someone you've never previously liked. I've never met anyone who's had a similar experience. Surely I can't be unique? During the next week, however, Melanie proved to be a more tenacious form of this virus; she hung around doggedly for much longer than my usual syndrome girls, and was still with me until I was distracted by a mild crush on a waitress. It was an inauspicious start to married life.

**Andalucia, 1992**. Southern Spain had long been on my wish list. As Helen and I stood in the Alhambra Gardens, she said that Granada looked as if it had been carved from ivory. I was miles away, she asked me what I was thinking about, and I made up something about Velazquez and Goya and the Spanish artistic temperament. I had actually been recalling my only previous visit to Spain, my last holiday with Mum and Dad. That was in 1974, a few weeks after I didn't go out with Lesley Linnell. I spent the rest of the Andalucian week wondering, once again, what had become of Lesley.

Was this the time I started thinking seriously about playing the Bunbury card with Helen? In my weak defence, I don't think it was that calculated. Bunbury had lain thankfully dormant during the first three years of our marriage. Helen might even have mentioned Bill

170

Patel once or twice ("didn't you say he lived in Birmingham now?") and I'd agreed that I ought to contact him.

During the autumn after we returned from Andalucia, Maurice Whittle called to say that he was going to an alumni event in Hereford. Did I fancy joining him?

The bugger never showed. He left a message at the bed and breakfast we'd booked into: "Sorry, Simon, Liv decided that on balance she didn't really like the sound of this event. Not worth the aggro of arguing the toss. Have to take a rain check."

I was gloomy at the prospect of a function in the university refectory to which most people had come with friends or partners. The meal was mass catering at its grimmest and the conversation non-existent. I sat next to an economics graduate whose name tag said he was Bobby Barlow.

"My friend Maurice Whittle did economics with history. He had planned to join me tonight. Remember him?"

"No, can't say I do," Bobby Barlow said, revealing no curiosity about the occasions that might have informed against Maurice, and conspired to keep him away.

"So what do you and Bobby do for a living?" I asked, trying my luck with his wife.

"We're in horses," she said.

"In what way?" I asked.

"Transport," she said.

In so far as I do pop and rock music, it's stuff that predates my graduation year. So the post-meal disco, featuring the sounds of 1979 such as punk and early new wave like Tubeway Army and Gary Numan, held no appeal.

I was surveying the scene with as much enthusiasm as my parents might have summoned up for a Rolling Stones night, and debating whether to make an early departure, when an elegant woman in her early 40s sidled over.

"Not one for the jazz buffs, is it?" she said, as the dancers were trying to work out suitable manoeuvres to accompany Are Friends Electric?

"Hello, Bebop Boy," she added.

"Wow, Yvonne Unger, hello there."

"Still smoking, I'm afraid," she said, holding up a packet of Silk Cut. "Why don't you keep me company while I nip outside for quick ciggie."

"Delighted."

"You here toute seule?" I asked as she took her first deep drag.

"Yes, currently unattached, divorce from husband number two imminent."

There was something about the way she said this that I liked.

"Any Mrs Waiters?"

"Yes, but not here tonight," I said.

"Quel dommage." She inhaled. "Frightful meal," she added, "I was sitting next to some peculiar chap with a sou'wester. He thought I was Anjelica Huston and said that that my dad had praised his unpublished novel about the second Bishop of Prague."

"You were probably lucky." I told her about Bobby Barlow, his wife and the transportation of horses.

"Actually," I added, "I was supposed to be meeting my friend Maurice Whittle, but he cried off at the last minute."

"Maurice? The funny little guy with the bum-fluff moustache who was so attached to you?"

"That's him," I said.

It was good to talk without competition from the pounding beat inside the refectory, although the music was still coming through loud and clear.

"What a choice of music," I said, "Don't You Want Me Baby?"

"Anachronistic, too," said Yvonne. "That was 1981. You know," she added, "I often wondered why you never asked me out, Simon."

"Sorry?"

"Was it because I was older than you and all the others? Well, two other reasons occurred to me."

"Yeah?"

"There was the pretty little blonde-haired girl in the Christian Union."

"Wendy. I did get myself in a knot over her," I conceded. "You could have asked me out, Yvonne. You were never slow coming forward."

"True. Or maybe it was something else put me off," she said. "Though I rather hope that the existence of a Mrs Waiters indicates that I was most woefully mistook, My Liege."

"All of this must make you some kind of lost girl to add to my collection," I said.

"Whatever collection that might be," she said. "Look, I'm here for a couple of nights. Wouldn't it be fun to catch up properly?"

This was the first occasion that Bunbury earned his corn. I called Helen and told her that as I was close to Birmingham ("Bill's still in Edgbaston, he loves being near the cricket, he was a very useful leg spinner," I said irrelevantly) it would be a good opportunity to catch up with him on the way home.

Okay, I know this is all very bad and inexcusable. But how many married blokes can say in all honesty that they would be able to resist such temptation if assured that there would be no payback time? Come on now; look at that TV sit-com where the bloke keeps going back to wartime through a door in a wall. Two women on the go but neither one could ever find out about the other. It's the ultimate male fantasy; that was the whole point of the programme.

"Now that *was* fun, Sirrah!" said Yvonne, when we parted company. "Pity we never did it earlier, and so much for my other theory about your reticence."

"Which theory was that?"

"I'd decided that you must be an item with Maurice Whittle."

**Rome, 1995.** My first trip to Italy, and the last holiday with Helen. I knew that it was time to quit school teaching. The realisation, while standing in the Colosseum, that my thoughts didn't stretch beyond the wretchedness of having to confront adolescent kids every day was decisive. My contretemps with Spike Gallagher, the lad who larged it over all his mates because his dad was doing life in Armley Jail for a gangland killing, was fresh in my mind. If the kids wanted him as a role model, I thought, fuck 'em, although this was a career derailment that had been a long time coming.

The other things I remember from that trip owed nothing to the glory of the Eternal City and the decadence of Ancient Rome; it was all about flies and spies.

1) Flies: I was plagued by midges. I smeared myself with potions but this only encouraged them.

"It's a display of machismo," I complained to Helen. "They're showing me that they are rock hard and can take anything I throw at them. The little buggers are wiping the stuff on their armpits."

"They're pregnant females who need the extra blood," she said.

"So I'm supposed to sympathise, then?" I said.

"What you need is one of those buzzing devices you can get these days that makes the sound of a male mosquito, and keeps the pregnant females away," she said.

"Sounds far fetched. Anyway, it's too late now," I said. "The damage has been done."

2) Spies: One day we took a train out to Frascati and I can still remember the back-street bar we were sitting in, with its old picture of Lazio over the till featuring Paul Gascoigne, when I opened my Guardian and read the story of Alan Tipping, "the package holiday spy".

Comrade Alan was a Soviet sleeper who'd arrived in the UK during the 1960s and merged seamlessly into English life as a clerk in the Civil Service; but then there was total silence from The Kremlin. The Russians must have forgotten him and why he'd been sent over in the first place. After Tipping's marriage broke up, he lost touch with his English wife and children for a while. When he had a cancer scare he became desperately homesick and wanted to see Mother Russia again.

Tipping's son had just published a memoir about his father's life, based on a diary he'd found. He revealed – this was the Guardian angle – that at some point in the late 1970s Tipping had been so lonely and homesick (and he thought, terminally ill) that he'd joined a couple of package tours from Manchester to Moscow and Leningrad.

*"I wanted to see a few places again before I died. I'd set my affairs in order in case anyone realised who I was and arrested me. For all I knew, they might have picked me up on arrival...they didn't of course and back home, thanks to the NHS and the Christie Hospital, I lived to fight on,"* he wrote.

"I must read this when we get back," I said to Helen. "Actually, it's a happy ending, reunited with his children, back on good terms with his ex-wife."

"Like your Uncle Andrew, the last bit," said Helen.

"I suppose so," I said, recalling Uncle Andrew's eventual, unorthodox accommodation with Auntie Laura and Tony Jessop.

"Perhaps you'll be in the book, Simon," said Helen, "seeing as you were on one those Homesick Russian Blues trips with him."

"Well, we didn't exactly get to know the chap that well," I said.

"Even so, he might just remember two young lads travelling together on one of his trips, you and Greg."

"It's possible, I suppose," I agreed.

# CHAPTER THIRTY

## Buy one get one free

Wendy was chatting to Mark, a good-looking teenaged boy on the check-out in the supermarket. This was something she wouldn't have done in the past. Elliot would have accused her of flirting.

The lad was calling over a supervisor to give him the go ahead to sell a bottle of wine.

"Must get irritating doing that all the time," Wendy said.

"Sorry?"

"Having to flag up the booze every single time."

"Bit of a nuisance," he agreed.

"It's a pity you can't do it first thing in the morning and then that would count for your entire shift if you see what I mean."

I smiled to myself; this was the kind of conversation that Helen would have had.

"This is the last week I'll have to do it, though," he said.

"New job?" I asked.

"No, I'll be 18," he said.

"Right, congratulations."

"Okay, Flo," said a supervisor, giving Mark a thumbs-up.

"Flo?" said Wendy.

"Short for Florenski. I've got my mum's surname, she's Polish."

As in the lost girl; no harm in asking, I suppose.

"You haven't got any relatives called Anna, by any chance?"

"Yes, my mum. As I say, Polish. Do you know her?"

"I did know an Anna Florenski. You could tell her that Simon Waiters sends his regards, in case she's the same one, although I don't suppose she would remember me."

I didn't see Mark Florenski again for a fortnight or so.

"Hi, Mark. Have a good birthday?" I asked when he returned. "Your eighteenth?"

"Sorry? Oh, yes, hi there," he said. "I've been to Warsaw to see some relatives."

"Pretty exciting."

"Yeah, cool. It's buzzing these days."

He leaned forward slightly as if to pass on confidential information.

"You were the fan of Thelonius Monk who lived in Hyde Park."

"Yes, I was."

"My mum did remember you, from when she was in Leeds. She says hello."

"Hello?"

"A-ha."

He looked at me shrewdly, knowing that this response disappointed me, that I'd hoped for something more.

"OK, thanks for that," I said. "I hope she's okay. Anyway, see you around, Mark."

"Yeah. Oh hang on, is this yours?"

He picked up a small tube of insect repellent from underneath a pile of carrier bags.

"No, someone else must've left it. Those things never do the trick for me. I think you need something more sophisticated if you're going to keep the midges at bay."

"Yes, there's better technology than that," he said. "You can get a buzzer that keeps pregnant mosquitoes away from you."

"Amazing," I said. "My ex-wife once told me about them and I thought that she was having me on."

I left Mark with a smile on his face and I had to laugh, too. All that anger and mystification over the girl who built me up and then

177

snubbed me within the space of 48 hours. I did the maths, based on Mark's age. Anna Florenski must have discovered that she was pregnant, maybe because of a one-night stand, somewhere in between meeting me in Leeds' Waterstones and that student party. I'd never have sussed that without Wendy's intervention. By taking on board one lost girl, I had discovered in the supermarket the simple truth behind my disappointment with another woman; that's what I call Buy One Get One Free.

Armed with this information, I decided what I would do about the beautiful Anna Florenski. Absolutely nothing. Perhaps I'm growing up at last.

# CHAPTER THIRTY-ONE

## Of friends and accountants

"I'm looking forward to meeting this Simone Waiters. Maybe she'll turn out to be a neat little French number."

Those were the first words spoken to me by the lad who was to become my best friend at university. He's not featured hugely in these chronicles; as I've said, we're barely in touch these days. It was a strange opening gambit because, as I've also pointed out, he never went on to show any interest whatsoever in any females at any time during our three years in Hereford.

Maurice Whittle and I were early arrivals at Dr Donald Pye's office for our first history tutorial of the academic year. Maurice, who was doing joint honours with economics, had been perusing the list of students' names on Pye's notice board.

"We're next to one another, Simone and I," he said. "Formidable, thank heaven for leetle girls."

I looked at the list for myself: Janet Crilley, Neil Killoran, Stephen Murphy, Geraldine Ryan, Yvonne Unger, Simone Waiters, Maurice Whittle. I pulled out my ballpoint pen and with a theatrical gesture removed the surplus letter, then held out my hand for him to shake.

"Sorry to disappoint, Maurice. Simon Waiters at your command."

"Oh, fancy that. Well, nice to meet you, Simon," said Maurice, looking not remotely crestfallen.

I told Maurice one day about how I'd botched things with Wendy Thomas. He was, unlike Greg Hammond, sympathetic but I might as well have been talking about non-destructive bridge testing for all it meant to him. I had him down as a representative of that rare breed, the asexual man, although (in the same way that I'd never come across bisexuals until I met Kevin Moody at the dairy) I wouldn't have put it that way at the time.

His sister, Bernadette, had said to me: "Is our Maurice still not going out with anyone?" then added, a little coquettishly: "What about you? Do you have a girlfriend, Simon?"

Yet Maurice, who became an accountant, was married within a couple of years of leaving Hereford. When the wedding invitation landed on our doorstep I did a double-take, not least because Mr and Mrs Jesper Widerberg were requesting the company of *Simone* Waiters at their daughter's wedding to Mr Maurice Whittle, in Oslo.

"So you've two good pals who are accountants," Helen said when she was about to meet Maurice for the first time, and I told her what my friend did for a living. "No just the one," I said. "Maurice". "Well, what about Bill Patel?" she said. "Well yes two, now you mention it, Maurice and Bill," I agreed. "Just as well you're not in that line yourself if you can't count beyond one," she said. I was never very good at guile and I'm surprised that I kept Bill Patel going for as long as I did before he blew up in my face as he was to do so spectacularly a few years later.

Anyway, Maurice and Liv settled in Leeds and we saw a lot of them until the split with Helen. I think Liv was one of those people (more often women, in my experience) who like to do things in couples or not at all. For whatever reason, they made little effort to keep in touch with me although I continued to get Liv's Christmas boast posts.

Every year I send out and receive a similar number of Christmas cards, around the 15-20 mark. Most just scribble their names and those of the current wife/husband/partner and any kids. As I never speak to any these people from one year to the next, it's an utterly futile activity. But it's painless, unlike Liv's annual round robin letter.

So each Christmas I get this note detailing everything that Liv, Maurice, Tom-Eirik and Anniken-Jane have done during the previous 12 months. They are horribly fascinating items, and I keep them in a Shaker hat box. I dug them out the other day for a cheap laugh. The most recent had its moments…

*It's almost Christmas time again. We had a little bit of snow the other week but (touch wood!) it's been mild since then. However, let's go back to the beginning of the year.*

A chronological account followed, with the family summer holiday lovingly recreated and due respect paid to the culture and history of places visited.

*"Tom-Eirik and Anniken-Jane were fascinated to learn that Rome, known as the Eternal City and once the centre of a Great Empire, is built on seven hills. They even managed to pick up a few words of Italian – but they didn't always get them right!! On one occasion, Tom-Eirik pointed to a cake in a shop and the woman serving wasn't sure which one he wanted. He pointed again – this time more accurately – and said: 'Questo, per favore', which means 'This one please'. The Italian lady behind the counter said: 'Ah, capisco', which means 'Ah, I understand'. We were so pleased that he could remember his please and thank you even when he was talking in a strange language, one other than English or Norwegian in which, of course, they are both fluent. Anniken-Jane thought Tom-Eirik's cake looked especially scrumptious and she said to me: 'I'd like one of those capiscos, too, Mummy.' So our Anniken-Jane was really saying: 'I'd like one of those I understands.' Well, we all laughed so much, but not unkindly, and Anniken-Jane, who has a great sense of humour, saw the funny side.*

*Next year it's MEXICO! Wonder what the little darlings will make of that!!"*

I could cheerfully have throttled Liv and had Tom-Eirik and Anniken-Jane put into care. The solitary contribution from Maurice was a hastily scrawled: 'Have a good 'un, Simon', followed by a reference to Manchester United's inferiority to Arsenal. If someone had warned Maurice of his destiny, before he set off on his trip to Scandinavia in 1979, he would have laughed in their face.

Maurice had picked up Liv, or more likely vice versa, in Oslo while he was Inter-Railing after our finals in 1979. She was a plump, cheerful

181

girl in her late 20s who didn't want to be left on the shelf. She homed in on Maurice while he was fumbling through his purse for notes in an Oslo bar (and probably, as a tightwad, wondering why he had come to one of Europe's most expensive capitals) and he allowed himself to be scooped up. Perhaps Maurice craved respectability; maybe he liked the idea of being a dad.

The last time I saw Maurice in his bachelor days was shortly before his departure on that fateful trip. I'd arrived late morning by train in his home town and decided that I might as well eat before knocking on his door. I found a small café where I was told to sit down and wait. When I asked for a menu I was told it was beef or omelette, with chips, and a mug of tea or beaker of coffee, 75 pence.

"That's it?" I said.

"Take it or leave it, pal. What were you expecting? It's not the Ritz."

A few blokes in overalls came in during the next ten minutes and seemed happy with the arrangement. I took the beef, it wasn't bad, if school dinner-ish. I paid up, got a weird look when I left a five pence tip, and made my way to Maurice's place. I couldn't explain where in town I'd found my café which Maurice, with his eye for a good deal, found frustrating. This became a standing joke between us and it was years later, by which time communication had been reduced to those Christmas cards, that the truth dawned on me. I must have drifted into a works canteen.

I think that Helen, when she came along, found them both hard work but kept it going for the sake of my friendship with Maurice. She struggled to cope with Liv's combination of banality and horrifying frankness, occasionally within a sentence or two of one another.

"The cornflower white's great for hanging pictures against but I just can't find the right curtains," Liv told Helen. "You know, Maurice and I have only had sex once since Anniken-Jane came along three years ago."

"That really is something I would have preferred not to know," Helen said to me later.

"Yeah, and Maurice would be mortified if he found out I knew that. Poor bastard, no previous form until he met Liv and then fuck all nookie after the bairns came along."

"That's one way of looking at it," said Helen.

"What's another?"

"Oh, for goodness sake," she said, "work it out for yourself."

"Some women just don't like sex much," I said.

"You can be blokeish sometimes. There's usually more than one side to that kind of story."

"What are you getting at?"

"Oh, come on, Simon, you must realise that Maurice has always been more than a little bit in love with you."

"Don't be daft," I said.

I didn't take this observation too seriously, in fact I was more focused on Helen's suggestion that I was blokeish. I'd never considered myself remotely in that light and I certainly didn't have lots of mates who I'd rather be with than my wife, which would be my definition of someone who is blokeish. And wouldn't really blokeish blokes use the definite article when talking about their wife?

I've done the numbers game before. I didn't have many male friends when I married Helen and I haven't acquired many more since reverting to the single life. I've got plenty of casual acquaintances through having lived in the same place for so long, and there are a few chaps I talk to in a couple of local pubs. Some of these people turn up in my dreams, together with folk that I'd forgotten I ever knew in the first place. The maths teacher who took the top stream will be running a corner shop; Greg Hammond's Uncle Jim, who once showed me his Manchester United scrapbook, will be a tour guide on my holiday in North Korea (not that it looks like North Korea), telling me to keep up with the party or face disciplinary measures by the Dear Leader. Our sub-conscious contains everyone and everything we have ever known, and anything can be brought out for an airing at any time.

The other night I dreamed I was back at the dairy for an old boys' reunion. Kevin Moody was telling me that, after a spell in the theatre, he'd gone into film production. He was making a "pioneering cross-generational gay movie" about the burgeoning relationship between John Brown and Maurice Whittle as both men finally come to acknowledge their sexuality. There's often a cinematic element to my dreams, which involves my watching a movie and taking part in it simultaneously. At some point, like The Purple Rose of Cairo in reverse, I stepped into the screen. John and Maurice were on a hill looking towards a town full of exquisite, mathematically perfect classical architecture, like something devised by Piero della Francesca.

"Fucking perfect, our Maurice," said John Brown. "Une città ideale. We'll give that whisky some stick on Saturday night."

John was standing behind Maurice now, arms around his waist. "This is all for you, Maurice," said John as he pressed firmly against his lover's buttocks. "On second thoughts," he added, seeing me, "here's mettle more attractive. It's my little friend Simon from the bottling plant."

I awoke in a cold sweat and thought about poor old Maurice, stuck in a 1990s' semi in Leeds, with Liv, Tom-Eirik and Anniken-Jane ganging up on him to book an all-inclusive holiday in Mexico, a 7,000 mile round-trip opportunity to turn lobster-pink while sitting by the side of a swimming pool every day, and to savour the eat-all-you-can-buffet every night, washed down by lashings of insipid lager with a lime attached to the top of the bottle.

I recalled his feeble reference to thinking about the girls; I remembered the possible semi pass when our legs touched for a nano-second while listening to Errol Garner; I reflected on Helen's suggestion that he'd been carrying a torch for me all those years and Yvonne Unger's theory that Maurice and I might be an item; but most of all, I thought about the wedding invitation with Simone Waiters written in his own hand.

Maybe that was a little in-joke, a reference to our first meeting. Or perhaps it was Maurice's way of telling me that he too had a lost love, his Sweet and Twenty to whom he'd never been able to declare himself; someone with whom there had never been the slightest hope of finding happiness. Maria Whittle had said to me: "So you're the famous Simon Waiters."

Maurice also had a love that never was; she was called Simone Waiters.

As my dad was to Archie Macash, so I was to Maurice Whittle. His lost girl.

# CHAPTER THIRTY-TWO

## Hunky Bobby Barlow

After the alumni event a postcard arrived, addressed to me. Helen got to the door first.

"Who do we know in Chichester? Oh," she said, turning it over. "Someone called Yvonne from your Hereford days."

I tried to grab it.

"Not so fast," Helen said playfully, waving it out of my reach. "Let's see what you got up to that weekend."

"She was a bit of a comedian, was Yvonne, I'd take anything you read there with a pinch of salt."

"If you don't want me to see the contents, that's hardly the way to put me off....well, well, Yvonne *is* a naughty girl, too, by the look of it," said Helen, finally handing me the card.

*"Lovely to meet up again,"* I read. *"Hope to see you next year for more of the same! Well, more of the same for Bobby and me, I should say. Yes!! After you went back to your hotel, I got together with that hunky Bobby Barlow we were talking to! Did you know he's into horse transport? Never thought that could be so enthralling! And do try to persuade Maurice next year – be good to catch up with your little friend again."*

"I suppose that there's going to be quite a lot of that sort of thing at a college reunion," said Helen. "Had Yvonne left some poor cuckold at home?"

186

"No," I said, "Recently divorced. Just looking for a quick trip round the wicket, probably."

"Well, she certainly found it. Just glad she didn't pick on you," she said, "without Maurice there to jealously protect your virtue".

Was this the point at which, encouraged by Yvonne's part in the subterfuge, former ditherer Simon Waiters gained too much swagger and sexual confidence and started to believe that he could be the Uncle Andrew de nos jours?

I enjoyed Alan Tipping's spy book. I bought it as soon as Helen and I returned from Rome to embark on what would turn out to be the final phase of our marriage. I liked the chapter about Tipping's trips with Thomson's Holidays to Moscow and Leningrad. Thank God I'd never painted the lily by claiming Bill Patel had been with us, too. Because, yes, Greg and I did get a mention and someone at Private Eye had also read The Forgotten Spook….

*Greg Hammond is on record as saying that he left the world of journalism too early. He must have loved Alan Tipping's book, then. Tipping recalls a riotous night with two young Englishmen, a couple of pretty Australian girls and a drunken Rasputin-like Muscovite who believed there was no such thing as a paid-for meal. 'I thought that one of the English lads, an engaging character called Simon, was on to me,' recalled Tipping, 'not least when I forgot I was supposed to know only a few words of Russian. But his mate was oblivious, too focused on the more attractive Aussie. And it paid dividends for him, I discovered later. This young chap, Greg, was toasting his absent friends Fox and Finder and struck me as a fantasist. He told me that his mate, Simon, had once met Yuri Gagarin which I thought doubtful. Looking back, however, I'm not so sure; there's nothing fanciful about the names Fox and Finder now.'*

*"Well," the Eye concluded, "Greg Hammond's long been known to have a wandering eye and no one disputes that he has a way with the ladies but it doesn't sound as though the world missed a great newshound."*

A few months earlier, the Manchester Evening Comet had reported the death of another ladies' man. Yvonne Unger had been in the city for a conference and I was on my way back to Yorkshire when I saw the billboard.

'North West Actor's Sudden Death' I read.

Albert Finney, Robert Powell, Frank Finlay? No, it was Andrew Tomlinson who stared at me from page five.

*A BUSINESSMAN who was one of Manchester's finest amateur actors died suddenly at home yesterday after suffering a heart attack.*

*Andrew Tomlinson, aged 56, of Wilmslow, was well known to local theatre-goers as a gifted performer who won several Evening Comet amateur dramatics 'Oscars'. During 30 years with South Manchester Thespians he played many major Shakespearean roles and was acclaimed for his performances in The Merchant of Venice, 20 years apart, as both Bassanio and Shylock.*

*Mr Tomlinson spent all his working life in the property business. He established a network of Tomlinson's Estate Agency branches in south Manchester and north Cheshire, recently selling the business due to failing health. He suffered his first heart attack more than 10 years ago and, following successful bypass surgery, continued to work and to act.*

*He died in the arms of his former wife, Laura – Mr Tomlinson spent the last few years of his life, following a second heart attack, living with Mrs Jessop and her second husband, Tony Jessop.*

*Mrs Jessop said: "He was a larger than life character and he lived life to the full."*

*Evening Comet theatre writer Michael McGinty said: "There is a tendency among us critics sometimes to look down on amateur dramatics. However, an accomplished actor like Andrew Tomlinson makes you reconsider your prejudices. He was a gifted performer who would have graced the professional stage, had the call of estate agency not been so strong.*

*"His first love was Shakespeare, but he was equally adept in lighter, comic pieces. For me, his Algernon in The Importance of Being Earnest and Marlow in She Stoops to Conquer, on both occasions playing opposite Katie Darling, with whom he enjoyed a remarkable on-stage chemistry, were highlights."*

*In a business capacity, Mr Tomlinson was a former chairman of the North Cheshire Chamber of Commerce, whose president Roy Sheridan said: "He brought a real sense of joie-de-vivre to our meetings. He used to say that property was his wife, but that acting was his mistress. He will be sorely missed."*

*Mr Tomlinson had no children. He is survived by a sister, Joyce Waiters, and a nephew, Simon Waiters, who as a young boy met Yuri Gagarin when the cosmonaut visited Manchester in 1961.*

I'd played the Bunbury although it wasn't really needed. Helen trusted me even though we were going through a creaky patch. And she was full of sympathy when I got home. I found her in the kitchen and she hugged me as if I'd been away for a month.

"Your mum's been ringing, she was upset that she couldn't get hold of you. If you'd bothered to call me at some point, you wouldn't have had to find out via your favourite newspaper. Isn't it time you got a mobile phone?"

I could tell she was seriously pissed off with me about this.

"Probably. Yes, okay promise I will."

"I know it must have been a horrible shock for you, finding out that way, love. I'm so sorry," she said, the default kindness breaking through again.

I'd been in Manchester where Bill Patel was visiting his parents. I felt an absolute heel and resolved to get rid of him for good.

"Some epic news about Bill and Suman," I said. "They're thinking of moving to the States. They've been doing a lot of sorting, before they put the house on the market."

"I hope I get to see them before they disappear," Helen said. "Funny that I've never met Bill, you two go back such a long way. I was beginning to wonder if he was a figment of your imagination."

Yes, I was resolved now that I had played my joker for the final time. From the Patels' holiday in Goa when we got married, to Suman's reluctance to do things as couples, to the Christmas card appearing on the mantelpiece magically but biennially so as not to do overdo it, I had felt for some time that I was pushing my luck. But for now I had to tough it out one last time.

"How are his youngsters doing?"

I painted an optimistic picture of Bill's life, in which Thomas and Julia Patel were chips off the old block, polite and respectful but full of character, and doing well at school. Thomas was more academic and planned to study medicine. Julia was practical, the sort of kid who would actually want to make those things on Blue Peter. She was very musical, too – highly accomplished on the viola, I decided ingeniously.

"That's nice," said Helen. "I think musical skill is a wonderful thing to have. I'd love a little one with that gift."

"You never know. Don't forget that I was the Meanwood Elvis, there must be some talent in the genes."

Once this would have made her laugh. Now she just smiled sadly. There had been no little Waiters. We'd had a few arguments about babies and my lack of enthusiasm for the project. I think that afternoon in the kitchen might have turned into one of those charged moments if it hadn't been for Uncle Andrew's departure.

Some time close to this event Helen dropped a real bombshell. When she was 18 she'd had a miscarriage, a secret she'd carried for almost two decades. I don't know why she'd suddenly chosen this moment to tell me; maybe something was loosened by our talk of the Patels and their achievements.

"I didn't even know I was pregnant. I just felt a sense of relief. It was a few months before A-levels, the father was a shit, of course, it would have been awful to have had a baby in those circumstances. Then I felt a terrible wave of guilt. A little life lost and all I could do was think about myself."

"Was Greg Hammond the father?" I said, failing to recognise that she was not commenting on men in general.

"Of course he was. I wasn't sleeping around. Nobody ever knew about this, other than my parents. Certainly not Greg. I miscarried shortly after that Valentine's weekend, when he had come home and finished with me. I don't think he had the slightest right to be told and I'm certain that, had he known, he would have said: 'Thank God for that.'"

It didn't take a great stretch of the imagination to hear Hammond uttering those very words before sending Helen to the bar for the next round.

I'd played the not-sure-I'm-ready-to-start-a-family card for the first two or three years of our marriage. After that, I relented with a lack of grace which must have given her pause for thought. I never made myself unavailable by feigning illness or going AWOL when her ovaries started to ping, and there was no C or Non-C behaviour of the kind my father had indulged in. Nevertheless, a lack of enthusiasm for babies was another characteristic I'd inherited from Dad. Yes, I know, I should have been more upfront about all that at a much earlier stage of our marriage.

If Helen had got pregnant I would have accepted my lot, but I did breathe a sigh of relief every month when she was disappointed or, if I'm going to be honest, tearful.

# CHAPTER THIRTY-THREE

## Ships in the night

Wendy thought that Hammond, to judge from his picture on the book jacket, was "still very dishy".

"Is he really that good looking?" she asked.

"It's his best side, but the girls always went for him rather than me," I allowed.

"Well, it's what's inside that counts," said Wendy.

"I'm afraid we're no longer in touch so I can't offer you an introduction."

"But he's married in any case," she said.

"I don't think that would worry him unduly."

"It might worry me a little," said Wendy. "What kind of girl do you take me for? Although it would be nice to meet him all the same," she added, not wanting to sound prim.

"We've been out of touch for some time, so it's not going to happen I'm afraid."

I did, however, know that Hammond was back, if only briefly, in the North-West. Private Eye had been on his case again.

*Our former man in Moscow, that ace Soviet spy-spotter Greg Hammond, has — or so we have been led to believe — a marriage every bit has harmonious as that portrayed in his Fox and Finder stories.*

*Friends say that Samantha is a fiercely loyal wife, but Hammond has been known to push his luck and everyone has their limits. It seems that Samantha might have reached hers after she found Greg comforting their Slovakian au pair who had, he claimed, received some bad news from home.*

*We understand that Egregious Greg, as he is known less than fondly in the literary world, is currently licking his wounds at a friend's house in Bolton, where he once worked on the newspaper, near his native Manchester. Whether the exile will prove permanent, it's too early to say.*

The lovely Samantha, dedicatee in several of the books. I'd seen a picture of the Hammonds in a national paper, talking to Christopher Eccleston and Susan Lynch, who played Tom Fox and Sophie Finder. Samantha was a posh and gorgeous blonde whose features were marred or enhanced, according to taste, by an ever-so-slightly turned-up nose.

I can honestly say that Hammond's success doesn't move me one way or the other. I'm glad I got out of the friendship with him when I did, so no one can accuse me of jealousy; I did tell him to get stuffed before he was famous. I wouldn't dispute that Hammond is smarter than I am. My intelligence is pitched badly. I should have been born cleverer or more stupid. I think too much, without thinking smartly. I can see that problems lie ahead, but I'm rarely astute enough to know what form they will take, or how I should deal with them.

To some extent, the Wendy Thomas-Carr dilemma concentrated my mind. I wanted to see her sorted out; I wanted to do the right thing for her. The trouble was my brain had all the clarity of a Citizens' Band radio set. All sorts of interference kept breaking in. Far from liberating me, Wendy had made me speculate ever more wildly on the different routes my life might have taken. Wendy, Lesley Linnell and Anna Florenski were the high-profile lost girls, but they were the tip of an iceberg....

What about those ships that pass in the night? I could fill a book naming the girls with whom the briefest encounters made me wish I'd had an opportunity to get to know them.

A few years ago, I went by rail from York to Lowestoft. All went well as far as Peterborough, where I faced a long delay because of line maintenance work or some such. Finally, a rickety-looking train trundled in. The most perfect looking woman I've ever seen read my thoughts as I got on board: "Welcome to East Anglia," she said.

We sat down on opposite seats and she instigated the conversation after seeing my Heinrich Böll novel. She was half-German and had been a student in West Berlin in 1989.

"That was well timed," I said. "Did you get a chip out of the wall?"

"I certainly did. And I'd been in East Berlin a few weeks earlier, on the day Honeker resigned as party secretary. Well, naturally I only discovered that after the event."

"You mean that you didn't spot the newspaper billboards: 'Our Erich Calls it a Day'"

"You know, funnily enough, I didn't. Must have had my head in the clouds," she said.

She wasn't conventionally beautiful; you might even have called her 'jolie laide' or whatever the German equivalent is. Put it this way, if we'd met at a party I wouldn't have done a freezing act because I was unworthy. She was a college librarian, again not an occupation to put her beyond my reach.

As the fenland went past we talked of everything under the sun or, at least, everything that mattered to us; there was a freakish overlap between our experiences and interests.

"Do you like Elvis?" Rather than the struggle for common ground that often accompanies a meeting with a stranger, I thought I'd try to seek out a source of mild discord.

"No strong feelings, but not a great deal," she said.

I told her about my Elvis-impersonating success, and how I'd done it to impress a potential girlfriend.

"Don't suppose it did you much good," she said.

"None at all."

About ten minutes from Norwich, she made a passing reference to her husband, who was picking her up at the station. I managed, I think, not to look too downcast as I continued our conversation about jazz before deciding as the train was pulling to a halt to give her something to remember me by, forever.

"Actually, my Elvis wasn't bad. My sort-of girlfriend rather liked it, we started dating properly from that moment and we've now been married for three years," I said.

"Dating properly? That's an interesting way to put it," she said. "Happily married?" she added. "No, better not answer that."

"This is going to sound very strange but, as we will never meet again, I'll say it anyway. I find you so attractive that, if you'd accidentally-on-purpose bumped into me in East Berlin during the 1980s, I would have assumed that you were a honey trap set up by the Stasi."

She didn't react as if I was mad and start seeking support from fellow passengers. She looked straight into my eyes and said: "That is one of the most bizarre things anyone has said to me. But I'll take it as compliment."

"How else?"

"You really are off the wall," she said.

"But quite harmless."

"Yes, I'm sure. I ought at least to know your name before we go our separate ways."

"Simon."

"Welch ein Zufall! Meine Nahme ist Simone."

"Simone? I've been called that by a friend."

"What, before you had a sex change? I wouldn't put anything past you."

"No, long story, a one-off, I've always been Simon."

"And I'm actually Janet, had you there. Well, hello and goodbye, Simon. It was nice to pass the time with you."

And that was it. I messed about with my bag for a minute or so to allow her to get onto the platform alone and into the welcoming arms of her husband.

Did she genuinely like me? Was she playing with me? If we'd been students meeting up this way, say while Inter-railing our way through a timeless Tuscan landscape of poplars and distant hill-top villages, would it have led anywhere? Was her relationship with her husband anything like mine with Helen?

I'll never know, but the woman who would forever be Half-German Janet provided a tantalising glimpse into what might have been. It would also have been the moment when I first stopped and really contemplated, other than as a passing thought, the utter randomness of when and where we pitch up on this Earth and our choice of partners. I arrived in 1958. My dream girl might have been born in 1928, or 1988. The old dear whose supermarket bags I carry to the taxi, the pre-pubescent girl to whom I'm invisible as she walks past chatting on her mobile: either might have been The One, if I'd been born 30 years earlier or later. Life on Earth started to evolve more than three billion years ago. To have missed the love supreme because you arrived a single generation out is too cruel to contemplate.

# CHAPTER THIRTY-FOUR

## A Nazi in the rock garden (I)

Natural history and horticulture might not be my bag, but there's a park and rock garden near my parents which I've always liked. The garden is steeply-banked and has a circular path running through it. I often take a stroll there on visits back home and occasionally meet a face from the past. So, when I heard a voice hailing me from the top entrance which led into the main park, I looked up in expectation of seeing an old acquaintance. But it was the Rev Lesley Linnell.

He waved to get my attention. Lesley might have been a boyish girl but as a man he verged on the effeminate; had he been born into that boy's body he'd craved, life would have been tough.

A punk dressed in black gave me a hard look as our paths crossed. His t-shirt had an evil message and I thought he was going to demand that I agreed with the sentiments. He was close enough for me to get a look at the swastika on his neck. He then slowed down near three strapping lads before, again, deciding not to engage.

His face had looked mild mannered and there was something suspiciously fresh about that tattoo. I reflected on this as I made my way towards the bench where Lesley was waiting. The punk had got there first. My clerical friend was now looking ill at ease at the contrast between the t-shirt's unpleasant communiqué and the Christian message of love and tolerance.

"Do you find that you have to prepare to listen to Mahler?" the punk was saying.

"I'd have to think very hard about that one," said Lesley, playing for time as she read the t-shirt's words: "Manc Nazis are motherfuckers."

The punk was standing very close to Lesley now.

"I do think August is such a gentle month," he was saying. "There's nothing more relaxing, surely, than the sight of some lovely garden plants in a perfect setting."

"Actually, I don't agree, pal," I said.

"I respect your inclination to differ, sir. A little healthy debate is fine with me, though perhaps we might yet tarry to strive for some common ground that we can share together."

"Well, try this for size, motherfucker," I said, felling him with a well-placed punch.

The thump as he hit the ground was pleasing, then alarming. It wasn't a soft fall; you could see why they call it a rock garden.

"Sweet Jesus, I think you might just have killed him," said Lesley.

"Dream or Reality?" I would have asked Helen.

# CHAPTER THIRTY-FIVE

## The natural and unadopted son

My mother had an Auntie Grace, who died in 1960, too early for me to remember her. Mum told me that Auntie Grace was a blue stocking. She never married, nor had a boyfriend to anyone's knowledge after her sweetheart fell at Ypres. She taught English and French, and she worshipped Charles Dickens. Uncle Andrew became the apple of her eye and when a teacher suggested that he was Oxbridge material, Auntie Grace began to look on Andrew with awe as well as affection. She lived round the corner from my grandparents and Uncle Andrew would pop in to see her several times a week on his way back from school.

Unfortunately, in the sixth form, Uncle Andrew discovered girls. His charm found a new target and Auntie Grace no longer had priority. His studies suffered, too. At 17, half-way through A-levels, Andrew announced that he was leaving school to work as a trainee in a local estate agents' office.

Auntie Grace never forgave nor forgot, and she took her revenge from beyond the grave. The bulk of her estate went to my parents and her best friend, apart from a few charity bequests and "£25 for Andrew Tomlinson, adopted son of my brother, Arthur".

"The bitch," he told me. "I wasn't that bad, I'd just been your average teenager and Grace's vicious last will and testament really hurt Mum and Dad. I blew my 25 quid on a trip to Amsterdam and a couple of blow jobs in the red-light district. I came back determined to show the old sow that I didn't need a leg-up from her."

Andrew reckoned that insult gave him the push he needed, although I'm sure he would have made it in whatever field he'd chosen. He took an interest in my academic successes and didn't take offence when I declined his offer to get me started in his business.

"You're not one of life's entrepreneurial types, are you Simon?" he'd say. "Teaching's a decent game to be in, even if it'll never make you rich."

When he died there was plenty of dosh to enable Auntie Laura to cruise around the world with Tony Jessop as often as she liked. And for Simon Waiters, "100 per cent natural and unadopted son of Harold and Joyce Waiters", there was £75,000.

This gave me the freedom to think seriously about giving up school work. When I got back from Rome I told my head teacher it would be my last year. I couldn't come up with any inspiring alternative careers when I did quit. I had a few days in Hereford, looked up the careers officer and did one of those questionnaires designed to reveal your aptitude and inclinations: "Would you rather A) command a small military unit on manoeuvres in the Hebrides or B) write press releases for an exciting modern dance group in Doncaster?"

A week later, a letter urged me to try my hand with the Army or the Police. This was followed quickly by a second communication, apologising that they'd confused my form with someone else's. "Too late," I replied, "On my way to Sandhurst now, then on standby for the next conflict in the Middle East."

What had Greg Hammond said? The best arts graduates go into publishing, the next best into journalism and the rest into teaching. I had no real idea what publishers did. But whatever it was, it seemed mainly to take place in London. I wrote to the local newspaper and asked if I could have some work experience. They put me into something called advertisement features, a department that lacked the alleged integrity of journalism and the alleged glamour of advertising. I wrote articles about shopping on the Yorkshire coast, homes and gardens, and booking early (very early, if I remember rightly) for Christmas. Advertisement-feature Land is a Happy Land; we live in a golden age. Everything is quite delightfully old-fashioned or up to date as Kansas City in exactly the right way. Thriving town centre shops are run by warm-hearted traders who have not forgotten, from the good old days, the holy trinity of quality, service and value. Museums, dusty and academic in the bad old days, are now enthralling hands-on affairs; pubs serve restaurant-quality food and today's cars no longer break down much (although if they do, highly-skilled mechanics, honest as the day is long, are on hand to give you a scrupulously fair assessment). It's the perfect antidote to the notion that Planet Earth is becoming a darker place but I exhausted very quickly all the creative possibilities this Panglossian world view offered.

I heard that a local prison wanted a part-time English teacher. Once the head of education had established on the phone that I had a degree and enough teaching experience to be out of my first flush of youth, I was in. The interview was a formality, although I thought it best not to reveal the final straw in my school teaching career.

I didn't make much use of my extra leisure time, other than reading Tolstoy, Dostoevsky and the Victorian novels I should have tackled at university, spinning out preparation and listening to lots of Radio 4. If Helen was disappointed not to return home to impressive feats of decorating, shelf construction or pie-making, she didn't show it and, in any case, I upped the hours at the prison gradually until I was going in four days a week. However, we were gradually moving apart. Neither of us liked to row and although we still got on tolerably well, we did far less stuff together.

My playing-away days were over though, and Bill Patel had gone forever. I was utterly shamefaced after his last outing, the week Uncle Andrew died, and my Bunbury had indeed headed off to a new life in Seattle.

One morning, a new lifestyle magazine was pushed through the door. Among the long-winded articles about Pilates, Indian head massage and wedding planners, I saw something that got me excited.

"Remember that time you came to see Greg at Hereford and we both met you in the Mappa Mundi bar?" I said to Helen.

"How could I forget? You and Greg were discussing Bill Patel."

"Er, that's right," I said. "But that's not what I'm thinking about. We were also playing the famous Belgians game. I came up with Paul Delvaux and Greg pretended that he knew who I was talking about, though he'd clearly never heard of him."

"Sounds like Greg."

"Well, there's a feature here about a local mural artist. He can paint a whole wall in your house."

"Yes, I know what a mural artist does, where does Paul Delvaux come in?"

"This bloke will do stuff any way you like, figurative, abstract, you name it. And listen to this: 'Terry Boston paints for his own enjoyment in a style occasionally reminiscent of the Belgian surrealist Paul Delvaux, who died recently.' I bet he'd be up for doing a mural like a Delvaux. Wow, that'd be something else to have here."

"No, it wouldn't," said Helen. "It'd be bloody awful. If you want to spend your money on a mural, I'm not going to stop you, but I want it to be something I don't mind looking at. I don't want to have to come down every morning and stare at a load of half-naked women going into a Roman temple."

I went to see Terry Boston. He was a small, bad-tempered middle-aged man with a mass of grey hair and a mad, reddish beard. Terry lived alone in a house decorated entirely with his own work. In the front room, a four-wall Turkish panorama evoked the decadence of the Ottoman Empire. At the back, a Cubist-style picture of New York featured the Empire State and Flat-iron buildings, and Brooklyn Bridge. The hallway was taken up with a nouveau-riche couple outside a neo-Georgian house, gazing adoringly at their 4x4 and Porsche.

"What do you make of that one?" he said, throwing down the gauntlet.

"It's not my style, I must say."

"It's modern life, innit? We're stuck with these fuckers, if that's what people want, I'll paint them. It's not my job to impose moral judgments, I'm just a tradesman for hire."

I hired him and explained that the Delvaux was to be a surprise for Helen. At £1,000 for a wall in the dining room, a job that he reckoned would take about four days, Terry Boston didn't come cheap, but it would be money well spent.

Terry was pencilled in for a week when Helen was going to Vienna and Budapest with a couple of girlfriends, so that the mural would be fait accompli when she returned. She would come round to liking it, I knew she would.

The mural was based loosely on a Delvaux work called The Meeting. Two women, one naked, one clothed, were greeting each other at a crossroads. The surrounding architecture was ancient Roman, but York Minster and the city walls could be seen in the distance. Two lines of women approaching the centre of the picture from left and right were wearing Manchester United kits, and Terry Boston had painted himself into the foreground carrying a candle and dressed as a referee.

"If you reckon I'm going to live with that for however long we are here, you've got another think coming," Helen said before she'd even taken off her coat.

"Just give it time, you'll grow to love it, I guarantee. How was Budapest?"

"Bugger Budapest. I loathe and detest Paul Delvaux. I will never grow to love this mural and I will leave you if you don't paint over it before the end of the month. That gives you two weeks to get every possible drop of pleasure out of it before it is, or I am, history."

The atmosphere was poisonous for the rest of the day and at ten o'clock I announced that I was going out for last orders. Helen was polite but cool when I returned, and a week passed with no further reference to the mural. That was when the postcard from Brussels landed on the doormat.

*Famous Belgians – Let's hear it for Van Dyck!*

*Whatever happened to Simon Waiters? Have you ever forgiven me? I was a bit of a bastard at times, I suppose you had a point.*

*Got the address from your parents. I've given them my cell number. Samantha would love to meet you – if there's no word from you, I promise that I'll piss off, and you'll never hear from me again.*

*Yrs non-conformistly, Greg*

*PS: I take it the Patel Bunbury has long been ditched!*

As Helen had picked up the mail, my first thought was: Did she know what a Bunbury was?

"You fucking bastard," she said.

"Look, Bill Patel…I can explain," I said, although I had no idea what form the explanation might take.

"Let me see. What did you say he was doing in Seattle? A senior accounts executive with Boeing?"

"It was just a joke that got out of hand."

"Perhaps you should have tried harder. You missed a trick or two in your little biog of Bill Patel."

Maybe I had missed a trick. Suppose I'd said that the Bunbury was Bill Patel's invention? That Hammond was wondering if Bill had dropped *his* Bunbury. Too late. In any case, I don't think it would have sounded convincing. I was on the ropes, bracing myself for the knock-out punch. I had no defences left and just wanted it over and done with.

"Yes, you weren't so clever. You could have told me that he used to be a plane spotter."

I looked at her blankly.

"As you sent him to a new life in Seattle, it would have added a terrific touch of veracity if you'd suggested that he was fulfilling the ambition of a lifetime. All those years spotting planes at Manchester Airport, dreaming of a job with one of the world's biggest manufacturers of aeroplanes…it would have made such a happy ending to the story…"

She took a breath while I took that in, before going on the attack again.

"…Then again, better perhaps to save such creativity for a more deserving case. You didn't need to be so clever with me. Stupid, trusting Helen swallowed the whole shooting match anyway."

She juddered to a halt, her eyes full of tears. Suddenly, she launched herself at me and pummelled my chest and face with feeble punches.

"You utter bastard," she finally managed to cough up. "Just how sick are you? You invent a character and you sustain the 'joke' for quarter of a century. You've used it to cheat on me and I've no doubt other women as well."

What could I say? "No, you were the only one I cheated on with Bill Patel, though he once got me in a bit of bother in an Indian restaurant." I collapsed on to the sofa and gnawed the back of my hand while further horrors occurred to Helen.

"Fuck, I've just remembered that time we met again in Halifax. I asked you about Bill Patel then and you couldn't resist. All you had to say was 'that was a daft joke between Greg and me' but, no, after all those years you had to keep it going."

And how could I have responded to that charge? She'd have thought I was weird if I'd stood in the Piece Hall and told her then that I made the whole thing up. Or how about this?

"Yeah, right, Helen. But I just saw it as a chance meeting with you at the time. I never thought I'd see you again after that. In fact, love, if you hadn't sent me that postcard from Crete, I wouldn't have given you another thought, and we would never have got together in the first place."

There didn't seem much point in telling her that I'd stopped misbehaving, that I'd 'only' had a couple of flings during eight years of marriage, and that Bill Patel had been despatched to Seattle to get him out of temptation's way. Better, I decided, to let the tide of anger engulf me.

Helen moved out to stay with a girlfriend in Harrogate. "Looks like Paul Delvaux has got a stay of execution," she said.

It was an easy divorce settlement. I bought Helen out of the mortgage on generous terms and stayed in the house. With Uncle

Andrew's dosh behind us, we could afford to be magnanimous towards each other. It's strange to think that someone can be such a big part of your life, and then be gone. Eight years of marriage; eight years of living together, sleeping in the same bed, living in the same space, breathing the same air, spending more time together than with anyone since I was a baby. And what was it all about in the end? Eight years of two people who liked each other on a good day, and tolerated each other on a bad one. If we were a football team, we'd have been a mid-table outfit. No glorious moments but little threat of relegation either, until one bad spell sends us down. We'd pursued a lot of separate interests. Nothing wrong with that, as long as there is trust; except that in the end the separation suited us better than the togetherness. And I betrayed that trust.

A year or so after the dust had settled on the divorce, Helen sent me a mildly conciliatory letter, more than I deserved. She hoped I'd sort myself out and find happiness eventually. She'd just teamed up with a nice-sounding chap called Paul, with whom she used to play squash occasionally, and they'd moved down south. As far as I know she never had a baby so there was no happy ending; I have to accept that the reason she had no kids could well be down to me, partly at least. I did have myself tested, sperm count a shade below the average but nothing to worry about unduly. So, I suppose my biggest mistake lay in not letting her go, to find a man who would give her what she really wanted. More honesty might have created a different story. I still feel guilty and I will carry that burden to the end of my days.

# CHAPTER THIRTY-SIX

## A Nazi in the rock garden (II)

How's this for an arresting opening to a newspaper story?

*...A six-foot four inches tall stand-up comedian got more than he bargained for when he tried out his routine on a diminutive transgender vicar....*

So, yes, Helen, wherever you are now, this wasn't Dream. It was Reality.

The report continued....

*After Dick Jefferson, aged 22, approached the Rev Lesley Linnell in Fletcher Moss Park, Didsbury, he was flattened by a blow from Simon Waiters. It rendered him unconscious for several minutes, long enough for Jefferson's 'victim' and 'assailant' to decide they should call out the paramedics.*

*Prison teacher Simon Waiters, 42, of York, admitted to the Evening Comet that he was too "quick off the mark" with the punch. However, he said that he thought the churchman was being seriously threatened. Mr Jefferson had a swastika tattoo on his neck, later revealed to be a temporary transfer, and was wearing a shirt with an obscene message.*

*Mr Linnell added: "It was pretty terrifying, and the encounter was in horrible taste but for all that I'm sorry Mr Jefferson had to end up in hospital. Mind you, it was quite a punch."*

*Manchester Metropolitan University graduate and part-time stand-up comic Mr Jefferson, who was kept in Withington Hospital overnight and released this morning, admitted: "This performance was intended as part of an ongoing post-grad study into split-second decision-making, in this case how people react to contradictory messages.*

*"In a way, Mr Waiters taught me a lot but it was certainly a more severe response than I envisaged. On reflection, I won't be pursuing any further this specific line of enquiry."*

*The Rev Lesley Linnell, also 42, has been the minister of two Methodist churches, Southlands and St Peter's, in south Manchester, for six months.*

*He has written extensively about his experiences of feeling trapped between both sexes and of undergoing the major surgery required for gender reassignment. He is hugely popular with his parishioners.*

*Mr Jefferson accepted a caution for displaying a message that could give offence and lead to a public affray.*

*Police did not press charges against Mr Waiters.*

I thought that was a fair summary of the proceedings. There's no doubt that I did pull the trigger too hastily. But I was also unusually quick off the mark by my standards in another way, working out the nature of Dick Jefferson's game. Lesley could see my point, expressed as tactfully as possible, that he'd been picked as a soft target. Jefferson was never going to run his routine past three beefy sixth formers who looked like contenders for the front row in their school's First XV. Lesley backed me up 100 per cent – always good to have a man of the cloth on your side – and the cops made it clear to Jefferson that he was the lucky one not be appearing before magistrates on Monday morning.

There was something else I liked about that addition to my cuttings file, and the version that found its way into my local paper via a freelance. Nobody called me Rocket Boy.

# CHAPTER THIRTY-SEVEN

## Trevor's final instalment

Wendy is an interesting work in progress, growing in confidence. Tina and her concrete man accepted my occasional presence when they realised I'd never tried to take advantage of a vulnerable woman; no need for them to know about Kath's timely intervention.

And Wendy's not really my type. I might have missed out on a nice relationship all those years ago but don't think it would have stood the test of time. Like D H Lawrence; enjoyed reading him then, not my thing now. I wonder if there are any women for whom this would work in reverse. Is there a Charles Dickens or a Thackeray out there waiting for me?

I've also got another new friend, having bonded with Lesley Linnell over the incident in the rock gardens. I've been invited to lunch with Lesley and George next weekend. I'm doing well out of reconnecting with the past, maybe I'm not the loser I thought although I'd be happier if I wasn't so lonely. I can't recall ever feeling so much the lack of a special someone in my life. Was I destined to become ever madder and more solitary, fearing the late-night door knock that could only be Trevor Smith arriving to renew our acquaintance?

In the teachers' staff room at the prison, the women were once more on about men. Men unlikely to buy their own underpants; men unfamiliar with how the washing machine works; men unwilling to let them watch Wimbledon if it coincided with a big football contest; men unhappy about leaning out of a car window to ask the way; men unable to go for a shit without taking a cup of coffee and extensive reading matter. My arrival usually prompted Vera Corbett to say: "We don't mean you, Simon." However, on this occasion, she was up for a fight.

"I've got a bone to pick. Our Diane is not a happy girl, she's been dumped."

"Sorry to hear that, Vera. How do I bear responsibility?"

"You were the one who suggested that she tries meeting someone through the Internet."

"Did I? I thought it was your idea."

"No, we discussed it and you said it was well worth a try," Vera insisted. "So that's what she does, she meets him a few times, really likes him and then what happens? He fails to turn up at the pub, his mobile's switched off permanently and she doesn't know where he lives. Strikes me he was only after one thing. Typical bloke."

"Men," a couple of them chorused as I left the staff room to take on Trevor, Frankie and the gang.

"You all right?" said someone, noticing that I looked distracted during a discussion about the week's news.

"Woman trouble, hey?" said Trevor, less sympathetically.

I pulled myself up immediately and tried to put a brave face on things. It wasn't de rigueur to take your troubles into the classroom; any issues you had were less than zero compared with those of the inmates. Then again, Trevor Smith would be out soon, and he loved watching me suffer.

Trevor had a wicked grin on his face at the end of the class.

"Just a couple more weeks, Simon. This is my final instalment, it's really helped me to get a few things out of my system," he said.

"Don't tell me. Is she called Irene Johnson?" I said.

"Bloody hell, Guv, that's not a bad guess. She's Irene Jackson, how d'you manage that?" said the Professor.

"Just a knack," I said, trying to put some bravado into my voice.

"Ta-ra, Simon," said Trevor on his way out, as if he'd already decided to duck out of his last few classes and was signing off for good. I might never see him again; at least I hoped I wouldn't. Unusual to be aware of that, at the precise moment the person walks away from you. Where had I read something similar, I wondered, and remembered that it was in Trevor's memoirs, talking about one of his lost girls.

I decided to stop at The Who'd 'a Thowt It, examine Trevor's ramblings, and see if the pub was any good. I was greeted by a bank of tables, all laid out and ready for diners. It wasn't much of a haven for the drinking man. I stopped on the way in to read a press review, although it turned out to be the sort of thing I'd tackled briefly myself during my month-long journalism career, with the words Advertisement Feature cunningly clipped off the top of the article.

*"Nothing is frozen, everything is freshly prepared and we always buy our meat from local farms," say Tom and Judy.*

A mural behind the bar took us back to Merrie England. Rustics had gathered in the market square to witness a series of improbable events. A cow soared above the moon, a dish and spoon were making their great escape, and the village idiot was successfully courting a comely dairy maid. The villagers, astonished at such sights, had bubbles coming out of their mouths. "Ee by gum," "Well, I'll be blowed" and, of course, "Who'd 'a thowt it?" The artist's signature lay in the bottom corner. It was my old mate Terry Boston.

"Yes sir?" said mine host, Tom presumably, materialising from a door to the side of the bar.

"Just a half of bitter, please."

"Will that be all, sir?"

"Go on, let's push the boat out," I said. "Packet of dry roasted."

"Certainly, sir," he said with a glacial smile.

"Business okay?" I said, meaning generally, as it was 4.30 in the afternoon and I was the only punter.

"They do say it's the lowest form of wit, sir."

"What is?" I said, though I knew what he was driving at.

"Sarcasm."

"Look, I was just making conversation, I meant…oh, forget it. This is a public house, I take it?"

"It's a gastro-pub, sir," he said with a nod of his head in the direction of the tables, chairs, knives and forks.

"Who'd 'a thowt it," I said.

Irene Jackson, I read, had been Trevor's sweetheart when he went down for handling counterfeit currency. A "pal" called Col, foolish enough to "sniff around" in Trevor's absence, was the victim of gut-wrenching retribution on our man's release. Col, like me, was guilty of an equally reprehensible crime, indifference to Elvis.

So would I receive that house call from Trevor pretty soon? Was this a wind-up, or should I ask for police protection? Yes, I could really see them agreeing to watch my house round the clock when Trevor Smith emerged from HMP Archway, a free man ready to renew his criminal career.

It took the edge off my smugness about almost getting Irene Jackson's name correct. Not that there was anything that much to be pleased about. I already knew she was Irene and his previous girls were AB, CD, EF and GH. Inspector Morse would have got there in two ticks.

What have I done to deserve this? All I've tried to do is to help Trevor. I have kept him in my class when I should have thrown him out, I've read his essays, and I've listened sympathetically to his tales of woe. Now he wants to put me in hospital or worse, because I don't love Elvis bleeding Presley, because I can't see that he did anything new, anything that the old blues and country guys didn't achieve. For me, The Elvis Wars have arrived a few decades early. One day, a sociologist will do a PhD on the link between an excessive love of Elvis and psychopaths. He will interview pensioner Simon Waiters, crippled survivor of a savage attack by one of The King's loyal henchmen.

To calm me down, I put on Thelonius Monk's Straight, No Chaser when I got home, one of the first jazz records I acquired. Auntie Laura had treated me, keen to encourage me to listen to interesting music. If

I applied Zen-like concentration, I could just about hear it as if I were 14 again; puzzling over the weird harmonies and complex rhythms, but realising that I had found the first item in a giant tuck shop to raid for years to come. I loved the title too, a pleasing combination of words that I had assumed to be entirely random.

I was brought back from the 1970s by a phone call. Michael Summerbell had a proposition for me, not very enticing, but he was adamant. He'd been press-ganged into meeting Greg Hammond for a lunch-time meal in Manchester and wanted me to come along.

"Things ended pretty abruptly between us and I ignored his last attempt at reconciliation."

"I know all that, Sim. But I think Hammond's feeling sorry for himself at the moment. He's been skulking around these parts for the last few weeks and his parents suggested I might like to meet up with him. I think they reckon I could be some kind of good influence, if that doesn't sound too ludicrous. It will be a less painful exercise if there are two of us."

"I could always bring Wendy with me. She's a fan, you know."

"Why not," said Michael. "A meeting should cure her."

# CHAPTER THIRTY-EIGHT

## Even the Worm (II)

Bob Hope said there were so many of his old films on television that he could flip channels and watch his hair-line recede. I pick up Fox and Finder novels now and then to see what kind of toll time's wingèd chariot is taking on Hammond. He'd written about a dozen books, but it was only with the success of the Christopher Eccleston TV series that he'd become really big.

I looked up Hammond on the Internet. I found a substantial colour publicity shot, the kind that publishers only use on serious-money writers. Hammond was holding a Champagne flute and wearing a shocking pink and turquoise striped shirt. He'd moved on a bit since his Younger's Tartan and Harp Lager days.

I looked at some of the names on his back catalogue: Photo Finish; A Scoop from Limbo; His Latest Flame, and the new one which was described as a bold departure. I read the blurb and felt sicker than I'd done since my afternoon in the marquee.

*Brian O'Toole and Jeremy Crowe have been best friends since they joined the Wolf Cubs on the same day. But it's an uneven relationship, one punctuated with random acts of cruelty by Brian, who is constantly astonished by his friend's ability to turn the other cheek. Is there nothing that Jeremy will not forgive?*

*The question is answered when they fall in love with the same girl. The winner, inevitably, is Brian. Jeremy sets himself on a course for a revenge that will be decisive and final.*

*This psychological 'why-dunnit' novel is a triumphant move into new territory by Greg Hammond, writer of the acclaimed Fox and Finder series....'*

The book was called Even the Worm.

What was it Trevor Smith said? "Are you in them, Simon?" This revelation did nothing to make the thought of a few more hours in the company of Smith an attractive one. The notion that he might be allowed to get away with skipping his last classes before release was, I knew, nonsense and why would he want to?

The following morning it was a courteous but subdued Good Screw who let me in, with no references to the catering industry.

I went into the staff room and all the man-phobes were sitting in a circle and looking shocked, presided over by Erika, the head of education, who hated everybody regardless of sex or creed.

"What's going on?" I said. "Shouldn't you lot be taking classes."

"They've been cancelled this morning," said Erika, a spinster in her early 60s and a teacher of the old school.

"Has there been a riot or something?" I asked.

"There's been a tragic incident," said Erika.

"What's happened?"

"An inmate's only gone and hanged himself."

"Blimey. Anyone I know?"

"Yes, he's in – he was in – one of your classes. Trevor Smith. It's very sad," said Vera Corbett.

A moment of ecstasy took me back to my betting days. It was as though my horse had won at fantastically long odds because the favourite had fallen at the final jump. The sensation lasted about two seconds. Then I felt shit, like someone who'd picked up his winnings and realised that it wouldn't make his life any better. I'd had my dark moments without ever contemplating suicide. How bad must Trevor have been, tearing up strips of an old shirt to make the necessary knots, all the while having time to reconsider, but not doing so? Michael had suggested that Trevor was probably "as weak and cheesy as the next bloke, probably more so" when I'd expressed fears about meeting him. As ever, Michael was right; maybe Smith just couldn't stomach his return to life on the outside as a total loser.

"Poor old Trevor," I said. "He was due to come out, you know. He was really looking forward to it, or that's the impression he gave."

"I think he'd got enemies on the outside," said Erika.

"I think he'd got one or two on the inside," said Vera.

"Wayne, for starters," said Erika.

"Who?"

"Wayne. Tweedle Dum," said Vera.

"Oh, you mean Speak, the Bad Screw," I said.

"*They* might call them screws, you don't," said Erika. "Anyway," she said, returning to her theme, "it seems that Trevor had a parallel criminal career. Petty thieving, and sexual offences involving minors," she said. "He'd, up to a point, managed to keep the second bit under wraps. I think some men had their suspicions about him but nothing was ever proven definitely."

"That must have been very frustrating for them," I said, thinking about Trevor's tendency to be accident-prone and the missing finger tip. "When he'd not been in my class very long he tried to show me a newspaper report of his court case. He said it was an armed robbery." I was just about to brag about how I'd uncovered his true level of literacy, then pulled myself up in time.

"I don't think Trevor's thieving career extended much beyond lead from church roofs and a few snatches from Woolie's," said Erika.

"This thing he showed me was armed robbery I'm sure," I said. "Someone was seriously injured. Not that I studied it closely," I added hastily. "I told him I didn't want to look at it."

"That case must have been another Trevor Smith," said Erika. "It's the only possible explanation. Our Trevor must have shown the article to everyone and claimed it was him. He must have carried it with him as a bogus badge of honour."

"Would you say you were friendly with Trevor, then?" Erika asked me.

"To tell the truth I don't think he liked me much at all, even though I tried to encourage him with his writing," I said.

"Well, he seems to be sorry if he caused you any problems," Erika said.

"What?"

"Only, they found an envelope in his cell, addressed to you. It got opened by mistake, us not seeing your name on it," Erika said artlessly. "Anyway, here it is. I'm sure you'll understand the message."

I read Trevor's note: "Apologies for the mind games, Simon. Great performance by you in those rock gardens…BRAVO!"

"Yes, well the less said about that the better," said Erika.

"A sad day, Mr Waiters," ventured the Good Screw as I departed.

A vicious sod, petty criminal and fantasist who liked under-age girls but I suppose Jesus loved him, I thought.

"Yes indeed. See you tomorrow," I said.

So why did he kill himself, I wondered? I played with an elaborate theory based on my new knowledge that there were two Trevor Smiths. The hard man gets wind of 'our' Trev's attempt to use the armed robbery court case to give him street-cred. No, even though Trevor had plenty of enemies, Michael's simpler explanation was probably closest to the truth.

At least I'd been liberated from that threat, I thought as I walked towards my car, although I dismissed as too triumphal the prospect of driving home to a tape of Sonny Rollins' Freedom Suite. In any case I wasn't free. Like Woody Allen in Hannah and Her Sisters, galloping cheerfully down the road after discovering that he wasn't terminally ill, I suddenly ground to a near halt. Reality kicked in as I thought about my gloomy and solitary future, 30 plus years as a lonely divorcee, libido gradually sinking below the horizon, together with any vestiges of my limited attractiveness to women.

Let's say 38 years, because that would make me 80. Old enough, although I accept that my dad wouldn't see it that way. I've got a method and date of departure in mind. Being zapped into eternity, like the over 30s in Logan's Run, wouldn't be bad although my exit plan is better: an assassigram, in 2038, carried out by Maria Grazia Cucinotta, revisiting her role as the earthy peasant from Il Postino. She would emerge from a huge cake, sing a brief message then provide a glorious fuck before killing me by painless lethal injection as I enjoyed a post-coital sleep; at 80, I imagine that would be very sound.

No happy ending like that for Trevor. I made a firm resolution – to find out where his parents lived, and to go to his funeral.

# CHAPTER THIRTY-NINE

## Even the Worm (III)

It's just tired looking," said Alison. "Why not splash out, you know, bit of a house makeover."

"What sort of things?" I said, although I understood what she meant. Helen had taken a lot of the better furnishings, I'd been left with the tat and had topped it up with hand-me downs.

"Decorate a couple of rooms, get a new sofa, a dining table, some throws. Nice cushions, maybe."

"Cushions?" I said, horrified.

"Fiddlesticks, pet. You won't turn horribly queer. They don't have to be pink squashy affairs. In fact, the right cushion can be manly," she said, pronouncing the y with a Mancunian acute e and flipping my knee playfully with the back of her hand.

"I could always go to see Melanie Cohen," I said, taking advantage of Greg Hammond's disappearance to the lavatory to raise the subject.

"The legendary Gill Todd's chum? Good move," said Alison. "But what can she do?"

"She went into the family's interior design business in Leeds."

"The Cohen Brothers. That's her? So she isn't saving the world or sorting out dysfunctional families?"

"Apparently not."

"I think we should get into your jalopy and pay her a visit," said Alison. "What larks, Simon!"

We were in Michael's favourite Italian restaurant. Wendy had arrived sporting a flattering hairstyle, a kind of wavy bob. She looked both younger and more grown up. Hammond was working hard to impress.

"Chris and Susan have signed up for two more Fox and Finders, and Granada's going into production soon. I'm writing two episodes myself rather than just being a consultant, it'll give me a lot more control over things, you know."

"Right," Wendy said, less awestruck than Hammond would have liked.

"What sort of car you driving these days, Simon?" asked Hammond.

"Hey?" I hesitated, because it seemed such a daft question. "Um, some type of Nissan, a Micra."

"Not a bad little motor, you can't go wrong with Nissans. I had a Primera, but I treated myself to a soft-top Beamer recently. Very tasty."

"I've never gone much on them," said Alison. I suspected that, like me, she didn't know what a Beamer was.

"You've got no soul," said Hammond.

"I'd have thought a good definition of having no soul might be someone who thinks that a person has no soul because she doesn't like a mass-produced metal box with a lethal and very large engine," said Wendy.

"You might just be right," said Alison, the first to untangle that observation.

Hammond ordered an expensive red without consultation.

"Twenty quid a bottle? I think you might just have run that one past us, we're not all made of money."

This was Wendy speaking again; she was loving not being the meek little lady.

As the evening wore on Hammond began to run out of steam, deflated by his failure to entice Wendy. I managed to get him on his own briefly when the girls, in time-honoured fashion, went off to the lavatory together and Michael disappeared for a quick roll-up.

"Think you might have bitten off more than you can chew there, Greg, with Wendy. Not the easy target you thought, hey?"

"Bit rich from you, Sim."

"I've never claimed to know how to 'handle the ladies' particularly well, if that's what you're driving at."

"Your problem, Simon, is that you don't know how to handle a real woman. Then again, you never knew how to handle any women."

"I never had much help from you at key moments," I said, somewhat feebly.

"Are you banging on about things from more than 20 years ago? Get a sodding life."

"Well, what about Lesley Linnell? You really shat on me there, didn't you?"

"I don't even remember anyone called Lesley."

"Come off it, remember that church conference in 1974, the girl from Flixton whose father was a doctor?"

"Very, very vaguely. We're talking about things from a quarter of a century ago now."

"You told her that I was interested in astrology."

"Astrology? Did I?...You know, I do believe that your status as the world's saddest man has been reconfirmed. There was a time when it was in doubt. When you told me to fuck off forever the evening we saw your Uncle Andrew with that floozy, I was impressed. You had a genuine grievance and, once I'd had time to digest it I thought, well done, Simon, you've finally stood up for yourself. I used to worry about you, you know, I thought you were too tender-hearted for this cruel world. I always liked you, although I could never resist tormenting you. But then you launched that attack on me outside the restaurant and I thought: hang on, old Simon, even the worm turns, hey? Perhaps he's going to be all right after all, he's toughening up. I got that one wrong."

With the girls chortling about something no doubt Hammond-related as they made their way back to our table, mirroring one another with their swinging handbags, there no time to pursue this argument. Hammond had wrong-footed me again. What surprised me was the way he'd taken the outburst in the Khyber Pass car park, at our last official meeting. Was that how he'd seen me? Was that how others still see me?

"As you pointed out once, the persistence of memory is a fascinating subject, we're all selective," I said.

"And there was me thinking we were both too civilised to make any references to the marquee, Simon."

# CHAPTER FORTY

## A visit to the Cohen Brothers

"So you've decided that it's hey-ho for the open road and the Cohen Brothers," said Michael.

"Yes."

"Wouldn't most people, in your shoes, choose just about anywhere else?"

"It's a good shop, apparently. No point in holding their daughter against the whole Cohen clan. I like to think I'm bigger than that."

"Okay, Simon, don't overdo it. I'll get Ali."

I played with the phone flex, pretending it was a skipping rope for a couple of Borrowers, while I waited for Alison.

"Well done," she said without any preamble. "I'd no idea you were taking any notice of what I said the other day, I thought you were too preoccupied with Greg Hammond."

"Wendy has asked if she can come along too," I said.

"Melanie will think you're operating some kind of harem. If she's there, that is."

"Oh, she will be," I said. "I gave the firm a call the other day to check if she'd be around."

"You really are a proper caution. No one can accuse you of being predictable."

"Well, she cropped up in a very strange dream the other night, not for the first time, looking rather nice and telling me it was time I grew up. I can't get it out of my mind and I'd like to see her. Call it some kind of attempt to seek redemption."

"For whom, Simon? You or her?"

The Cohen Brothers' store advertised itself as offering the best of British, Irish and Italian design and manufacture. The shop was set up in a series of rooms, starting with an entrance hall then moving on to sitting and dining rooms. Everywhere, things were dressed with rugs and throws, vases of flowers and large pieces of pottery. Each room area lit up in three different ways, changing every two minutes to display the range of shades, spots and wall lights. It was vast, taking up two floors of an old woollen mill whose great cast-iron pillars and roof struts soared above.

"Some stylish stuff," said Wendy, as we did a preliminary orientation walk through the rooms and I watched for Melanie's arrival.

"Absolutely."

"Absolutely what?"

"Absolutely stylish."

"Just checking you're still at home. We've come to look at furnishings."

"Right," I agreed, knowing that Melanie would be around the next corner.

She was, and my legs began to turn to jelly when I saw her in one of the bedrooms, talking to a couple of young sales assistants. What would be my opening line? Something sardonic about 1977? Melanie could have stepped straight out of my dreams. Her chic black hair had a few silver highlights and she looked trimmer than in student days when carrying a few extra pounds was a feminist statement. I tried to look interested in a huge bed made up with beautiful, crisply plain linen. I wondered if this was the sort of thing Melanie slept in every night.

Then Melanie saw me. She was walking over. The funny thing was, she looked more embarrassed than I was. The smile came as much from the eyes as the mouth, and she still had perfect teeth.

"Is it Simon Waiters?"

"Good grief, it is," I stammered, putting a hand on a bed head for support. "I mean, good grief it is you. It is Melanie Cohen."

"Yes. It is. It is me. I've often wondered what happened to you. Well, well, what a surprise though I was told you were coming so not quite such a surprise," she said. Alison made some remark about having heard a lot about her while I tried to regain my powers of speech.

"Anyway, how can we help you?"

"He wants to do some room improvements," said Wendy firmly, when I struggled to respond. "He's starting from scratch in the living room and he wants a two-seater sofa, a rug, maybe a couple of throws and a decent book case. Oh, he'd like to see some lighting too."

"I'm sure we can help him, can't we ladies?" said Melanie.

"It's not a ménage à trois," said Wendy.

"Is there anything you don't sell?" I asked.

"Oh, we're not too ambitious. No kitchens, bathrooms, children's furniture. We have to draw the line somewhere, in fact we're thinking of letting kitchen specialists handle that as more people want to eat in the dining room and dropping the dining room furniture," Melanie said, a little breathlessly, her syntax not so clever.

"But as I say, I'm sure that we can sort you out," she added, regaining her composure. "Why don't I get one of the sales team to show you a few things, discuss colour schemes and the like and maybe we can talk again later?"

"Well, she seems okay," said Alison, and Wendy agreed. Melanie had disappeared in search of her most ruthless sales assistant.

"You didn't meet her in the seventies. Anyone can be nice if they're trying to flog stuff," I said.

"Don't be so cynical, she's genuinely warm. She certainly likes you."

"Ha."

The sales assistant played a blinder, helpful but not pushy, and we drew up a shortlist. I was going to have to make at least one more visit as I hadn't even begun to think about lighting.

"Melanie wondered if you would like to go up to her office, at the far end of the second floor," the assistant said. "For coffee and biscuits…er, that's just you, Simon."

"Sure."

"Supping with the devil now. Take your time," said Alison.

Melanie had a small, functional office with a couple of contemporary watercolours of Leeds on the wall. On her desk was a picture of a teenaged boy. Behind her, just a couple of feet above floor level, was a small pair of maroon velvet curtains with bright yellow tassels, perhaps hiding a picture or plaque. It was so oddly placed that I looked twice to convince myself that I hadn't imagined it.

"Hello again, Simon," she smiled. "Your friends still looking round?"

I confirmed, as economically as I could, my connections with Wendy and Alison. She got flustered again, then we did some personal history – divorced no kids, divorced one kid and husband went off with one of her friends just about covered it – and then Melanie decided she had to get something off her chest.

"It's going to sound strange apologising about something twenty-odd years ago but here goes."

She was sitting there and assuming, with no lead-up, that I'd know exactly what she was talking about, even though we were going back to 1977. Mad, but right.

"Well, I don't think my behaviour was what you might call exemplary, talking about Pakis and all."

"A simple tut-tut would have sufficed, I knew you weren't a red neck. I'd discovered some unpleasant truths about Gill Todd, to be honest," she said. "Some of her attitudes I mean, and she always seemed to find the nice guys, get bored with them in double-quick time, then spit them out. It used to annoy me that they couldn't work it out for themselves. I wanted to grab them by the throat and say: 'For God's sake can't you see what's coming.' Don't know why, but I decided to take it out on you, and your Paki moment was the opportunity. The funny thing is, there I was trying to be all right-on

226

and I didn't have a single friend who was Asian, Caribbean or whatever."

"Are you still in touch with Gill?" I asked.

"After our Roman holiday, you've got to be joking. We had this massive row in the first few days, issues which were just surfacing when we last met."

"In the Piazza Navona?"

"Er, no, back at our pensione, I think, what odds is it where it happened?"

"Just an image that came into my mind," I said.

"We'd been going to head north but then she met this Italian bloke with a flash car and she decided to go down to Calabria with him. Needless to say, I wasn't invited."

"The end of the friendship?"

"Too true, I moved out of that house in Moss Side as soon as I got back."

"You don't seem to have much luck with your friends."

"I think I sometimes get close to the wrong people, or send out the wrong signals to the right people."

She paused for a second, adjusted the picture of her lad to her satisfaction and debated with herself just how confessional to get.

"You did annoy me at times, Simon. I thought you were too in thrall to Gill and demeaning yourself. You were too good for her."

"You might have a point on the first bits, not so sure about part two."

"Anyway, I certainly got my come-uppance," she said.

"How so?"

"Going out with Greg Hammond. I suppose it's an interesting talking point now as he's well known, but it wasn't a pleasant experience."

She ran her hand through her hair and did more desk adjustment. She thought that she'd said enough for now.

"When are the Lord Mayor and corporation band coming, then?" I asked.

"Sorry?"

I nodded to the maroon velvet curtains.

"Are you sure you're ready for this, Simon?"

"I've no idea, until I find out what it is."

"You realise it's not everybody I would allow to see this? A few folk might take serious offence."

"Go for it, as they say these days," I said.

"Whatever," she said, mock-gormless, leaning down to reach the curtains and revealing a nice bit of thong. "Good work by Levi the tassel-maker, don't you think?" she added, pulling on the cord to reveal the hidden portrait.

"Jesus, Melanie, I hope you didn't show it to the Yorkshire Post reporter."

"Certainly not. Shocking, isn't it? But there are some things from your youth that you just cannot let go."

# CHAPTER FORTY-ONE

## Trevor's sensitive side

Helen and I would amuse ourselves at weddings by trying to work out who the guests were. The genetic thread running through some families was so strong that you couldn't help but suss the connections. The shabbily-dressed bloke at one table had to be the groom's funny bachelor uncle we'd heard so much about, while the flash chap at another with the snooty Home Counties girlfriend might be that high-flying cousin on the bride's side.

You couldn't play that game at Trevor Smith's funeral. Sitting with his mum and dad were just two older people, probably grandparents. Two young women were separated from the family by a few pews. One of them, the governor's PA with whom I was friendly, had given me Trevor's parents' address. The other woman might have been a probation officer. Trevor must have got through a few of them over the years.

The vicar was doing his best, talking about small acts of kindness that Trevor had carried out as a boy: shopping errands, helping folk across the road and the like. It was a self-conscious address, as if he realised that the banality of these titbits, the few crumbs of decency that he'd managed to scrape together, merely exposed Trevor's wasted life for what it was. However, the Rev had something more positive to say. He'd saved this nugget, and was suddenly more animated: "Many of us struggle to find our niche in life, perhaps through lack of self-confidence or opportunities. It was a great pity that Trevor never found a good path to pursue despite the encouragement he received from his parents. Lucy and Neil have told me how much he enjoyed writing compositions when he was at primary school. When he moved on to the secondary, English remained his best subject and the teachers said that his efforts showed, when he tried, a vivid imagination at work.

"At Archway Prison, he revived this interest in writing. He wrote a series of pieces about what he referred to as the girls that got away. Lucy and Neil showed me a couple of examples, and I was touched by what I saw. I am told that Trevor never had a proper sweetheart. Lucy and Neil said that they were astonished to find that he had yearned after girls, but lacked the confidence to ask them out. Could Claire Daniels or Annabel Barnes, as I think two of them were called, have taken Trevor down a happier path? We will never know.

"As it is, Lucy and Neil tell me that they drew great comfort from these pieces. They showed a better side to Trevor, a certain sensitivity which other people around him, including fellow inmates, probably failed to see. They were also touched by the trouble that Trevor's teacher, Simon Waiters, had taken. Lucy says that when she read Simon's observations, she wept. Again, who knows what might have happened if one or two of Trevor's school teachers had been as positive and caring."

The conveyor belt on which the coffin lay came noisily to life. The box shuffled slightly, as if Trevor was making himself comfortable before his final journey. After the first few chords of a taped, church-organ version of an old song, which I guessed must be by Elvis, the belt began to move. Trevor was on his way. As the dark velvet curtains parted for him, I thought about the curious little arrangement in Melanie's office and the hideous face that lay behind it.

"And you must be Simon," said the vicar, shaking my hand warmly as we left the church. "I've heard all about you from Lucy and Neil."

"You must come back to the house for some tea," said Lucy Smith.

"You can follow us, Simon," said Neil Smith. "It's very straightforward, if you lose us. Half a mile to the crossroads, then the second turning on the left after you pass the Toby Carvery."

He was an amiable, if bureaucratic-looking cove, solidly built and with a thin moustache which was comical rather than petty. He could have stepped out of an old-fashioned children's book, of the kind you might have seen in the 1950s, in which father returns home to a well-ordered house and a family-round-the-table meal, followed by an hour watching an enormous television set with a tiny screen, or listening to the wireless.

Shortly after passing the Toby Carvery I turned into a narrow street. Once again, as with Tina, we were in West Yorkshire, millstone grit country and the terraced houses were golden or black, depending on whether or not they had been sandblasted back to the original colour. Lucy and Neil Smith lived in a neat house marred by a mean PVC front door. The downstairs rooms had been knocked into one. A full-sized table tennis table was laden with sandwiches, cakes and ale.

"I used to play table tennis myself, at the local church, Mr Smith," I said.

"Neil will do nicely, lad," he said. Although he talked to me as if I belonged to a younger generation, he couldn't have been more than a decade older than I was.

"Trevor liked the game, it was the only sport he ever showed any aptitude for. It used to upset him when he was the last to be chosen for football and cricket."

The grandparents hovered around me, occasionally putting a hand on my shoulders, as if touching a lucky mascot. Lucy Smith, slight and with a pinched, careworn face, looked like a woman who hadn't taken life's knocks too well.

"Those pieces Trevor wrote showed him to us in a new way, Simon. We loved them, we had no idea that he ever thought like that," she said. "I suppose we'll never know where we went wrong, we just never understood him. All he ever wanted to do was hurt us, even when he was pretending to be nice. In his teens he got his first tattoo done, with my name on it. I thought it was a joke, I've always hated tattoos. Then he wet his fingers and rubbed it hard, to show me that it was real."

"We all go through life fighting contradictory impulses," I said, glad that Lucy and Neil had never had the opportunity to see Trevor's final piece for me, about the fate of the Irene Jackson-fancying Col; the man who, like me and Half-German Janet, wasn't much bothered about Elvis one way or the other. "As the vicar said, the right woman might have put Trevor on a happier path."

The room was a hotchpotch of old and new. There was a cheap, modern sofa of the kind soap stars advertise on afternoon TV, pushed back against the window to make way for the ping-pong table. The carpet was a garish, swirling mixture of dark reds and greens, and the wallpaper, bright floral designs on one side and plain woodchip on the other, looked like a compromise to keep both Lucy and Neil happy. A glass-fronted bookcase contained a Bible and some old-fashioned adventure novels of the type that nearly put me off reading for life when my parents tried to force them down my throat: She, Lost Horizon, Coral Island. Next to a 1970s stereogram, Herb Alpert snuggled up to sunny Alma Cogan, the girl on whom, I'd read somewhere, Paul McCartney tried out Yesterday after he'd dreamt the tune and wanted to know if it already existed.

In the back yard, there was a small shed. This would be where Neil Smith, jacket off and wearing braces, had leaned over a bicycle, showing Trevor how to mend a puncture and telling him that footballers didn't know how to use a knife and fork.

I remembered the name of the Elvis tune which piped up as the conveyor belt had whirred into action at the crematorium: In The Ghetto. A gloomy affair but a better choice than Return to Sender or, even worse, His Latest Flame.

Nature versus nurture. Some children are doomed because of where and when they fetch up in this world. But Trevor Smith was simply a bad 'un who would have turned out that way if his mum and dad had been warm-hearted social workers in 1950s Sweden.

Before I left, I went upstairs to the lavatory. I stopped to examine the plaque on a bedroom door. Beneath a picture of a bicycle and a space hoppa were the words 'Trevor's Room'.

"I hope you will be all right driving home, Simon," said Lucy, as I was leaving. "You look as if you've been crying."

# CHAPTER FORTY-TWO

## The Goy With The Thorn In His Side

When I was a kid I used to wonder where writers got their ideas; all their experiences must be grist to the mill, someone explained to me. As a features journalist on the Bolton Evening News, Hammond interviewed a famous novelist. He asked her if it was okay to use a small tape recorder, and just take a few notes for background information. The batteries in the recorder were flat, so he changed them while she waited patiently, but the replacements weren't much better, and he could see that the cassette kept slowing. Hammond glanced anxiously at the machine to watch its progress and took ever more copious notes as he realised that technology was letting him down.

He said to me: "She could see I was getting anxious because she was such a fast talker that my shorthand just wasn't up to it. And I'll swear she speeded up deliberately, she must have got up to 150 words a minute. I thought to myself 'bet she uses this incident some time in one of her books.'"

I've read Even the Worm. I'd be lying if I said I didn't recognise some aspects of my personality in Jeremy Crowe. There's more than a little of the unappealing Brian O'Toole in Hammond, and I've got to give him credit for self-knowledge. I bet our curry nights feature in another of his books, in some form or another, and I'd wager that somewhere there's an unsympathetic character based on Melanie.

234

When I called the Cohen Brothers a week or so later, I was put through to Melanie as soon as I gave my name. She suggested lunch and I agreed enthusiastically.

"For a wine bar, they serve a good pint," she said, as we sat in a small place a few blocks from the store. "I'm assuming that your conversion to real ale stuck."

"At least I can thank Gill for that. I've been doing some past-times stuff recently, thinking about old flames, missed opportunities," I said, making it sound like a harmless hobby for a winter's evening reflection by the fireside.

"Have you now?"

"Yes. I even got to thinking about someone I knew in 1974, when I was not quite 16. More than a quarter of a century ago. The memory plays strange tricks."

"I can top that. I go back to 14. He was a gorgeous boy called Ethan Tinner, known to his mates as Can Man, and he came to my brother's Bar Mitzvah. He asked me to dance with him and I said no. Maybe I thought you had to play hard to get."

"And he never asked you again?"

"No, he just asked someone else. I'd misread how things are supposed to work between girls and boys and I'm not so sure that I've ever cracked it. That's just for starters though I won't bore you with details. There's plenty more, I call them my lost boys."

"How long have you been doing that?" I said, almost choking on my pint of Landlord.

"About ten years. Just after Howard left, I was feeling down, and I took Martin to see Peter Pan. It's kind of stuck around ever since. So, yes, I've been through some of that sort of thing," she added, "It's maybe inevitable at our age."

This was the moment I might have got more confessional, but I simply said, as if dismissing the subject: "Perhaps we shouldn't set too much store by it."

"No. Maybe not."

She ran her index finger around the rim of her glass in a slightly distracted way.

"I bet you thought I was a right madam back then," she said at last.

"I was terrified of you."

She looked hurt.

"I saw Greg Hammond recently, first time for 20 years or so," I said, to get the conversation moving again.

She gave me another wounded look. Her hand, resting on the table, was very close to mine and I almost reached across to reassure her, then thought better of it. I could feel myself blushing, and my ears burning red, as they used to do when I was an adolescent.

"Ever read any of his books, Melanie?" I asked with a clumsy lurch into safer territory.

"In a word, no," she said. "You know what D H Lawrence said about trusting the tale, not the teller? Well, there are limits."

"It wasn't a happy courtship?"

"It was a brief one."

"He never told me you were going out together. I was back at university and I only knew because my mum mentioned it in a letter. When he'd just started his first job, wasn't it?" I said, omitting Mum's description of Melanie.

"He was a good-looking boy but the main reason I agreed to go out with him was that he wasn't Jewish."

"Was *not* Jewish?"

"I was trying to give my parents a hard time, I didn't think they'd want me to get involved with a goy. I mean that's not the only reason I…" she said before drying up.

"Did you succeed, in shocking your folks?"

"Yes, and it was even worse when they actually met him. Er, it wouldn't be an issue now, the gentile thing I mean," she added, and then bit her lip.

"So you were a rebel."

"Not really. I was a middle-class kid who was going to become an accountant and maybe work later in the family business, which is what I've done. I was just trying to show a bit of chutzpah."

"What about all that sociology stuff? That was the chic subject of choice for young hard-liners in those days."

"Your memory's good, Simon, but maybe not perfect. I was also doing economics. I'd decided to drop the sociology and Gill said I was selling out, which was bloody sanctimonious of her…Were you really terrified of me?" she added after more fumbling with her wine glass.

"No, that's way too strong. You were, at least I thought so, the most radical person I'd ever met, and I just didn't have the terms of reference to handle you. I mean, there was me, only just sleeping with a girl for the first time and there was you, mocking me for being politically somewhere centre of centre. Meanwhile you were advocating free love, protests against the Chilean junta, and banning the Black and White Minstrels."

"And where do you stand now, politically?"

"Same as it ever was," I said, trying to sound like the Talking Heads record. "Once an imperceptibly Left-wing liberal, always an imperceptibly Left-wing liberal."

"Wow, you're so dangerous! I used to get cross with you over your lack of engagement with politics, but the notion that I was getting through lots of blokes comes as a surprise. I was a virgin, as it happens," she said, not lowering her voice in time to prevent a couple of people at the next table looking across at us.

"I must have made up the thing about free love, decided that it probably came with the territory," I said. "I used to imagine that one day I'd come across a big headline about you in the Daily Mail."

"Is this the most dangerous woman in Britain?" she said, loudly enough for a few more customers to become interested in us.

"Exactly," I said, "Red Mel brings the nation to its knees."

"One reason I only lasted a few weeks with Greg Hammond," she said when she had stopped laughing, "was because his single interest was in getting me into the sack. I was ready for a serious relationship when someone good came along but I thought 'I'm not throwing away my virginity on you.' So, I wasn't as alternative as you thought. In fact, I was as innocent as you in many ways. It makes me want to weep when I think about how useless I was. But we shouldn't be too hard on ourselves. We were only 19, remember, only a couple of years older than Martin is now."

"That's teenagers for you," I said, as I had to Lesley Linnell, another former angry young miss. "How's yours shaping up? Nice looking lad, by the way, to judge from that pic."

"He's lovely," she said. "Very equable for his age."

"Not too much so, I hope."

"Well, he has his moments. You'd really like him, and so will a lot of girls when he cottons on to the idea that he isn't totally repulsive to look at."

"The torments of being young."

"He tells me he's off to see a Jewish Smiths' tribute band tonight, Schmorrissey and Schmarr."

"Best cover version The Goy With The Thorn In His Side?" I said. "Or Goy Friend in a Coma."

She laughed again. "Yes, he'd like that."

It turned out that, despite the regrettable love of The Smiths, the young Martin Lucas – he'd got his father's surname – was getting into jazz. Melanie remembered that was my thing.

"We had a conversation about Jelly Roll Morton, didn't we?" I said, "Before…"

"Yes, before we talked about careers I think. My dad's still got those 78s. You remember that do you, and the careers stuff?" Melanie didn't say this harshly, but she wasn't on the back foot any more.

"Gill said something strange about you."

"She said I'd make lots of money, I think we know what that was code for. I was hoping you'd say something to her, I was looking to you to stick up for me."

238

"I'm so sorry, Melanie. I was desperate not to fall out with Gill...but that's exactly what I did anyway. In a manner manufactured by her, that is, because it turned out she'd lost interest in me by then."

She put her hand on mine.

"I think I might even have called you Rocket Boy, I was so cross."

"You did."

"Sorry about that, the last thing I want to do now is fall out with you again."

"Rather Jelly Roll Morton than Gary Glitter," I said. "I was amazed by that picture of him in your office."

"Gary Glitter, a love that dare not speak its name," she said. "I bring him out for a laugh when I'm down. I know he's totally beyond the pale, but it reminds me of when I was young. First love never dies, does it?" she added, after a pause.

"Perhaps not."

"I was just thinking," she said, then looked uncertain of her ground and didn't seem sure how to continue.

"To be honest," I said, filling the gap. "I'd no idea that you genuinely liked Gary Glitter. I thought it was some kind of pose."

"Why would I do that?"

"Dunno, as you said we were so young. I guess I thought you were trying to show that you had a sense of humour underneath all the talk of black media stereotypes and the politics of Latin America. You know, underneath it all."

"Underneath it all," she repeated. "Was I really that bad?"

Neither yes nor no struck me as particularly good responses.

"You were going to say something before, you were just thinking something or other."

"It was nothing," she said, smiling a little sadly because this trip into the past, and the talk of lost friend Gill Todd (who had, she'd heard, made it to the USA) and lost love Gary Glitter had induced a touch of melancholia. "Time I was getting back, Simon. Give me a call tonight and we'll fix up a proper date."

"Right."

"Oh, two other things. That was the only occasion I ever called you Rocket Boy and I was misquoted in the Yorkshire Post. I might have sold my soul, but I have never ever in my life used the word lifestyle!"

She kissed me as we said goodbye at the front door of Cohen Brothers. I still felt the sensation of her hand touching mine and I finally twigged that Melanie knew we were too old to let opportunities slip through our fingers. And that, when she talked of first love, she didn't mean Gary Glitter.

As for me, I'd completed the set of lost girls: Gill Todd, Wendy Thomas, Anna Florenski, and Lesley Linnell: too bad, too-not-quite-my-type, too pregnant, too male.

# CHAPTER FORTY-THREE

## Scene in another restaurant

I've read the agony columns, and I know a few people in the same boat as me so I'm not totally ignorant about the difficulties of courting for the over 40s, especially after a long break.

If you filmed my life it could slip comfortably into a list of movies with foodie themes; alongside – though perhaps not for artistic merit – Eat Drink Man Woman, Babette's Feast and Tampopo. Some key moments have taken place in restaurants. Trips to Indian eating houses with Greg Hammond gave me two dark nights of the soul; following the second, I made a decision I should have taken after the first.

I'd not been so nervous about a first date for two decades. It was lunch as she'd wanted to come to York for some work-related reasons, but we were both aware that this didn't make it any less of an actual date. Walking to my favourite restaurant we were equally tongue-tied, as if both scared of making a wrong move or saying something stupid.

The waiters greeted us cheerfully; they always remember me.

Before we entered, Melanie had looked approvingly at the black and white Art Deco exterior. She was clearly taken, too, with the restaurant's chic, minimalist look, warmed up by large, dark teak tables and colourful abstract wall paintings, 'knocked together', I'd been told, by the owner's daughter.

Melanie picked up an expensive, well-balanced fork, then put it down self-consciously, as if not wanting to appear to be an arbiter of good taste. She looked super, and I tried to keep feelings of unworthiness at bay.

"You take all your first dates to the best places?" she said.

"There's a good transport caff up the road, but I decided to push the boat out for you."

"You got a warm welcome when we walked in," she said.

"That's the Waiters effect."

"And so modest."

"No, what I mean is, everyone remembers me because of my name. There aren't many of us around."

We were drinking a vermouth aperitif. We'd ordered a bottle of New Zealand sauvignon and were waiting for our starters.

"Yes, I know you're a rare breed."

"It surprises a few people. I think I'm the only Simon Waiters in the country."

"I can believe it," she said and suddenly pulled a semi-gurney, as if not sure whether to reveal something.

"I might as well tell you this," she said, confirming that I'd read her correctly. "I felt really bad about that night with Greg Hammond, although I was more fed up with Gill than with you. I knew our friendship wouldn't have survived, even without the business in Rome."

"I sort of cottoned on that might be the case."

"I haven't finished," she said. "The thing is I knew I'd been harsh on you and I found myself thinking about you from time to time. Very occasionally I'd look up your name in a telephone directory."

"When you visited somewhere new?"

"Yes."

"Would you have called if you'd found me?"

"God, no. I was sure you'd have thought I was crazy. I've always had enough insight to pull myself back from the brink of anything truly bonkers. I figured that I was the last person you'd want to see again."

I hid for a few seconds, pretending to take a few sips from my already-empty vermouth glass. So many alternatives were going through my head at once that I couldn't decide which one to select.

"Well, you know now that the last bit's not true. And we all do strange things," I finally managed to say. "When one girl ditched me, I drove ten miles out of my way the next weekend just to see her house for one last time."

This wasn't quite accurate. I did all that in my head but, because I'd been running late, never carried it through. Still, it was true in spirit. I wanted Melanie to know that I didn't think there was anything in the least crazy about her. Unless you counted a serious soft spot for me.

Any impediment in our relationship would come from young Martin. Armed with the self-belief he had yet to acquire, he would have no problems with the girls: good looking in an amiable rather than out-and-out chiselled kind of way, slim and a natty dresser to boot. Not for Martin the trousers falling off the backside full-nappy look.

Martin Lucas, for all Melanie had talked him up, didn't strike me as an especially communicative teenager, and he was indifferent to my attempts to court his mother. If we'd been applying a five-point Likert scale on his mum's new beau, ranging from strongly approve to strongly disapprove, I would have sat right in the middle. "I have no opinions on this man, despite our shared interest in jazz, and his presence makes no odds to me one way or the other."

Melanie was disappointed by his indifference to me, or recent lack of concern for anything else.

"I don't know what's got into him."

"Lovesick, maybe?" I ventured.

On my next visit, a girl waved enthusiastically to him as we stood by the window.

"She looks okay, Martin."

"Huh."

"Oh, bit of a cow, hey? Not so nice."

"Rebecca Goldman, certainly not," he said, affronted.

"So…nice enough then. But attached."

"Huh, attached?....Oh, see what you mean. Not that I know of. Though…"

"Yeah?"

"Actually, a friend of mine did ask her out recently."

"But no joy?"

"No, she wasn't off about it. But she said that she didn't want to get involved with anyone for a while."

"You know, that sounds suspiciously like something that was reported back to me when I was your age. Take it from me, she doesn't mean a word of it. I'm right on this and I'll bet you a Dizzy Gillespie album to a packet of crisps."

"So, you're saying I should try my luck."

"What have you got to lose? Apart, if you like, from the thrill of spending the next ten years waking up in the middle of the night thinking why the hell didn't I at least give it a go. You know, there was a great girl I once knew who asked me if I wanted to go with her to see the Electric Light Orchestra. Know what I said?"

"Sorry, not my kind of music?" said Martin, latching on quickly.

"Almost word for word. I think I actually said 'not my bag'. As if it mattered a flying fart whether I liked the sodding Electric Light Orchestra or not."

"Can we watch our language in here, please," said Melanie walking in on our conversation.

"Sorry, I'm giving your lad a serious talking to. I'm trying to establish beyond any doubt that I'm coming through loud and clear."

"And is he?" said Melanie to Martin.

"Yes, Mum."

I hoped I was right; for good or ill, any Likert-scale central tendency bias in Martin's attitude towards me would now be swept away.

# CHAPTER FORTY-FOUR

## My Dickens and Thackeray

It's almost December; it'll soon be a year since I sat in the bath contemplating a bleak 2000, and reading about Melanie and the Cohen Brothers. My obsession with the past has burned itself out, because the future could be so good. It's natural enough at my age to start taking stock of the cupboard. If you decide that the contents are unsatisfactory you ask why; then you put a negative spin on the past, blaming yourself for everything, especially the wrong turnings, and giving yourself credit for nothing. But I seem to have rediscovered a glass-half-full outlook, encouraged by Melanie's upbeat approach to life. If Wendy's my D H Lawrence, then Melanie is surely my Dickens and Thackeray rolled into one.

"You live in a beautiful place," she said the other day, as we walked past the Minster.

"Yeah, full of aggressive street urchins riding stolen bicycles on the pavement, and pissheads who accuse you of dissing them if you look at them for a nanosecond too long," I countered.

"Well, yes," she admitted. "But every age has its problems, Simon. It's better than living in a time when kids were sent up chimneys or died in air raids. Look at that. The Baptism – Piero della Francesca on the pavement."

"Yes, but…" I said, looking at the tapes round the picture, holding it in place.

"But what? You've got some reservations?"

Yes, to me it's the artistic equivalent of miming but I decided to say nothing.

We've been in all the medieval guildhalls, to the top of the Minster and she's threatening to get me in a hot-air balloon; I'm rediscovering my own patch.

I got lucky when I went to the Cohen Brothers. I could have ignored the beige taunts and I didn't have to obey my subconscious, which dragged me there in the first place.

I feel uncomfortable about, if not ashamed by, my immediate reaction to Trevor Smith's death but we're all entitled to harbour the occasional unsavoury item in a dark corner of the brain, so long as we keep it to ourselves. I suppose I did the decent thing in going to his funeral. I'm not thrilled about the manner in which I became an accidental hero to Lucy and Neil Smith but if those essays have brought them comfort where's the harm in it?

Things become set in stone during our 40s. When we're young, we can always brush aside disappointments, knowing that there will be other opportunities. Then at some point in our life everything changes; we go through a border crossing into a land where the laws are different. For most people, that's no big deal, especially if ambition is no longer such a burden and the kids are well balanced, on the cusp of going solo and fighting their own battles. The less fortunate among us are doomed to live with a sense of loss, the realisation that time is running short, and that the roads we never travelled will remain unexplored.

So it's a lucky man who has the opportunity to find out where some of those roads might have led him, especially if he can see that they would have gone nowhere you'd want to visit.

Melanie was the single genuine lost girl, the only one of whom I can say that I missed out on something special. Then again, maybe the ultimate lost girls, and boys, are the ones we'll never meet. I could be reincarnated forever as Simon Waiters and, by taking just a few different steps each time, have endless, unrecognisably different lives, filled with almost entirely different people. We can only scratch the surface during our four scores. I never met, nor will ever now come across, the girls who would have topped Melanie, Lesley, Anna and Gill.

Or Wendy. She's doing fine, even been on a couple of dates, she tells me. Elliot has indeed turned out to be the classic bully who backs down. When the lawyers have things sorted she'll be comfortable enough. I'll never forgive myself for what I did to Helen, but at least I have played a small part in getting Wendy's life back on track.

I've never gone in for Schadenfreude but I like to think that Greg Hammond had a few disappointing weeks around the time of our brief reunion. His competitive spirit must have taken a bashing when Wendy snubbed his advances, and a national paper used the line about his being "asleep at the wheel when he met a Soviet sleeper". But he's back with Samantha and is a man whose womanising days are surely over; that's something we've got in common, at least. "We're stronger than ever now," he told a woman from the Daily Mail, although the forced grin on Samantha's face didn't indicate domestic harmony.

Martin was a trifle fazed by the contrast between the effortless style of his mum's city centre apartment and my place, where work is still in progress, but he was impressed when he heard his Jan Garbarek albums on a really good sound system. He bought me a packet of cheese and onion the other day, accepting that I'd won our little wager. Soft touch that I am, I gave him Dizzy Gillespie's Afro-Cuban Jazz Moods anyway. And he's looking forward to sharing his first Christmas with a girlfriend; Rebecca Goldman is not destined to become, in 2030, his version of Lesley Linnell.

"Hey, Simon," he said to me one afternoon, "did you ever find out what happened to that girl you didn't go out with?"

"The Electric Light Orchestra one?"

"No, the girl who said she didn't want to get involved with anyone else at the moment."

"Yeah, she moved away from Manchester, but she came back eventually. Anyway, she's had a sex change. She's a bloke now. And an excellent chap, too, but after a manoeuvre like that there was no real way back for us as a potential item."

"I guess not," said Martin. "Just as well you didn't tell me that before I asked Rebecca out. Might have put me off my stroke."

There's no great drama to report with Melanie and me. We're one of those couples who should have got together a generation earlier. We've only had one tiff so far; she was less than complimentary about the Delvaux mural.

"I don't find those naked women very appealing, but it's more than that. I just think the whole thing's a dog's dinner. The perspective's all over the place, for starters."

"I think you'll find that Terry Boston's playing with perspective, just like Delvaux used to do."

"Did he? I'm not so sure, I reckon that Terry's just got it wrong. Aren't you thinking of Giorgio de Chirico? Let's face it, Simon, it's a bit crude."

I sulked briefly, but decided that she might be right; the mural didn't bring back happy memories.

"Any house doctor would tell you it's got to go," she said.

"That's true, I've sometimes thought the same myself," I admitted.

"You never know," she said, choosing her words carefully. "Just suppose you were thinking of moving from here at some point, it might be an idea to get rid of it sooner rather than later."

Yesterday, I applied a coat of emulsion. It will need at least one more. You can make out faint details here and there, including the red of a Manchester United shirt, but it's fading fast.

# Acknowledgements

I would like to thank Alan Smith who read two versions of this book and made some hugely helpful suggestions, particularly regarding ideas worthy of further exploration. Thanks also to Brian Thompson for his observations on an earlier draft, and of course to Rose and Alan at Stairwell for once again taking me on board.

Other novels, novellas and short story collections available from
Stairwell Books

| | |
|---|---|
| Carol's Christmas | N.E. David |
| Feria | N.E. David |
| A Day at the Races | N.E. David |
| Running With Butterflies | John Walford |
| Poison Pen | P J Quinn |
| Wine Dark, Sea Blue | A.L. Michael |
| Skydive | Andrew Brown |
| Close Disharmony | P J Quinn |
| When the Crow Cries | Maxine Ridge |
| The Geology of Desire | Clint Wastling |
| Homelands | Shaunna Harper |
| Border 7 | Pauline Kirk |
| Tales from a Prairie Journal | Rita Jerram |
| Here in the Cull Valley | John Wheatcroft |
| How to be a Man | Alan Smith |
| A Multitude of Things | David Clegg |
| Know Thyself | Lance Clarke |
| Thinking of You Always | Lewis Hill |
| Rapeseed | Alwyn Marriage |
| A Shadow in My Life | Rita Jerram |
| Tyrants Rex | Clint Wastling |
| Abernathy | Claire Patel-Campbell |
| The Go-to Guy | Neal Hardin |
| The Martyrdoms at Clifford's Tower 1190 and 1537 | John Rayne-Davis |
| Return of the Mantra | Susie Williamson |
| Poetic Justice | PJ Quinn |
| Something I Need to Tell You | William Thirsk-Gaskill |
| On Suicide Bridge | Tom Dixon |
| Looking for Githa | Pat Riley |
| Connecting North | Thelma Laycock |
| Virginia | Alan Smith |

For further information please contact rose@stairwellbooks.com
www.stairwellbooks.co.uk
@stairwellbooks